Garrett cringed inwardly as the pieces fell into place

"You and my buddy Josh work together?" Disbelief was evident in his voice, but the woman standing before him—who sported a tattoo on her neck, a pierced eyebrow and blue-tipped hair—didn't look like any of the high school teachers he'd had. Of course, his teachers had all been Catholic nuns.

"I teach freshman English at Paducah Tilghman." A subtle rise of one of her eyebrows seemed to add, *"So there."*

Apparently the mention of Josh's name loosened his son Dylan's tongue. "What happened to your hand?" He pointed blatantly at her disfigurement.

"Dylan—" Garrett started to correct him.

"No, it's okay." Tara gave him a small smile, but then sobered when she looked back at Dylan. "Motorcycle accident."

"Cool!" Dylan's voice was filled with awe.

Bona fide crazy, Garrett thought.

Dear Reader,

I'm a Francophile...smitten by France, its language and its culture since childhood. My uncle, a World War II veteran, gave me the French phrase book he carried while stationed there, and that small book started me on a love affair that has lasted a lifetime.

A few years ago, my husband and I had the chance to rent a flat in Paris for two weeks—one of those rare, dream-come-true experiences that pop up when you least expect it. I always keep a journal when I travel, and that one I filled cover-to-cover with wonderful observations of what it felt like to be Parisian for a short time.

The flat we rented had a large terrace shared by one other flat, which was unoccupied in real life. It was, however, *very* occupied in my imagination by a young widower, Garrett Hughes, and his son, Dylan.

When I was writing *The Summer Place* (Harlequin Superromance April 2013), Tara O'Malley introduced herself to me, and, as I got to know her better, I realized the preacher's kid from Taylor's Grove, Kentucky, was the perfect person to share that terrace with the Hughes men. I hope you enjoy their story!

And, by the way, I happen to have firsthand knowledge that nothing is more romantic than being kissed under the moonlight in Paris!

Until next time,

Pamela Hearon

PAMELA
HEARON

—

Moonlight in Paris

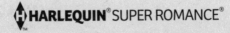

Recycling programs
for this product may
not exist in your area.

ISBN-13: 978-0-373-60828-7

MOONLIGHT IN PARIS

Copyright © 2014 by Pamela Hearon Hodges

All rights reserved. Except for use in any review, the reproduction or utilization of this work in whole or in part in any form by any electronic, mechanical or other means, now known or hereafter invented, including xerography, photocopying and recording, or in any information storage or retrieval system, is forbidden without the written permission of the publisher, Harlequin Enterprises Limited, 225 Duncan Mill Road, Don Mills, Ontario, Canada M3B 3K9.

This is a work of fiction. Names, characters, places and incidents are either the product of the author's imagination or are used fictitiously, and any resemblance to actual persons, living or dead, business establishments, events or locales is entirely coincidental.

This edition published by arrangement with Harlequin Books S.A.

For questions and comments about the quality of this book, please contact us at CustomerService@Harlequin.com.

® and TM are trademarks of Harlequin Enterprises Limited or its corporate affiliates. Trademarks indicated with ® are registered in the United States Patent and Trademark Office, the Canadian Trade Marks Office and in other countries.

Printed in U.S.A.

www.Harlequin.com

ABOUT THE AUTHOR

Pamela Hearon grew up in Paducah, a small city in western Kentucky that infuses its inhabitants with Southern values, Southern hospitality and a very distinct Southern accent. There she found the inspiration for her quirky characters, the perfect backdrop for the stories she wanted to tell and the beginnings of her narrative voice. She is a 2013 RITA® Award finalist for her first Harlequin Superromance, *Out of the Depths* (August 2012). Visit Pamela at her website (www.pamelahearon.com) or on Facebook and Twitter.

Books by Pamela Hearon

HARLEQUIN SUPERROMANCE

Other titles by this author available in ebook format.

To my precious daughter, Heather...
the one true masterpiece of my life.

Acknowledgments

Writing a book requires gleaning information from many sources and sometimes becoming annoying in the process, I'm sure. I'm always amazed by the willingness of people to share their knowledge and experiences that add authenticity to my story...and I'm filled with gratitude.

As a small show of my appreciation, I'd like to thank the following people: Coroner Phil Hileman for his expertise on accidental death and suicide; Susan Barack for her contact in Paris; Steve and Jackie Beatty for sharing the opportunity for a Paris vacation; Sandra Jones, Angela Campbell, Maggie Van Well and Cynthia D'Alba for their suggestions, ideas, plotting help and patience; Kimberly Lang for always having the time to talk me through the loopholes and gaps; Agent Jennifer Weltz for her wisdom, insight and approachability; and editor Karen Reid for her gentle guidance, fabulous editing and her innate ability to just "get me."

Above all, I want to thank my loving husband, Dick, who stays beside me through it all and encourages me to continue following this dream.

CHAPTER ONE

"I'VE ALWAYS HEARD life can change in an instant. Guess I'm living proof, huh?"

Tara O'Malley threw a glance out the window to the tangled mass of metal that had been her motorcycle. It sat on prominent display today in her parents' front yard—a grim reminder to passing motorists that motorcycles travel at the same speed as cars. Tomorrow, it would be junked.

Her mom sat the butter dish in the middle of the table and dropped a quick kiss on the top of Tara's head. "*Living* is the important word in that sentence."

"Yeah, I know." Tara focused her attention back to the app on her phone where she was entering all the family's medical history. Her accident had made her aware of the need to have such information at her fingertips, but it was Taylor Grove's blood drive in her honor today that made her finally sit down and fill in the blanks. "What was Thea's blood type?"

"A…same as mine," her mom answered absently. "Do you think Emma would stop and get a bag of ice on her way into town? I'm afraid we might run low."

"I'll call her." Tara pulled up her favorites list and thumbed her best friend's number.

"Hey," Emma answered on the first ring.

"Hey, would you stop and get a bag of ice? Mama's afraid we'll run out. And while I'm thinking about it, would you resend that class schedule for this week? I couldn't get the one from the office to open, and I keep forgetting when the junior high students are coming for their tours." The last full week of school was always crammed with so many activities that it was hard to fit in a lesson.

"Sure. I'm just leaving Paducah. Does your mom need anything else? Paper plates? Paper cups?"

"Do you need anything else, Mama? Are we using paper plates?"

Faith shook her head. "No, I'm doing Memorial Day like Thanksgiving in May this year. I just need enough people to eat all the food."

"She says to bring people." Tara relayed the message.

"I haven't eaten all day, so I'm bringing a three-meal appetite," Emma promised. "Be there in forty-five minutes or so."

"Okay. See you then." Tara pressed the button to end the call, and, before she could think, reached to rub the burning itch on her right hand. As had happened so many times over the past two months since her accident, her breath caught at the empty space her pinkie and ring fingers had occupied, and she sent up a quick prayer of thanks that two fingers and a spleen were all she'd lost. She traced the bright red scar that stopped halfway up her arm. "I'm thinking

I might get another tattoo. Maybe some leaves that will make this look like a vine."

That got her mom's attention. Faith shot her daughter a pointed look. "Your dad will disown you. He took your first one pretty well only because it's hidden, and the second with a grain of salt, but he threatened to write you out of the will over the last one."

Tara didn't mention the two they knew nothing about. She grinned, remembering the aggravated look on her dad's face when she'd shown off the Celtic symbol for life just beneath her left earlobe. When she'd explained it was in memory of Grandma O'Malley and their Irish roots, he'd held his tongue, but the hard set of his jaw had indicated his displeasure.

Tara often referred to her dad as the closest thing to a saint she'd ever known. As the preacher at the lone church in Taylor's Grove, Kentucky, Sawyer O'Malley sought to lead a life above reproach, and for the most part, he'd been successful. A loving and faithful wife…three relatively good kids.

Thea and Trenton had both gone through some rebellious stages during their teenage years, but it was just regular teenage stuff—a little drinking, some partying. But Tara, the "good girl," had been the surprise to everyone, including herself.

Five years ago, her fiancé, Louis, returned from a mission trip in Honduras with a brand-new wife—an event that threw Tara's world into a tailspin. Louis, her boyfriend of eight years, had been the only guy she'd ever dated. They'd even signed pledge cards that vowed chastity until marriage. Then he'd shown up with a wife, leaving Tara as an oddity—that rare twenty-three-year-old with her virginity still intact.

She'd made quick work of making up for all the lost time.

"Are Louis and Marta bringing their brood?"

Her mom answered with an affirmative nod as she slid the giant pan of macaroni and cheese into the oven.

Tara's ex and his wife hadn't lost any time, either. Three children in five years. And though it had taken a couple of years, Tara was glad she and Louis were friends again. She liked his family—especially Marta and her quiet, kind ways.

Tara set her phone down, feeling guilty that her mom was so busy, and she was doing nothing of great importance. "I'm not an invalid, Mama. Can I at least set the table?"

Her mom chewed her lip for a moment. "All right, you can set the table. But I'll get Lacy's china myself." She disappeared into the other room.

Tara took the hint. Grandma O'Malley's Belleek tableware was too precious to risk being carried by someone with newly missing fingers.

Trenton came in through the back door, arms laden with cartons of soft drinks and bottled water. With the blood drive in Tara's honor going on, the annual O'Malley Memorial Day Dinner had swelled to triple the usual number of people. The entire day had been very humbling.

"Hey, pinky."

Tara snorted and rolled her eyes at her brother's twisted sense of humor. He'd labeled her with the new nickname before she'd even gotten out of the hospital.

"Would you help me with the chicken?" He found an open spot on the drink-and-dessert table, and unloaded his arms. "I've got to get all those pieces turned and basted, and the ribs need a close eye kept on them."

"Sure." She eased out of her chair, still aware of the tightness from the scar where her ruptured spleen had been removed. "But I need to know your blood type first. I'm filling in an emergency app for our family."

"AB," he answered.

Tara keyed in the information, and then frowned as she glanced down the chart. "What's with this?"

Her dad came in from the garage just in time to hear her question. "What's with what, lovebug?" Slipping an arm around her shoulder, he gave her a quick hug and a peck on her temple.

She pointed to the chart. "It doesn't make sense. Trent's AB like you. Thea's A like Mama. I'm the only O negative in the bunch."

Her mom came in from the dining room with Grandma O'Malley's china stacked to just below her chin. Sawyer moved quickly in her direction, ready to alleviate her of the load as Tara continued voicing her thoughts to no one particular. "Is that even possible? Can an A and an AB produce an O?" She laughed. "Maybe we need a paternity test, Dad, to see if I'm really yours."

Faith's loud intake of breath drew everyone's attention. Her eyes went wide with a horrific look of mingled shock, pain and undeniable guilt an instant before twelve of Grandma O'Malley's treasured china plates crashed to the floor.

FAITH ISABEL FRANKLIN O'Malley had never wanted to die before, but the past seven hours had convinced her that death would be preferable to the excruciating pain she was presently feeling. It was as if she was dangling from a cord attached through her heart and the organ was being ripped slowly from her body. She'd been aware of every second of every minute of every hour that had brought her closer to this time when it would be just the immediate family.

Time for her confession.

People had started arriving before the broken china could be disposed of, so the mess and loss of family heirlooms made a convenient cover for the tears she couldn't bring under control. Sawyer, Tara and Trenton watched her with guarded expressions throughout the afternoon, and even Thea, soon after her arrival, began questioning the family quietly about what was going on.

Their looks of pain had been almost more than

Faith could bear, but Sawyer's blessing for the food had been her major undoing. She'd lost it completely when he gave his thanks for the spared life of Tara, his beloved daughter. His voice had cracked at the words, and Faith and the rest of her family knew the reason behind the falter.

She knew that he knew. They all knew.

She also knew the next few minutes could bring her family crashing down around her. The china had served as a warning.

Her hands lay on the table in front of her. She clenched and unclenched them, twisted her fingers, then her rings. She swallowed hard, trying to clear the way for the words, knowing in her heart there were no "right" ones—none that could ever make this anything but what it was.

"His name was Jacques Martin," she said at last, finding no preamble that could ease her into the subject. "He was from France. Paris."

Tara's eyes widened at the news. She sat up straighter in her chair and rubbed the side of her hand vigorously—a common gesture for her since the accident.

Faith shifted her eyes to her husband. "We spent one night together. Graduation. He left to go back to Paris the next day."

Sawyer rubbed his temples as his eyes squeezed closed, and she felt the squeeze in her heart. Was he praying? No. More likely he was running through the timeline, letting all the pieces fall into place.

Their college graduations had been on the same day, hundreds of miles apart. He'd been in Texas while she'd remained in Kentucky. By the time he moved back home ten days later, the pregnancy test had already read *positive*. Another test ten days after that had been all it took to convince him they were going to have a baby—together. They'd eloped, to no one's surprise after four long years apart.

Deception had been easy. But twenty-eight years had woven the lie tightly into the center of the fabric of their lives. Now, it was starting to unravel.

No one said anything. Everyone was avoiding eye contact with her except Tara, who sat staring with tear-filled eyes, pulling at her bottom lip. That gesture was unadulterated Sawyer, but Tara's wide, curvy mouth was the spitting image of her biological father's. Faith had always found it ironic that Tara's mouth served as the constant reminder of the lie that remained a secret.

Until seven hours ago.

Trenton stood up quickly, the force sending his chair backward across the wood floor. "I don't think I want to hear this," he announced. "Whatever happened back then is between you two." He folded both arms around Tara's neck and rested his chin on her head. "Pinky's my sister. Wholly and completely with none of that half stuff. Nothing's ever going to change that." He clapped his dad on the back and planted a quick kiss to the top of Faith's head before strolling casually from the room.

Thea scooted over into the seat Trenton had vacated, weaving her hand under Tara's thick mane of red hair until she located her sister's shoulder. She pulled her close—cheeks touching, tears mingling—as she shot Faith a "how could you?" look. "I feel the same way," she said. "We've never been just sisters. We've always been closer than that. There's no way anything can make us any different than what we are."

Tara's chin quivered as she nodded.

Faith's spirit lightened momentarily at the show of solidarity. Maybe things were going to be okay after all. But one glance at Sawyer told her that wasn't so. Her husband was a preacher. A man who made his living talking. He'd counseled hundreds of couples with marital problems through the years, always knowing exactly what to say to clear the air of the fallout from unfaithfulness.

His silence grated her heart into tiny slivers like lemon zest.

"So whatever became of this…Jacques Martin?" Tara's voice held the same strained edge it had when she realized her two fingers were gone.

"I never saw, never heard from him again," Faith answered, then added, "I never wanted to. I had all I needed and wanted with you all." Blood pounded in her temples. How could she make them understand? "Jacques was…" Someone she'd had too much alcohol with that night. Someone she'd gotten carried away celebrating with. Someone who'd helped her bear the loneliness of not being with the person she loved on one of the most important days of her life. "He was someone I barely knew."

Sawyer swerved around to face Tara and gathered her partial hand into both of his. "You're my daughter, lovebug. The daughter of my heart. Like Trenton said, nothing's ever going to change that." He pressed their knotted hands against his chest. "I hold you right here, and nothing will ever break that grip."

Faith watched the tears overflow from her daughter's eyes, unaware of her own until she felt a drop on her arm.

Tara nodded. "I love you, Dad." She paused and Faith held her breath and prayed that those words would be repeated to her.

They weren't. Instead, Tara stood, pulling her hand from Sawyer's grip. "I really, really need to go home. I need time alone to process this."

Thea followed her to her feet.

A different fear gripped Faith's insides, a familiar one since Tara's accident. It recurred every time one of her children left her house to drive back to their own homes. "Will you be okay making the drive back to Paducah? You want me to call Emma?"

"I'm leaving, too. I'll take you home," Thea offered.

Tara shook her head. "I don't want to be with anyone. I'll be okay."

Faith stood and reached for her, and her daughter hugged her then, but her arms felt limp and lifeless with no emotion behind them. Her parting hug with her dad had a bit more vitality, but not much.

Faith's breathing grew shallow when Thea didn't hug her or Sawyer, but she did take Tara's hand to lead the way out.

As Tara slid the patio door closed behind her, Faith turned her attention back to her husband. They stood beside the table where their family had shared thousands of happy mealtimes. Would those be enough to blot out the anguish of today?

She took Sawyer's hand and tilted her head in silent question.

"It's not the action, Faith. It's the deception. The betrayal."

He pulled his hand away and headed for his study, locking the door behind him.

CHAPTER TWO

"But how are you handling it, really? And none of that 'I'm okay' stuff. I held your hair when you threw up your first beer, so I've seen you at your worst." Emma blew on her spoonful of tomato soup, waiting for an answer.

Tara reached behind her chair to shut the door to Emma's office, pondering how to put her feelings into words. "You remember that weird, uneasy feeling inside you the first Christmas you no longer believed in Santa Claus? It's kind of like that. I remember knowing the presents were still downstairs, waiting to be opened. But the magical quality was gone forever. That's the way I feel. Like some kind of wonderful something has slipped away, and I'll never be able to get it back."

Emma's eyebrows knitted. "But you haven't really lost anything. Your dad is still your dad…."

"But I've lost who I thought I was. Everything I accounted to my Irish heritage—my red hair, my fair complexion, my love of Guinness. I've only talked myself into believing they had significance." Tara popped a grape into her mouth. "And that makes me wonder what other things I've believed in that were actually of no significance."

"Well, maybe you need to talk to somebody." Emma tore open a package of oyster crackers and sprinkled them over the top of her soup. "You know—" she shrugged as she stirred them in "—a professional."

"You're a professional guidance counselor with a master's in counseling. I'm talking to you."

Tara watched her friend's eyebrows disappear beneath her wispy bangs. "Doctors don't operate on family members, and counselors don't counsel family."

"But we're not—"

"We're just as close."

"Who I really want to talk to is Jacques Martin." Tara blurted out the idea that had kept her awake most of the night. "I just want to take off for Paris and find my birth father."

"And what good would that do?"

Tara thought about that question while she nibbled on a carrot. What good *would* it do? "Mostly it would satisfy my curiosity," she admitted. "I can't stop wondering what he looks like, what his personality is like. Do I have his nose? His laugh?"

"Your mom can tell you that."

Tara's throat tightened around a bite of carrot. She dropped the rest of it back into the plastic container, her appetite suddenly gone. "I can't talk to her any more about him. At least, not yet."

"I understand." The sympathy in her friend's voice made Tara's throat tighten again. "So what difference would it make if you found out those things about him?" Emma gave a quick nod in Tara's direction. "You rub your lip when you're thinking about something just like Sawyer does. No matter where those little things come from, they make up *you*."

Self-consciously, Tara dropped her hand from her mouth. "I just want to look Jacques Martin in the eye and say 'I'm your daughter' and see his reaction."

Emma eyed her warily. "Can't you just let your imagination play out that scene for you? Paris is way too big a city to find somebody with only a name to go on. And it's very expensive from what I hear."

Tara shrugged and glanced out the window to avoid eye contact. "I have my inheritance from Grandma." She cringed at Emma's outraged gasp.

"You're serious! You've actually given this some thought…and have a plan. It's a crazy idea, Tara— one you need to get out of your head right now."

Emma's gray eyes bored into her, causing Tara's cheeks to burn. "Thought you weren't going to counsel."

"I'm not counseling. I'm giving my best friend a verbal shake to wake her up." Emma ran her fingertips through her short bob, fluffing the soft, chestnut ends. "Finding him would take a feat of magic. He might've moved. Might not want to be found. Some people don't. Or…or he might be dead. Have you thought about that?"

"That's another thing. Family medical history is important." Tara held up her half hand. "Emergencies happen. Diseases strike. It would be great to at least have a hint of what else I might come up against in the future. Mama's family doesn't have any heart disease, but what if it's in his genes?"

"Then you do all the right things to keep your heart healthy no matter what."

Tara looked at her friend in earnest. "Even if I didn't find him, I could learn about my French heritage. The Irish thing I've always been so proud of has been jerked away from me, and now I want to replace it with *something*. I want to find out who I *am*."

Emma looked at her long and hard, the steel in her gaze softening to a down-gray. "Know what?" She reached across the desk to place her hand on top of Tara's. "I'm wrong. If it means that much to you, I think you should do it."

"Really?" Tara jolted at Emma's change of heart. "Because I'm thinking I want to do it soon. Like as soon as school is out."

"That's short notice. Can you make all the arrangements that quickly?"

Tara shrugged. "I don't know. Maybe through a travel agent."

"That will run the cost up even more. Do you know anyone who might know somebody over there?" Emma drummed the desk with her spoon. "What about Josh Essex?"

Tara hadn't gotten far enough in her planning to

consider that the French teacher might have connections in Paris, but it was a good idea—he did usually take students to Paris during the summer.

"He was eating lunch in the teachers' lounge when I got my soda." Emma got up quickly, abandoning her soup and crackers. "Let's go talk to him now."

"CAN WE PLAY some catch, Dad?"

Dylan had disappeared a couple of minutes earlier, and now stood in the doorway of the flat holding a ball and wearing the St. Louis Cardinals ball cap, jersey and glove that had arrived from his grandmother that day.

Like I could refuse. Garrett gave a wry smile. "Sure. Just let me get the dishwasher loaded."

Dylan set the ball and glove in the chair he'd vacated earlier and picked up his plate to help clear the table, something he rarely did. No doubt he was anxious to try out his new equipment.

"Watch your step," Garrett warned as the six-year-old caught his toe on the frame of the sliding patio door.

When the Paris weather permitted, they ate every meal possible out here on the terrace. The wide expanse of concrete wasn't anywhere near as large as their backyard had been in St. Louis, but life had its trade-offs. For a second-story flat, the extra living space the terrace afforded was well worth the small amount of extra rent. Although several other flats had windows that looked out on it, only one other had a door leading to it. And that one had been empty for over a year, so Garrett and his son had gotten used to having the entire space to themselves.

They made quick work of loading the dishwasher, and then Garrett grabbed his own glove as they headed back out to their makeshift practice field.

Dylan punched the new leather with his fist. "I'm ready for a fastball."

That drew a laugh. "One fastball comin' up." Garrett made a wild show of winding up, watching his son's eyes grow huge in anticipation. At the last second, he slowed down enough to toss the ball toward the boy's padded palm.

Dylan kept his eye on the ball, stretching his arm out to full length and spreading his glove open as far as his short fingers would allow.

The ball landed with a *thump,* and a pleased grin split Dylan's face as he hoisted the glove and ball over his head in a triumphant gesture. "Freese makes the play!" he yelled.

"How 'bout we send a picture of you and your new stuff to Nana and Papa?"

"And Gram and Grandpa, too."

Garrett snapped the picture and messaged it to both his parents and Angela's. Then he laid the phone down within easy reach to listen for the calls that were sure to come.

His mom and his deceased wife's mother called every time he sent a picture of Dylan, which was often. The distance was hard for them.

They'd all done their damnedest to talk Garrett out of the voluntary move to Paris three years ago when the brewery he worked for was bought out by a Belgian company. Only his dad had fully understood his need to escape from the constant reminder of his wife's suicide. And his guilt.

No matter how they felt about it, the move hadn't been a mistake.

Dylan mimicked Garrett's windup, minus the slow down at the end. The ball he released sailed wide past his father, who broke into a run to catch it on the bounce. His timing was off. He missed and wasn't able to catch up to it until it hit the back wall.

"Dad! Your phone's ringing," Dylan called.

By the time Garrett got back to answer it, he was winded. *"Allô."* He breathed heavily into the phone. *"C'est Garrett."*

"Well, your French has definitely gotten better, but the creepy heavy breathing makes me wonder if I've caught you at a bad time. My math says it should be around dinner time there."

Garrett laughed, recognizing the voice of his teammate from college Josh Essex. "Actually, it's pitch-and-catch after dinner, Josh."

"Is that the new French phrase for hooking up? 'Cause, if it is, my seniors will want to know."

"By the time I get around to..." Dylan was within hearing distance, so Garrett veered away from what he'd been about to say. "To needing *that* information, the *deed* will probably be obsolete."

"I can't even bear that thought." Josh chuckled. "How's Dylan doing?"

"Growing too fast for me to keep him in jeans. We've resorted to rolled cuffs and belts."

"Well, let's hope cuffs, belts and, of course, the *deed* never go out of style."

"I hear you," Garrett agreed. "And to what do I owe the pleasure of this call, Monsieur Essex? Especially in the middle of your work day."

"I have a friend—a colleague—who's wanting to come to Paris in a couple of weeks and plans to stay a month. Does your building have any short-term rentals?"

Garrett's eyes cut to the flat across the way, and then wandered on around the terrace to the window boxes devoid of flowers—a dead giveaway in spring and summer that spaces were empty. "Yeah, probably. Hold on." He fished his wallet out of his back pocket and thumbed through the cards until he found the one he wanted. "You have a pen handy?"

"I'm just waiting on you."

"Here's the number to call." Garrett read it off slowly. "That's the main office of the company that owns my building. They'll have listings of what's available."

"Got it. Thanks."

"Will we be seeing you this summer?" For the past three years, Josh had brought groups of his students for ten-day tours of the City of Lights. The visits had certainly been the highlight of the summer for

Garrett, who tried to deny to himself how much he missed the U.S.

Josh's sigh was fraught with frustration. "I don't have too many interested, and a couple who were had to drop out. June 20 is the cutoff, and I'm still not sure."

Garrett didn't know who was more disappointed, he or Josh. "That's too bad."

"Yeah, well, it's the damn economy. How about you? You and Dylan planning a trip stateside any time soon?"

Garrett had been thinking this might be the year to go home for Christmas, but he was keeping mum on it in case he backed out. "Economy here's just as bad. I might have to hock Dylan to buy tickets."

Dylan perked up at the mention of his name, but not enough to tear his concentration away from his task. The ball he was bouncing off the wall shot back at him. He missed it, but not for lack of trying. Garrett took that as a sure sign his boy was meant for the big leagues, and the thought made him smile.

The familiar jangle of a school bell reverberated in the background. "Gotta go, man." Garrett could tell his friend was on the move. "It's the last week of school, and I'm showing *The Diving Bell and the Butterfly* to my third-year students."

"Great movie." Garrett motioned a thumbs-up to Dylan, who'd made a successful catch. "I hope you get enough students to make your group, so we'll get to see you."

"Me, too." The background sounds heightened as lockers slamming joined the mix. "And thanks for the number. Maybe I'll see you in a couple of months."

"We'll look forward to it. See you, man."

"Later, dude."

The call ended before Garrett realized he hadn't asked who needed a flat for a month—hadn't even asked if the interested party was male or female. Man, he was slipping.

While he liked the idea of having someone from close to home in the building, he hoped whoever it was wasn't interested in the flat across from them. He and Dylan would hate to give up their private recreation area. Would hate to give up their privacy, in general.

After the years of chaos with Angela, this terrace had become his and Dylan's oasis of tranquility. Beyond the walls was one of the most exciting cities in the world, but here was quiet space.

He didn't want anything to interfere with that.

Not even for a month.

CHAPTER THREE

Tara breathed a relieved sigh as the key turned in the lock. Getting lost twice in the maze of dark, windowless corridors had her convinced she'd entered some kind of Parisian warp zone and might never find the flat she'd rented. The lights in the hallways were on a timer, and didn't stay on very long. Just finding the switches was like being on a treasure hunt…blindfolded…with no map.

Elbowing the door open, she rolled the duffel into the small foyer, dropping it and her shoulder bag as she took in her new surroundings.

"Well…thank you, Josh…and whomever you got that number from." Tara tried to recall the name—some college friend of Josh's. It didn't matter. What did matter was that this place, with its warm wood floors and modern furniture, was cheery and chic and perfect for a month's stay. She would have to pick out a nice thank-you gift for the French teacher.

A quick tour found the rest of the apartment much to her liking, too. The bathroom seemed antiquated with its pull-chain to flush the toilet, but the living room and the bedroom both looked out on a terrace rimmed with ivy-covered lattice work and flower pots brimming with color.

A notebook lay prominently on the dining table. Lettering across its front spelled out the word *tenant* in several languages. She flipped the book open to the section labeled English. Coming to Paris had been such a quick decision that there'd been no time to study the French language in any depth. She'd hoped her two years of high school and college Spanish would help, but it hadn't yet.

Everyone she'd been in contact with so far had spoken at least a little English, except for Madame LeClerc at the front desk. Hand gestures had been the language that had landed Tara the key to the flat. There were a few other gestures she'd wanted to use with the awful woman, but she would have hated to get kicked out before she got moved in.

Inside the notebook, Tara found a note of welcome, which she scanned for important information. "Oven temperature displayed in Celsius…shutters on a timer, which can be reset to your schedule… take key when you leave as the door locks automatically…terrace shared by one other flat…call if you are in need of any assistance."

The words blurred on the page. The excitement of being in Paris for the first time and facing the opportunity to find her birth father was fast losing ground to jet lag. What she needed was a breath of fresh air, and with rain imminent, she'd better make it quick.

She unlatched the sliding door and stepped outside into the heat of the sultry morning, careful to close the door behind her so as to not allow any of the precious air conditioning to escape.

Latticework placed strategically around the large concrete patio gave some definition to what area belonged with each of the flats. Her section was a bit smaller than the other, but still quite large.

The sliding door to the other flat directly across from hers was open as were many of the windows of other flats. Vague sounds of morning with families and children drifted through.

Around the corner from her door and several yards away, a railing hung with flowerboxes added an explosion of color to the gray day. Below lay a courtyard with a lovely formal garden and a huge wooden door that looked as if it was left over from the Middle Ages.

She heard a shout, and a boy who looked to be eight or nine ran through the courtyard below, trying to make it to the wooden door ahead of something—or someone. At that point, the first drop of rain hit the top of her head.

Maybe the boy was trying to beat the impending downpour?

But then a second shout filtered up toward her, and two more boys appeared, larger and older than the first, who was frantically working to open the massive door.

One of the older boys pounced on the child from

behind, pinning his arms behind his back while the third boy approached menacingly.

Tara's schoolteacher persona pushed to the forefront. She had to do something, but if she vaulted over the railing, she'd break her neck. And there was no way she could find her way back downstairs to that area in time to save the boy from whatever the ruffians had in mind for him. In desperation, she used her teacher voice and yelled over the railing, "Hey! Stop that! Leave him alone."

The older boy paused midstride and turned toward the voice. He looked up with a sneer and made a gesture toward her that needed no translation. When he started back toward the younger boy, the child started to shriek and thrash about.

A whirring sound nearby jerked Tara's attention from the tableau below to the sight of metal shutters closing over the windows of her flat. *Mechanical storm shutters. Thank heavens!* They would buy her more time here.

A shout obviously from an adult male came from below, and then a short, burly guy appeared, and the big boys immediately stopped their attack. With the rain coming harder, Tara could feel her curly hair growing bushier by the second, but she had to stay long enough to make sure everything was okay.

Even without understanding the language, she caught the word *papa* from all three boys often enough to figure out they were siblings and *Papa* was taking care of things. And just in time, as the sky opened up then, and rain pelted her full force.

Relieved that she was no longer needed, she sprinted in the direction of her door and rounded the corner, letting out a shriek of her own. "Eek! No!"

Storm shutters had been installed over the door, as well. She got there just in time to see them clamp down tightly, a metal fortress barring anything—or anyone—from entrance.

Frantically, she looked for a button. Surely there was an override. Lifting a metal flap exposed a numerical keypad, but, try as she might, she couldn't recall anything about a code in the note she'd read. She tried a few random numbers…0000…1234…but soon gave up, realizing the futility. She wasn't even sure it would be a four-number code.

"Damn it!" She gave the metal a swift kick. The barrier didn't budge, but the action bruised her toe and her ego.

She was already soaked. The lemony, cotton sundress, which had made her feel so chic, now clung to her legs, directing the water flow into sodden ballet flats. She squished back around the corner, checking the windows, hoping for a breakdown somewhere in the system, but finding everything in dismally perfect working order.

She would have to wait it out. Crossing her arms, she leaned against the wall, and she was surveying her surroundings when the open door gaped at her from across the terrace. How many times had her dad preached about the open doors in life and choosing the right way?

Shielding her eyes from the pelting rain, she studied the door. No movement came from that apartment. The owners might be gone...might be trusting souls who left their back door open because they usually had no neighbors.

If she cut through their flat, she could find her way back down to Madame LeClerc—not a pleasant thought, but standing in a downpour wasn't exactly the way she'd pictured her first hour in Paris, either. She could get...*beg*...the spare key, come back up and let herself in through her own front door.

While she pondered the plan, the sky grew blacker, and despite the heat, she began to get chilled.

A crack of lightning nearby made the decision for her. She loped across the terrace toward the safety of the open door, praying the occupants had left for work...or at least had a good sense of humor.

She paused for a few seconds just inside the door and knocked on the wall. *"Bonjour?"* she called. She was met by silence, but the luscious aroma of fresh coffee told her that the owners were out of bed...or awake, anyway. The scent had a magnetic pull that drew her a couple of steps deeper into the room.

"Bonjour?" she repeated, at a total loss to say anything else in her limited French. She cocked her head and listened, becoming aware of a sound only when it stopped. Running water, which she'd initially

attributed to the rain outside. But this was inside. Someone who was in the shower had now gotten out.

Good Lord! Her predicament thudded into her stomach full force. What if the owner wasn't sympathetic *or* amused? What if he or she called the police? She was in a foreign country where she knew no one.

Wouldn't that be a lovely way to meet the father who didn't know she existed? *Hi there. I'm the daughter you didn't realize you had. Would you mind coming to the police station to bail me out?*

She shivered—not from a chill this time.

Thunder was coming right on top of the lightning, so going back outside was unthinkable. She'd choose arrest over electrocution any day.

Most people paused in the bathroom to put on lotion or shave after a shower. Maybe she could still make it out the front door without getting caught.

She started to tiptoe across the floor when the squish between her toes reminded her how wet her shoes were. Toeing out of them, she clasped the soggy slippers in her hand.

She crossed the room and turned down a hallway only to find light creeping from beneath the door along with a shower-fresh scent.

An about-face focused her on the door at the other end, where the hallway widened into a small foyer with a desk and, obviously, the front door.

She tiptoed as fast as she could in its direction,

not even hesitating as the floor creaked and groaned beneath her.

A little boy appeared through a doorway to her right, rubbing the sleep from his eyes.

He took one look at her and let out a terrified shriek.

HIS SON'S SCREAM propelled Garrett out of the bathroom with the towel he'd been drying himself off with still in his grip and his brain moving at warp speed to assess the situation before him.

Dylan's eyes lost some of their terror as he scampered to safety behind his dad, but the same look remained fixed in the eyes of the stranger standing in their foyer—a young woman…obviously deranged.

Garrett scanned her quickly for a weapon but didn't spot anything. The way the yellow dress plastered against her body would make it difficult to hide anything. She looked as though she'd just stepped out of the shower herself…fully clothed. The bright red bush of hair that sprouted from her head was tipped in blue and had an undeniable Medusa quality about it. The hand she used to push it out of her eyes was only half there.

Nine years with Angela made him a freakin' expert on handling crazy women. No sudden moves. No shouting. But he gripped the towel tighter, thinking he could throw it over her head, then tackle her and keep her pinned while Dylan called the police.

"Pardon." Her voice shook on the word as she

raised her hands to shoulder height, one palm out in a show of surrender, the other clutching a pair of shoes. "Um…*bonjour?*"

Garrett tilted an ear in her direction to pick up more of the weird accent.

"*Je…Je* got locked out of my flat in the rain." She kept her hands up, but flicked her fingers in the direction of the door that opened onto the terrace.

The accent dropped a pin on the map in Garrett's brain—America…and most definitely the South. His guard dropped a smidgen by sheer reflex. "You're American," he said, at last.

"Oh, you speak English. Thank God." The woman's shoulders sagged and her eyes closed momentarily as if she were actually in prayer as she said those words. Her hands dropped limply to her sides. "I just got here." Her eyes flicked from him to the terrace door. "I'm renting that apartment over yonder." As she made jerky movements with her head in the direction of the terrace, the words came streaming as fast as her drawl would allow. "The automatic storm shutters closed, and I don't know how to get them open." Her eyes came back to him, flitted downward and upward just as quickly before a crimson flush started to steal its way from the neckline of her dress into her cheeks. "And I left my key inside on the table, so even if I get back to my apartment, I can't get in." She gave a frustrated sigh, running her fingers through her hair and squeezing the roots. "I'll have to beg another one from Madame LeClerc, which won't be easy because I'm pretty sure she already hates me."

The Southern accent had started to lull Garrett into complacency. He relaxed completely when she called Madame LeClerc by name. Nobody got by Ironpants LeClerc without a confirmed reason to be in the building. He dropped the idea of using the towel to subdue the young woman, and used it instead in a more appropriate manner by wrapping it around his middle. "So you're our new neighbor? Which flat are you in?" he asked as a final test of her veracity.

"Four C," she answered, somehow making the phrase three syllables long. "We share the terrace."

"She talks funny, Dad." Dylan had moved around to stand beside Garrett—not clinging, but Garrett was aware of the shoulder pressing into his thigh.

The woman squatted down to be on eye level with his son. "Bless your heart. I'm so sorry, scaring you like that." She offered her half hand for Dylan to shake. "I'm Tara O'Malley, by the way."

Garrett felt his son tense as he gazed at the three fingers extended in his direction. Tara O'Malley didn't move forward, just waited patiently as if she expected him to sniff it first. Finally Dylan stepped forward and took the hand, shaking it vigorously. "I'm Dylan Hughes."

Pride swelled in Garrett's chest. He offered his hand and helped Tara up as they shook. "I'm Dylan's dad. Garrett Hughes."

"Oh!" Tara's face broke into a wide smile. "You're Josh Essex's friend. The one who gave him the number I used to find my flat."

Garrett cringed inwardly as the pieces fell into place. "That's right." He was at least partially responsible for the crazy woman being here. "You and Josh work together?" Disbelief was evident in his voice, but the woman standing before him—who sported a tattoo beneath her ear, a pierced eyebrow and blue-tipped hair—didn't look like any of the high school teachers he'd had. Of course, his teachers had all been Catholic nuns.

"I teach freshman English at Paducah Tilghman." A subtle rise of one of her eyebrows seemed to add, "So there."

Apparently the mention of Josh's name loosened Dylan's tongue. "What happened to your hand?" He pointed blatantly at her disfigurement.

"Dylan—" Garrett started to correct him.

"No, it's okay." Tara gave him a small smile, but then sobered when she looked back at Dylan. "Motorcycle accident."

"Cool!" Dylan's voice was filled with awe.

Bona fide crazy, Garrett thought.

Tara continued to address Dylan. "Yeah, motorcycles can be very cool, but they can also be very dangerous. Sometimes people driving cars don't notice them, or they think of them as a bicycle. So don't ever get on one without a helmet, and don't ride too fast."

"I won't," Dylan assured her.

"Well." She sighed, and Garrett followed her eyes to the rain that was coming down so hard that her flat across the way was barely visible. "I've been enough trouble to y'all this morning. I'll just mosey on back to my place."

"Stay and have breakfast with us!" Dylan blurted, and Garrett's jaw tightened at the suggestion.

"Oh, no, I can't. I'm soaked to the skin. My hair's a mess."

Garrett's logical side urged him to let her go on her way, but his emotional side, which was being suckered by the sultry, Southern accent, chided him for even entertaining the possibility.

"You can't go out in this," he said, ignoring the warning sirens blaring in his brain. "Although we're just across the terrace, we're actually on opposite sides of the building. You'd have to go literally half-way around the block to get back to the main entrance."

"Well…"

She chewed her bottom lip as a visible shiver ran through her, making her suddenly appear delicate and fragile. Garrett felt a stirring below and realized he was still standing there wearing nothing but a towel.

"I'll go get dressed and find you some dry clothes to put on. I think this rain has set in for a while." He motioned to the pot of French-pressed coffee on the counter in the kitchen. "Help yourself to some coffee. We'll be right back."

"I'll bring you some clothes!" Dylan was obviously excited to have an unexpected guest for breakfast. He ran ahead into Garrett's bedroom.

Garrett lost no time rifling through a bottom drawer for the long shorts he shot hoops in. No doubt they would swallow Tara, but they had a drawstring that might, at least, help her keep them up. He grabbed a T-shirt from another drawer and thrust the pair toward Dylan, who was still in his pajamas. "Take these to our guest, sport, then go get dressed."

A smile spread across his son's face. "I like her, Dad. She's cool." He ran from the room, clutching the bundle.

"Of course you like her." Garrett muttered under his breath as he closed the door. "She's crazy. Just like your mom."

He wasted no time getting dressed. Time alone between his son and the crazy woman wasn't going to happen.

CHAPTER FOUR

PEOPLE STAYING AT bed-and-breakfasts do this all the time, Tara told herself as she passed the plate of croissants to the little boy who'd insisted on sitting beside her. Of course, it would probably have been easier to convince herself there was nothing weird about eating breakfast in a new country with total strangers if she hadn't seen one of them naked a few minutes earlier.

She tried to focus on the inch-long scar that cut diagonally through the left side of Garrett's upper lip—the one that disappeared almost completely when he smiled—rather than let her mind wander to the footlong one on his thigh that pointed like an arrow to his masculine assets.

"I finally decided it was time to see Paris." She answered Dylan's last question just shy of the complete truth. "How long have you lived here?"

Dylan piped up before his dad could answer. "Three years. We moved here when I was three, but I'll be seven soon, so I guess then I'll have to start saying we've been here four years."

Garrett used his spoon to point at his son. "Quit talking so much, sport, and eat your breakfast."

With a grin that could charm the sweet spot from a Louisville Slugger, Dylan opened his mouth wide and shoveled in a spoonful of Greek yogurt and fresh berries.

The boy's grin was a replica of his dad's, as was the sandy color of his hair. But the jade-green hue of his eyes was a far cry from the walnut-brown of his elder's.

No mention had been made of a wife or mother. And something about Garrett Hughes's manner seemed standoffish, despite the fact he'd invited her to stay for breakfast. If he'd kidnapped his son and moved to a foreign country, Josh Essex would've let her in on that, wouldn't he?

"So you're originally from St. Louis?" Tara probed, trying to get Garrett to continue where he'd left off before Dylan had started in with questions again.

Garrett held up the carafe as a question, and Tara offered her cup in response. "I grew up in St. Louis," he said, "and moved back there after college. Not too long after my wife died—"

Ah, a widower. "I'm so sorry." She took another sip of the incredibly strong brew and settled a hand on her chest to check for any hair it might cause to sprout through the T-shirt.

"Thanks." Garrett acknowledged her condolences with a curt nod. "The brewery I worked for was bought out by a Belgian company that was expanding. Dylan and I moved here with that expansion."

"How exciting that must've been."

Garrett shrugged one of his broad shoulders, and even though a sport coat now covered it, Tara's mind flashed back to how it had looked unclothed and damp from the shower. "It came at the right time," he answered.

The concoction Garrett called coffee had chased away any effects of jet lag and set her mouth to chatty mode. "And what do you do at the brewery?"

"I'm head of the marketing department."

The formality of the country she was visiting struck her as she wiped away the last remains of the buttery croissant from her lips with the linen napkin that had been part of her place setting. "Were you already fluent in French before you moved here?"

Her question brought a low chuckle from Garrett that tickled at the bottom of her spine. "Whether I'm fluent *now* is still debatable." He jutted his chin in his son's direction. "Dylan's the language wizard. He speaks it like a native."

Dylan paused, the spoon halfway to his mouth. *"C'est vrai, Tara. Je parle le français très bien. La langue n'est pas difficile."* He cocked his head and grinned, looking like the cat that ate the berry-and-yogurt-covered canary.

Garrett shook his head as his mouth rose at one end. "And he's obviously quite modest about it."

Tara smiled, her heart touched by the endearing relationship between these two. Would she and Jacques Martin ever have anything that approached this? The thought caused her hand to tremble as she set her cup back on its saucer. "How did you get so good, Dylan?"

"Only French at school. Only English at home."

"And speaking of school, we need to be on our way." Garrett stood and started clearing the table. "Go brush your teeth and get your stuff, bud. We'll walk Tara down to the front entrance."

Hearing her name from Garrett's lips sent an unexpected, pleasant zing through Tara. She gathered her and Dylan's dishes as the child hurried to the bathroom.

"With our key, we can get in the courtyard below and take the shortcut through the building." Garrett loaded the dishwasher while he talked, and Tara stored the items that needed to be refrigerated. "Madame LeClerc is quite taken by Dylan. If she balks about giving up the extra key, he'll be able to talk it out of her."

Tara glanced around, noting that everything was done. "I'll change back into my dress as soon as Dylan gets out of the bathroom."

"Don't bother." Garrett's eyes met hers, and then darted away as he waved at the outfit she had on. "You can return those…whenever."

Tara's stomach did a quick flip. She'd just been given an invitation to come back. A little offhanded, maybe. But, nonetheless, an invitation.

"Earth to Faith. Can you hear me?"

Sue Marsden's annoyed tone broke through the

deep fog of Faith O'Malley's thoughts. She glanced around the small circle of women who made up the Ladies' Prayer Group, noting all twelve eyes were on her.

Being the preacher's wife, she was used to that, but she still hated it…had always hated it. Living in the glass house had taught her to never throw rocks, but that wouldn't stop the community from verbally stoning her if word got out of what she'd done.

Sue Marsden would be the first to start flinging.

"I'm…I'm sorry. What did you say?" Even that comment was an admission that she hadn't been listening and would give Sue something to gossip about later.

Sue gave that laugh of hers, which wasn't really a laugh at all but more of a *tsk-tsk*. "I asked if you had any prayer requests. We are a prayer group. Remember?"

We don't have enough time for my list, lady.

Prayer requests from the group too often gave Sue her weekly start on new items of gossip.

Time and again, Faith had seen it happen, had warned the group that what was shared within the group should stay within the group.

But Sue's pious contention was that the more prayers rallied on a person's behalf, the better the chance of God's listening. She'd back her ideas with much Bible-thumping and scripture quoting. And, yes, the prayer chain she'd formed after Tara's accident had been much appreciated.

But to have the matters of Faith's heart bandied about Taylor's Grove like an item in a tabloid was unthinkable, and even the slightest hint of turmoil in the O'Malley household would start the rumor mill turning.

On the other hand, if she didn't share *something,* the ladies would think she was being either secretive or uppity. She'd walked this tightrope for years and knew well how to perform on it without losing her balance.

"Tara called this morning," she said, at last. "She got to Paris last night around midnight our time. I'd like y'all to remember her in your prayers…her safety."

Nell Bradley spoke up. "I've worried so about her ever since I heard she was gallivanting off to a foreign country. And in such a hurry about it. I'll never understand why kids these days have to have everything right now."

"Well, I'm not at all surprised." Sue waved her hand dismissively. "Ever since she and Louis broke up, Tara's been a different person. She has a capricious nature that none of us had ever seen. She needed someone like Louis to keep her reined in."

The comment jarred Faith's composure, causing it to slip. "Tara's twenty-eight. She doesn't need anyone to rein her in. Certainly not a man."

"You can't be okay with all her shenanigans, Faith. Motorcycles and tattoos." Sue rolled her eyes. "Last

Sunday, she came to church with her hair tipped in blue, for heaven's sake."

That brought out the lioness in Faith. No one was allowed to attack her cubs…her pride. "Sue, I am very proud of my daughter," Faith said quietly before she gave a swipe, claws extended. "And, yes, her hair might be tipped in blue, but, at least, she was *in church* last Sunday."

The astonished looks of amusement told her that everyone picked up on the thinly veiled reference to Sue's daughter Quinn, who made it a habit of sleeping in on Sunday.

Faith's cheeks burned with shame that she'd stooped to Sue's level and had given everyone a story to repeat this week.

Well, at least the talk would focus on her and not Tara.

A muscle twitched in Sue's jaw, proof that she'd felt the stinging blow. "Let's pray," she snapped.

Faith bowed her head and took deep breaths to slow her racing heart.

Another week had passed and her secrets were still secure by all indications.

No one had mentioned the increase in Trenton's visits home as opposed to the decrease in Thea's.

No one had brought up the haunted look in Sawyer's eyes, or the despair that Faith felt was surely reflected in her own.

No one knew that they hadn't touched each other for going on four weeks now. That the happy faces they put on in public dissolved once they stepped through their door at home. That Sawyer pulled away every time she tried to reach out to him. That their conversations were cordial, but lacked any kind of intimacy, as if they were acquaintances meeting on the street.

That he'd moved into Trenton's room.

That her family was fractured just like she was on the inside.

That she was searching desperately for something to hold them together. To hold *her* together before she fell apart completely.

No one knew what she was going through.

No one could ever know

Amen.

CHAPTER FIVE

HENRI LEANED FORWARD in his seat across the table and lowered his voice to a conspiratorial whisper. "Now that we are alone, perhaps you should share with me some details about your *unsettling* morning, eh? Is Dylan well?"

"Damn, I'm sorry." Guilt took a swipe at Garrett's insides. He should've realized that his friend would jump to the conclusion that the unsettling morning he referred to in their meeting might mean something had happened to Dylan. "Yeah, he's fine. But we both got quite a scare."

"*Pourquoi?* What happened?"

The approaching media blitz for Soulard Beer had the head of production wringing his hands, but Garrett's marketing staff and Henri's IT staff had been treated to a well-earned lunch with the company's owners. They'd be working late again tonight, so they'd been told to take their time getting back to the office. Garrett and Henri intended to do just that.

"I'd just gotten out of the shower, and I'm standing there buck naked, when all of a sudden, Dylan lets out a scream that would've made even your well-lacquered hair stand on end."

Henri smirked at the mention of his perfect coif. "Jealousy does not sit well on you, *mon ami*. Now, quickly, tell me what happened to Dylan."

"Dylan was fine. But I go running out with a towel in my hand—" Garrett held up his napkin in his fist "—and there stands a woman in my foyer, who's also dripping wet, but she's fully clothed."

"Did Dylan allow this woman into your flat?"

The threat of a lecture to Dylan lay in Henri's tone, so Garrett hurried on to reassure him. "No. She came in through the terrace door, which I'd left open. Turns out she's an American who's renting the empty flat that shares our terrace. In fact, she's a friend of Josh Essex. You remember Josh?"

Henri nodded, and Garrett continued his tale. "She just arrived this morning, and was on the terrace when the rain started, and her storm shutters closed. She was locked out in a downpour, so she came over to our place."

"But what made Dylan scream?"

"Well, for one thing, she startled him. He'd just woken up. But, damn, Henri, you should've seen her. She looked like something out of a slasher movie."

The side of Henri's mouth twitched. "*Oui?* A woman in a wet T-shirt? I am thinking that is not so terrible."

Garrett shook his head. "No, you're not getting the picture. She had on this yellow dress that's soaked and clinging to her, and she's got bright red hair—"

he held his hands out beside his head to indicate how far Tara's had stuck out "—with the curls tipped in blue. Her eyebrow's pierced, and she's got a couple of tattoos. One on the side of her neck, and one right above her ass."

Henri's head cocked in interest. "And how do you know this?"

Garrett gave a sheepish grin. "The wet dress was practically transparent, so I noticed that one when she walked past me."

"Ah, *oui.* It is always a man's duty to check out a woman's ass if it is presented."

"Exactly," Garrett agreed. "But the really freaky part was, on top of all this other stuff, half of her right hand is missing. She lost it in a motorcycle accident."

"*Mon dieu!*"

"Yeah, exactly. And, of course, Dylan goes from being terrified to being fascinated in about fifteen seconds and invites her to stay for breakfast."

Henri laughed. "So, did she behave herself at breakfast?"

"Oh, yeah…sure. She was very nice, in fact. She's from Kentucky, and she's got this strong Southern accent."

"Mmm." Henri smacked his lips appreciatively. "Two very sexy things, *oui?* An American woman speaking French with the American accent, and a woman from the southern United States saying anything at all."

Garrett didn't respond. He shifted in his seat, uncomfortable with the ideas of Tara and sexy being linked.

Henri dabbed the sides of his mouth with a napkin-swathed finger. "I see you brood all morning and now I have to wonder why an unexpected breakfast with a-little-wild-yet-nice woman would make you do that?"

Garrett twirled the demitasse spoon between his thumb and index finger. "She made me uncomfortable."

"But you said she was very nice." Henri's bottom lip protruded in the quintessential French pout. Garrett had noticed Dylan doing the same thing lately.

"Oh, I don't think she's dangerous or anything…"

Henri pressed him more. "Then what is it about this woman that bothers you?"

"I don't know." Garrett was beginning to wish he hadn't brought up this morning's escapade. He'd only meant to entertain his friend with the story, and now Henri was trying to turn it into some deep analysis that Garrett was in no mood for. No doubt, the woman had dug up some buried emotions, but it was better to leave them in that dark hole within his psyche.

"Then you are in luck, my friend. I am the world's greatest expert on…" Henri gave a vague nod in the direction of a middle-aged brunette wearing a power suit with a one-button jacket and, by all appearances, nothing underneath. "A-little-wild-yet-nice women—this new neighbor reminds you of Angela, *oui?*"

"No, not really." Garrett shifted his gaze away from Henri's knowing smirk. "Maybe a little..."

"Mais...?"

"When Angela went off her meds, there was no telling what she might do. She might disappear for hours with no hint of where she was and come home with a new piercing or another tattoo." Garrett tossed the spoon on the table. "And once, after Dylan was born, when she wouldn't take her meds and was swinging from one extreme to the other, she dyed her hair a hideous shade of pink."

Every time he thought he was over his pity and his anger toward his wife, something would happen and those emotions would wash over him, drenching him and making him feel just as exposed as Tara had been in that damn transparent dress. He picked up the spoon again so he could have something to squeeze and transfer the emotion to.

"Many women have colored hair and piercings and tattoos, Garrett." Henri checked his reflection in his own spoon and adjusted his tie. "This woman. This..."

"Tara. Tara O'Malley."

Henri leaned forward again, peering closely at Garrett. "This Tara O'Malley is not Angela."

"But she's obviously got some of the same idiosyncrasies."

Henri's face broke into a wide grin. "You like her."

Garrett saw where this was going. "Don't. Don't even start with all your matchmaking nonsense. Even if I liked her, which I don't, at least not like you're thinking…she's only here for a month. I don't want Dylan getting attached to anyone who's just going to leave."

"Pfft!" Henri waved away his argument. "You have already picked up on something within her that attracts you." He wagged his finger "And *you* don't want to get attached to her, either."

Garrett opened his mouth to stretch away the tightness in his jaw. "You're such a damn know-it-all, Henri. But you're wrong this time. I'm not worried about getting attached to that freakin' woman. She's not my type." He ran his hand through his hair. "The thing is, despite all my efforts to be everything he needs, Dylan misses having a mom. He's vulnerable with women. I sure as hell don't want anybody who's just passing through—be it Tara O'Malley or someone else—to get close to my son. He doesn't need another major loss in his life."

Snap!

Garrett opened his hand and sheepishly dropped on the table two pieces of metal that *had* been a demitasse spoon.

"We will charge that to the company, *oui?*" Henri calmly adjusted his starched cuffs until the perfect amount showed from below the sleeve of his suit coat. "A spoon that is broken can be quickly replaced. The heart that is broken requires a longer time."

MOTHER NATURE PROVIDED Tara with the perfect excuse to give in to the jet lag and slightly delay both her exploration of Paris and her search for Jacques Martin. She napped the rainy day away until late afternoon gave way to clear skies at last.

Calls were made to her family and Emma to let them know she'd arrived safely. They'd all been entertained by her tale of the morning's adventure. And they'd all mentioned how typical it was for her to have such a strange thing happen, as weirdness seemed to keep her in its sights—but she'd only shared with Emma the splendid details of Garrett's atypical nude appearance.

Need for sustenance finally prodded her out to rue du Parc Royal in search of a market, but not before she double-checked to make sure the key to her flat was in her possession. With no Garrett or Dylan in tow, it was doubtful that Madame LeClerc would give up the extra key a second time without requiring a pound of flesh as a deposit.

The third *arrondissement*, part of the area commonly known as le Marais, was every bit as charming and quaint as Josh had described. Narrow, cobblestone streets were lined with small, yet elegant boutiques and art galleries. Cafés occupied nearly every corner, and entire blocks were taken up by sprawling apartment buildings, whose ancient courtyards were protected by electronically locked wrought-iron gates that allowed spectacular views but no access.

Cars parked willy-nilly along the curb—and some

up on the uneven stone walkways—gave the area a delightfully chaotic touch. Pedestrian traffic was heavy, and since the sidewalks were too narrow to accommodate two people passing, most people walked in the streets, stepping aside to let the occasional automobile by while dodging the plethora of bicycles.

A market turned up just two blocks from her building, but she passed it by for the chance to explore a bit longer with empty arms. A few more blocks brought her to a wide avenue—boulevard Beaumarchais—with one specialty food shop after another lining its sidewalks.

A variety of savory sausages hanging in the window of the *charcuterie* made her mouth water, enticing her to give it a go.

"Bonjour, mademoiselle," the elderly butcher called as soon as the bell heralded her entrance.

"Bonjour," she answered, to which he immediately replied something she didn't understand. *"Je voudrais..."* She didn't know the word for sausage, so she simply pointed to the kind she wanted in the case.

He smiled. "English?"

"Oui. Yes." She gave a grateful nod.

He pulled the sausage from the case and cut off a small piece for her to try. The bite filled her mouth with a salty, savory burst that begged for a chardonnay to wash it down. Her accompanying "Mmm" brought a proud smile to the butcher's lips.

"Is very good, *oui?"*

"It's delicious. I can't wait to have a glass of wine with it."

"But of course." Obviously, the wine was a given. "How much would you like?"

"A quarter pound?"

His eyebrows drew in. "No pounds in France. Kilos."

Tara cringed. *Kilos?* She had no idea. "Um…" She hesitated.

The butcher picked up on her distress. "How many people?"

"One. Just me."

He tilted his head and gave her a glance as if sizing her up. "No, *mademoiselle*. You are too beautiful to eat alone. This is Paris!" He gave a dramatic sweep of his arm toward the street. "Find someone to share."

Tara's cheeks warmed. She'd already laundered the borrowed clothes and had thought about inviting Garrett and Dylan over for a light meal to repay their hospitality when she returned his things—having bought too much food for just her would be the perfect excuse.

The butcher's mouth turned up in a knowing grin. "Ah, I see you have someone in your thoughts. *Bien*." Using his knife as an appendage, he pointed to where he thought the cut should be made. "Enough for two, *oui?*"

"Actually, three." Tara held up three fingers. "But one is a little boy with a big appetite."

He laughed pleasantly and moved the knife over a couple more inches before making the cut and wrapping the portion in the quintessential white paper. He insisted she try some of the fresh pâté, which was exquisite, and she bought some of that also.

Before she left, he gave specific instructions on what to pair the purchases with. "Serve with *le fromage,* the honey, *une baguette, les cornichons* and, of course, *le vin.* If you do this, you will never eat alone."

She thanked him and left the shop feeling as if she'd made a new friend. He'd given her advice on where to find the best of everything on his list, even pointing out the specific shops that were his personal favorites, so those were her next few stops.

Everyone who waited on her immediately switched to English as soon as she started trying to speak French. Josh had told her that just the effort on her part would be appreciated, and that seemed to hold true. The Parisians, it appeared, would rather speak English than hear their beautiful language butchered by her American tongue.

The two cloth totes provided with the apartment filled up quickly with the butcher's suggestions and the fresh produce from the open-air market. After tasting the samples, she couldn't pass up the tender asparagus spears or even the turnips, which she would never have considered serving raw at home.

She had to rein in her sweet tooth at the *pâtisserie* with its shelves crammed with decadent, scrumptious-looking pastries. She escaped with only three items by promising herself she could have one treat each day.

Who was she kidding? Everything she ate for the next month was sure to be a treat. Like the butcher said, this was Paris!

She purchased a small bouquet of daisies from a wizened old woman who stood on the street corner with two pails of flowers—they would be perfect for what she had planned. And two bottles of wine—one white and one red—from the wine shop filled her second tote to the top, giving her arms as much weight as they could bear for the walk home.

Once she moved away from the wide avenue, the side streets all looked the same. Twice she lost her bearings and had to backtrack to the park with the rose garden surrounding the statue of the man on the horse, but eventually she found her way back to the apartment building and surly Madame LeClerc.

This time, Tara would follow her dad's lifelong advice to win over the enemy with love. She held out the bouquet of daisies and said the little speech she'd looked up in the phrase book and memorized before she left to go shopping. *"Bonjour, madame. Merci beaucoup pour votre aide ce matin."*

The woman looked stunned, her eyes moving from Tara's face to the daisies and back. For an uncomfortable moment, Tara thought she was going to refuse them. But then, the woman's demeanor changed.

She smiled a smile so sweet, Tara would've thought it impossible a few minutes before.

"Merci, mademoiselle." Madame LeClerc's voice shook a little as she spoke. *"Merci beaucoup."* She lifted the flowers to her nose for a quick sniff as she buzzed Tara through.

Thanks, Dad.

The thought closed her throat as she headed up the stairs. She hoped her mom and dad had worked out their problems. Oh, they'd tried to act as if everything was okay when she and Thea and Trenton were around. But there was a heaviness that pervaded the atmosphere around them, as if the elephant in the room was sitting on everyone's chest. How long would it take until someone from the church took notice? If Sue Marsden got the slightest whiff of the juicy tale that lay within her grasp, she would burn up the telephone lines.

Tara unlocked her door and entered her flat, her shoulders now heavy with guilt. She tried to distract herself by putting her purchases away. It was too late for regrets. She was here to find her birth father, and she was prepared to face any ramifications that may come.

Her good friend Summer Delaney had once talked to her about the ripple effect—how every action is like a rock thrown into the pond of our lives. The first ripple causes a second, then a third. They multiply and spread, yet they're all connected at the source. And there's no stopping any of them.

Her mom and Jacques Martin had thrown a rock into the water one night, and twenty-eight years later, the ripples just kept coming.

She poured herself a glass of wine. Grabbing her laptop, her handheld GPS and the phone book from the apartment, she headed out to the terrace to kick off the official search for the stranger who gave her life.

CHAPTER SIX

"HI, TARA!"

Dylan sprinted across the terrace, a baseball glove clutched to his chest and a delighted grin on his face. When he came to an abrupt stop beside the table she was working on, Tara saw the ball nestled in the glove.

"Hi, Dylan. Have you been playing ball?"

"Not yet. My dad's not home."

An uneasiness gripped Tara's insides. "Do you stay home alone?"

Dylan shook his head. "Monique stays with me."

Ah, there's a Monique. Why she was surprised—maybe even a tad disappointed—by the news that her sexy neighbor had a woman in his life? He hadn't mentioned anyone that morning, but she should've figured a guy like him would be attached...on some level.

Right then, a petite young woman—maybe even a teenager—stepped onto the terrace. Her glossy black hair was pulled into a high ponytail and she had a cell phone to her ear.

"That's her." Dylan waved.

The woman spotted him and gave an answering wave, then went back inside.

"She talks on the phone a lot to Philippe. They're going to get married soon."

Tara scolded herself for the little flutter that news caused. "So Monique is your babysitter?"

"Yeah." His attention made an abrupt swerve to the small GPS device she held. "Whatcha doing?"

"Well." Getting into personal details wouldn't be prudent, but the child's curiosity was natural. "I may have some family in Paris. So, I'm looking up names in the phone book, then I'm using the laptop to map where that address is, and then I'm putting the address in my GPS to get directions in case I decide to visit…um, that location."

"Cool! Can I see?"

She handed over the small device and watched the child's unabashed wonder as he examined it thoroughly. The kids at the summer camp where she'd been a counselor had the same reaction, and that memory gave her an idea. "Have you ever been geocaching?"

Dylan shook his head. "What's that?"

"Here. I'll show you." She logged into the geocaching website she was a member of and typed *Paris* into the search box. A list, several pages long, appeared instantly. She pointed to a few of the items. "Each of these gives a description and the location of something that's been cached—that means hidden—here in Paris. But the location is given in latitude and longitude." When Dylan's bottom lip protruded in thought, she reminded herself he was only six. Precocious, but still only six. "Those are just numbers like addresses. Anyway, you put those numbers into the GPS, and it leads you to the thing that's hidden."

"Like a real treasure?" The child's jade eyes glowed with excitement.

"It's sort of a treasure—a small one, though. Usually, it's a little box with various items inside, and a notepad and pen. You get to choose an item to keep, and you leave behind one of your own. Once you sign and date the notepad to prove you were there, you hide it back where you found it."

"I want to do that! I want to go geochashtering!"

"Geocaching," she corrected. "And maybe we'll go sometime if it's okay with your dad."

"Can we go tonight? Right now?"

Tara chuckled at the child's enthusiasm. "No. We have to wait for your dad to say it's okay. Plus, he'd probably need to go with us, too, since I don't know my way around very well."

"He has to work late tonight, but he said he'd be home in time to play some pitch-and-catch, so maybe we can go when he gets home." The boy's exuberance had taken over his mouth, which was moving a mile a minute.

Tara held up her hand to slow him down. "Tonight's probably not a good night, Dylan. Your dad will be tired after working late, and y'all will have to eat."

"What's y'all mean?"

"You all. All of you, or in your case, both of you. But what I'm saying is, we can't go tonight, but we'll definitely try to go sometime while I'm here…if it's okay with your dad. Deal?"

"Deal." The glum look only stalled his face for a few seconds. "You want to play some catch?" He held up his ball and glove.

It was plain that she wasn't going to get much more done tonight. Besides, she'd been at her research for over two hours and was ready to stand up and move. "Sure. Do you have a glove I can use?"

"You can use Dad's." Dylan laid his gear on the chair and headed back to his flat in a run while Tara gathered her material and deposited it on the coffee table in her living room.

By the time she got back outside, the child had returned. He handed her a ball and a worn glove. "Will it hurt your hand to throw?"

What a sweetie—showing concern for her hand. Tara picked up the ball with her two fingers and thumb and wiggled it in front of his nose. "It will give me a mean curveball, I think."

His face relaxed in a grin, and he backed away a few feet and took his stance.

The man's glove swallowed her left hand. "Ready? Here it comes," she warned Dylan, and tossed the ball lightly.

He caught it easily and tossed it back. "You need to wind up." It was clear by his tone that he'd meant what he said to be an admonishment—he was not to be thought of as some wimpy, little kid.

Tara blew the dust off her high school softball career and wound up like a pro for the second pitch. She didn't let loose a fastball, but still threw one hard enough to bring a gleeful laugh from her opponent when he found the ball once again lodged in his glove. Dylan wound up and threw it back with surprising force for a kid his age.

"You've got a good arm, buddy."

His eyes gleamed with pleasure. "My dad says I've got his arm. He used to play in the minors."

Tara tucked away that interesting tidbit for conversation with Garrett later. "Well, no wonder you're good. It's in your genes."

Dylan's mouth drooped at the corners, and he pointed to his cotton shorts. "I'm not wearing jeans."

Tara laughed as she threw the ball back to him. The child's mastery of the language made her forget he was only six. "Not the kind of jeans you wear. The things you inherit…um, you get from your parents. That kind of genes."

"Oh, like my eyes. Dad says I got my mommy's eyes."

His words caught in Tara's chest, making her next breath heavier than the last. "Well, she must've had beautiful eyes. They're very handsome on you." She coughed to clear away the sudden congestion in her throat. Which of her own physical characteristics came from Jacques Martin? Eyes? Height? Build? She would have an answer soon perhaps.

Dylan's next pitch went a little wild, and she had to chase it down. When she got back into place, she moved the conversation to a less emotional common ground. "So, tell me about your school. Where do you go?"

"I attend *L'école primaire publique ave Maria.*" He was obviously enthused about the subject because for the next hour of pitch-and-catch, with frequent breaks, Dylan educated Tara on the French education system.

She learned that students only attended school four days a week, with Wednesdays as well as weekends off. But school days were long, lasting from eight-thirty to four-thirty.

This was the last week of school, and then Dylan would be on summer break for the months of July and August. Monique would be staying with him most days. And some days, he would go to Pierre's house. Pierre was his best friend and a baseball enthusiast, also.

During their game of catch, Monique came out to check on him occasionally. "She doesn't like to play catch," Dylan explained. "I usually just throw the ball against the wall until Dad comes home."

"What time is that?" It was already past seven-thirty, so Garrett was putting in a really long day.

"He's working late this week, but he'll be home

by eight." The words were hardly out of his mouth before a deep voice brought their game to a halt.

"Dylan!" As if their conversation had transported him to the spot, Garrett stood in the doorway of their flat. The sport coat and tie he'd worn at breakfast were gone, and his white dress shirt and khaki pants accentuated the broad shoulders and narrow waist of his athletic form.

An image of his naked torso flashed across Tara's brain, and she felt her face heat in reaction.

"Hey, Dad." Dylan ran to meet him with a hug, which Garrett greeted with a smile.

But, as she headed his way, Tara watched the facial expression transform into a scowl when Garrett's eyes shifted up to meet hers.

DAMN IT! GARRETT cursed his own shortsightedness. He should've told Monique not to allow Dylan to bother Tara. But he'd been so absorbed with work when she called to tell him they were home, he hadn't given it a thought.

A quick glance at the happiness on his son's face told him an attachment was already forming...and it was easy to see why.

The woman headed toward him held little resemblance to the freaky one he'd had breakfast with this morning. The wet yellow dress was gone, replaced by a pair of cream-colored shorts that showed off a set of long and toned legs. A peach T-shirt was the perfect complement to her fair complexion. No makeup disguised the adorable smattering of freckles that dotted her cheeks and nose. Had those even been there this morning? And what about the pierced eyebrow? Oh, yeah, there it was…. Her red curls—and a few of the blue ones—curved softly around her face and neck.

The entire effect was light and feminine, and Garrett fought down a wild urge to search among the curls for the tattoo nestled under her ear…with his mouth.

"Tara's a good catch, Dad."

The words stunned Garrett speechless for a couple of seconds, by which point she was already upon him.

Caution dimmed her bright eyes as she gave him a tentative smile. "We were just playing around some. I hope that's okay."

Garrett gathered his composure and shoved his sexual awareness to a deeper, safer place in his psyche. He took the glove she held out, searching for the appropriate words that wouldn't sound overly harsh in front of the boy. "Dylan shouldn't be interrupting your private time."

Her wariness gave way to a relieved smile. "He didn't interrupt anything. I had a good time." She held up what remained of her right hand, stretching the fingers apart. "It was good therapy—mentally and physically."

Garrett's spine stiffened at her words. If she

needed mental therapy, she needed to get it from someone other than Dylan.

Her thumb caught her middle finger, leaving her index finger pointed to the sky. "Oh, be right back." She turned and jogged across the terrace to her flat.

Garrett had no idea what she was up to, but he used the time to get Dylan out of hearing distance. "You need to go get washed up for dinner."

"Can we invite Tara to eat with us?"

Oh, hell. The entreaty in Dylan's eyes solidified that Garrett's fears were justified. He squatted down to eye level with his son—time for some damage control. "No, bud. Tara didn't come to Paris to visit with us. She's only going to be here for a month, which isn't really too long, so we need to leave her alone, and let her do what she wants with her time."

Dylan's bottom lip protruded in advance of his protest. "But—"

"No buts. You're not to bother Tara. Understand?"

Dylan sighed. "Yeah." He dropped his glove and ball inside the door and slunk off toward the bathroom, looking like a whipped puppy.

Garrett watched him until the bathroom door closed. When he turned back, Tara was headed toward him from across the terrace. He stepped out to meet her, sliding the door closed behind him.

The clothes he'd loaned her this morning were arranged in a neatly folded bundle, which she held out to him. "I figured out the washer and dryer, so these are clean."

Garrett took them from her. "Thanks. You didn't have to do that."

She slid her hands into her back pockets, which stretched her shirt tighter across her breasts. "Well, y'all didn't have to help me out this morning, but I sure did appreciate it. I…um…" She cleared her throat and tossed her head in the direction of her place, flashing the tattoo under her ear in Garrett's direction. "I picked up some sausage and cheese and wine and a few nice pastries. I plan to have a light supper on the terrace, and I was wondering if you and Dylan would like to join me? Give me a chance to pay you back for breakfast?"

Her accent coupled with the expressive, vivid green eyes battered at Garrett's resolve, but the cautious voice inside him whispered its repeated warning about getting too friendly. "It's nice of you to offer, but I don't think we'd better. I work long hours, so dinnertime is special for Dylan and me. *Alone* time, you know?"

"Oh, sure." A deep blush crept up her neck into her face. "I should've thought of that."

The disappointment in her voice was palpable, but the first snip was made, and Garrett was determined to stop any more buds of friendship before they blossomed. "Well, there isn't a lot of privacy around here, so we'll try to respect yours as much as possible while you're here." A movement from the corner of his eye told him Dylan was headed back toward them. Garrett laid his hand on the door handle.

"I'm sure you'll do the same for us," he added before sliding the door open and stepping back through it.

His escape wasn't quick enough to keep him from catching the hurt look in Tara's eyes—the same look that was reflected in his son's eyes when he met them.

"Now, how about some dinner?" Garrett clapped his hands together in a fake show of enthusiasm.

Dylan shrugged, looking like lead weights were attached to his shoulder. "I'm not very hungry."

Garrett's gut twisted at the words.

But they also told him without a doubt he'd done the right thing.

CHAPTER SEVEN

FAITH PUSHED THE beige dress to one side, and studied the next one carefully—a sleeveless shift in a pretty shade of mint green that Sawyer had always liked on her. But, like everything else in her closet, it was modestly cut and gave no hint that the creature clothed in it had a clue that such a thing as sex existed.

Just once, she'd love to wear a dress that was a little provocative…that showed a little cleavage or more of her back than was strictly proper. Nothing vulgar. Just something feminine and sexy. Something that would remind her…and Sawyer…who she was at her center. The way God made her before the congregation of Taylor's Grove Church had molded her into who it wanted her to be.

The green dress was her best option for tonight, though.

Changing out of her white slacks and navy blue knit top into the new pink lace and satin bra and panties gave her a rush as if she was doing something scandalous…and fun. She paused to look in the mirror and evaluate the effect. A subtle attack was what she was going for. Just a touch of sexiness that would spur Sawyer on if she got him to the stage where he wanted to undress her.

The idea came to her after prayer group this morning. She'd never had to seduce her husband before, so shopping for sexy underwear this afternoon with that motive had been venturing into foreign territory.

Until four weeks ago, Sawyer had pursued her with a vigor that sometimes made her question all the jokes about middle age. She'd counted herself blessed to have someone who'd always made her feel attractive and desired despite the frumpy clothes and the weight gain that had crept up on her in her forties. They both understood that the preacher's wife had to be appropriately dressed at all times. They'd accepted that fact and had made ultimate use of their private time. And when all the kids finally moved out, she and Sawyer had had plenty of…how did the younger generation put it? *Bow-chicka-wow-wow?*

Well, this *chicka* was going to try her darnedest to coax the *wow-wow* out of the *bow* tonight.

She swiped on just a touch of foundation, and a light application of mascara defined her lashes. The salesperson had assured her that the pink lip gloss would make her lips irresistible. It looked like any other pink lip gloss, but maybe the extra price indicated it had some esoteric qualities perceived only by men. If the manufacturer truly wanted to make it irresistible, it would've been bacon-flavored.

A quick brush-through to fluff her hair, a squirt

of cologne and a pair of beaded flip-flops finished the look that she hoped was casual yet sassy.

Back in the kitchen, the timer indicated it was time to put the cornbread in to bake alongside the meatloaf. The green beans were done, tomatoes sliced, and ears of fresh corn were buttered, wrapped in waxed paper and ready to be popped into the microwave.

New sexy underwear. Sawyer's favorite dress. His favorite meal. Fresh strawberries waited in a bowl on the counter, but she hoped she would be his dessert of choice.

Her heart skipped a beat when she heard the door open.

"Hey," he said as he entered the room.

She watched his eyes skim over her. "Hey," she answered, trying to keep it casual. "Supper's almost ready. You hungry?"

"Famished." He paused, and she saw his Adam's apple bob in his throat. "You, uh...you look pretty."

That's a start. Don't scare him away. "Thanks." She started the corn cooking in the microwave and pointed to the plate of tomatoes. "I was out in the garden—you can put those on the table—and I got sweaty and itchy. I had to take a shower to cool off. By tomorrow, we should have a nice mess of okra."

The light came on in his eyes—the one she hadn't seen in far too long—as it dawned on him that tonight she wasn't going to try to talk about their problems. She watched the transformation as his shoulders relaxed and the lines disappeared from between his eyebrows. With an easy, compatible fluidity, they fell into their routine of her dishing up the food and him setting the table, and for the first time since Memorial Day, her hopes ran high that perhaps the dry spell was over.

After supper, she set the second part of her plan into action. "Let's walk down to the park. Are you up for that?"

His hand hovered motionless for a moment before he placed the dish into the dishwasher. "Yeah. Sure. If you want."

Faith's pulse quickened. That he was willing to face the park together was a positive sign. She adjusted the strap of her new bra and smiled to herself.

Sawyer wiped off the countertops while she swept, and when the kitchen was clean, they started their stroll to the park at the center of town.

They'd managed to stay under the radar because, since Tara's accident, their park visits had become more sporadic rather than a daily occurrence. One or the other of them would show up a few times each week, armed with plausible excuses about the other's absence. Tonight's two-minute walk was a journey of a thousand miles as it was the first time they'd made it together since the Memorial Day Faith would never forget.

The park, which had no other official name because it was the only one in town, was the official gathering spot for the whole community. On any given night, you could catch up on the happenings of the day within a ten-minute period.

It was the park where everyone came after weddings to celebrate, after funerals to mourn and after births to pass out cigars and roses.

It was the park where Sawyer had proposed to her in the gazebo under the stars after everyone had gone home for the night.

It was the park where Tara had taken her first step in an endeavor to join the children playing on the swings.

The park at the center of town was the center of the town's life. The heart of Taylor's Grove.

As they approached, the sweet strains of "Gentle Annie" being played by Ollie Perkins on his violin met Faith's ears, and the poignant tune encouraged her to slip her hand into Sawyer's and pull him in the old man's direction. He didn't protest. While macular degeneration was doing its best to steal away the last vestiges of Ollie's sight, his ability to make the violin sing seemed to increase in an indirect proportion to what he lost. His renditions of Stephen Foster tunes could squeeze a tear from the devil himself.

Bobo Hudson vacated his seat beside Ollie and motioned for Faith to sit down. She could hardly refuse, but felt the sting of disappointment when she had to let go of Sawyer's hand.

Ollie finished his song. "Ev'nin', Faith." He turned his head slightly and nodded in her direction.

"How'd you know it was me?"

The disease had wiped out Ollie's central vision almost completely, but left a bit of the peripheral. He wiped his forehead with his trademark red bandanna. "I recognized your cologne."

She patted his knee affectionately. "You gonna play my favorite?"

She always requested "Shenandoah," and he always obliged, but, this time, he shook his head and tucked the bandanna between his chin and the chin-rest on his instrument. "Nope, not yet, anyway. Got something different tonight. I was thinking today about Tara, and how she'd always ask for something Irish she could dance a jig to. Well, since she's in *Paree,* I thought we might just join her there, in-stead."

Faith cringed inwardly and cut her eyes to Saw-yer, who blanched at Ollie's words as "Pigalle" rolled off the strings. The subject of Tara's being in Paris still cut Sawyer to the quick. He barely lasted until the song was over, then hurried away to join a small knot of men who always discussed the county's poli-tics while they refereed the checker game between Johnny Bob Luther and Kimble Sparr. Faith, how-ever, was stuck in Ollie's audience for a while longer.

She tried not to despair…hoped the mood of the evening hadn't been spoiled completely by Ollie's innocent comment.

When Al and Mary Jenkins walked up, Faith gave up her seat to them and found her way back to her husband's side. He and Tank Wallis were discussing how badly the crumbling steps on the front of the church needed repair. The project had been at the top of Sawyer's list for months now, but he couldn't get the maintenance committee, which Tank was the chairman of, to get off dead center with it.

"Some of those cracks are getting so big, it's just a matter of time before somebody catches a toe in one and breaks a hip," Sawyer declared.

"I hear you, Preacher, but it's not time to fix them until Sue says it's time."

The mention of Sue's name reminded Faith of their little verbal skirmish that morning, and with it came a flicker of irritation. The woman's power over the church, over the town and, yes, over Sawyer, was sickening.

Sue hadn't earned that power. Her daddy, Burl Yager, was the one who sold a huge tract of land on Kentucky Lake to a developer. And it was Burl who built the Taylor's Grove Church out of that money and set up the trust fund that paid for the upkeep of the building, as well as the preacher's salary. Burl had been a fine man who loved the church and wanted it to thrive.

When Sawyer, as a teen, had surprised everyone in town by accepting God's call to become a minister, it was Burl who'd paid for his college and seminary study. But, when Burl died, Sue had inherited everything, except his benevolence. The church had tried to circumvent her ways by forming committees. But that had done little good. Sue held the purse strings.

"I'll talk to Sue again," Sawyer said, but his tone indicated he doubted that would do any good.

A chuckle rolled out of Tank's big belly. "Maybe you ought to send Faith this time." The big guy gave her a knowing wink. "Word from the prayer group says it's one to nothing in Faith's favor."

Sawyer sent her a questioning glance. He hadn't heard yet. Good. At least she could give him her side first.

She smiled and rolled her eyes. "No scorekeeping in Taylor's Grove. We're all playing for the same team." Turning her attention to Sawyer, she added, "Strawberries are going to get mushy if we don't get back and eat them pretty soon."

He nodded. "Can't let that happen. See you tomorrow, Tank." He patted his friend's shoulder in parting. They crossed Yager Circle and headed down Main Street before he finally asked, "So are you going to tell me what happened at prayer group?"

She dreaded bringing up the subject of Tara's trip, and related the incident to him as innocuously as possible, stressing Sue's general displeasure of Tara's nature.

Just as she'd hoped, his eyes flashed anger at Sue's snide comments, but his guarded chuckle about her own retort came with a warning. "You know she's not going to let you have the last word."

"I don't care." Which wasn't exactly the truth. She *did* care…too much. About Sue's opinion, and everybody else's in this antiquated fishbowl of a town.

She and Sawyer turned up their driveway, bypassing the front door and going around to the patio doors in the back. "I just get so tired of her holier-than-thou attitude."

"You know better than to let Sue get to you." Sawyer opened the door, letting her pass through first, then followed her in. "She means well."

The irritation that started with the mention of Sue's name flickered higher. "You always take up for her."

"I just try to understand where she's coming from." He got two bowls from the cabinet and set them on the kitchen counter.

Faith clutched his arm, and pulled him around to look at her. "How about me? Have you tried to understand where I'm coming from?"

His look lasted a long moment, his lips pressed together in a thin line. "We're not talking about prayer group anymore, are we?"

"We're talking about the fact that you haven't touched me for nearly a month. Are you even trying to understand?"

The cloak of sadness that had been absent in his eyes during supper dropped back into place. "Faith, I can't—"

"Can't or won't?" Emotion sent a tremor through her body. "Why *can't* you understand? Why won't you *let* yourself understand?" She reached behind her and jerked the zipper of the shift down. "I love you." She pushed the dress off her shoulders and arms, exposing her breasts clad in pink. The dress caught on her hips. She hooked it with her thumbs and shoved it free to pool around her ankles. "You always forgive Sue. I want you to forgive me. I want you to want me." She stepped into him, sliding her arms around his waist, plastering her body against his.

His hands found her shoulders, and he pushed her gently away to hold her at arm's length. "I want that, too, Faith. I pray for that every night." He let go of her, his arms dropping like heavy weights to his side. "But, it's not happening. My prayers get clogged by other thoughts like, what if I lose Tara completely? What if she finds Jacques Martin and chooses him over me?"

"That's not going to happen, Sawyer."

"It could happen. The man was able to lure *you* away from me." He turned his gaze away from her toward the back window. "Oh, I know it was only one night and alcohol was involved. I get that. But your night with him caused a major change in us. It changed the way you relate to me. I tell myself that he gave us Tara…and she's so precious to me…but what if finding him changes the way she relates to me?"

Faith stayed quiet. She would let him talk and get it all out. Surely, that could only help.

He wiped a hand down his face, leaving a glistening dampness below his eyes, and turned back to her. "And every night I try to talk myself into going to you in our room." He looked her up and down, his face contorted with anguish. "You're a beautiful, vibrant woman, Faith."

She stepped into him again, pleading with her eyes. "Then do it. Make love to me. Please."

The anguish settled into a look of despair. "I can't." He took her hand and moved it slowly to his groin.

It was a familiar gesture, but it took on a surreal quality as her hand groped for something that wasn't there. Nothing. No detection of even the first stirring of an erection. The bulge she'd expected was instead a small mass as soft and pliable as putty.

His whisper was coarse and strangled. "I. Can't."

He released her hand, and she stepped away from him quickly. Her eyes blurred as she leaned over to gather her dress, snatching it up and making a dash for the bedroom.

She slammed the door and locked it behind her, then collapsed against it onto the floor as the wave of understanding washed over her.

Sawyer—the only man she'd ever loved—couldn't get an erection for her.

He didn't want her.

And maybe never would again.

TARA SAT AT the café in the shadow of the Eiffel Tower, still ogling the beauty of Paris's quintessential landmark while practicing her lines. The addresses of forty-three Jacques Martins were programmed into her GPS, and, though she was aware of the challenge she faced linguistically, she was armed emotionally for whatever happened. Or so she hoped.

Garrett Hughes's stuffy behavior last night had been good practice, reminding her that first impressions weren't always reliable. What a surprise he'd turned out to be—and not the pleasant kind. She'd been looking forward to some occasional American conversation while she was here, and yeah, maybe a little casual flirting, as well. But the guy had turned out to be a contrary curmudgeon who obviously resented her staking a claim to part of the terrace that he used like it was his sole dominion.

Well, he could go piss up a rope. She'd paid the rent for a month, and that gave her terrace privileges. Much as she liked the apartment, she wasn't going to spend all her time inside when she could be taking her meals and her books outdoors.

Besides, Dylan was a delight. He made her feel at home. And from where she was sitting at the moment, looking out over a park that could very likely hold a huge chunk of Taylor's Grove, it was obvious she wasn't at home anymore.

She signed the receipt the waiter brought and picked up her things. The GPS dangled from her wrist, where she could check it often. She punched up the set of coordinates for the maybe-father closest to the Eiffel Tower and began her first search, following the map toward the blinking dot. It was just like the geocaching she'd explained to Dylan yesterday, but with what could be a priceless treasure as the find rather than a box of trinkets.

The exquisite beauty of the city with its wide, tree-lined avenues and perfectly proportioned balances of lines and curves, man-made and natural, tempted Tara to forget the hunt and give in to the desire to explore. But her mind kept running ahead to her destination, and her heart pumped fast to keep up.

The map guided her around the final turn to a street filled with small boutiques rather than homes. The internet search had yielded all addresses—business and residential—that had a Jacques Martin linked to it, but she was surprised nonetheless…and maybe a little relieved…to see that the first address was that of a shop. Walking into a store was easier than ringing a private doorbell.

She stopped outside the address and took several deep breaths before pushing the door open and stepping inside. The strong, pervasive scent of formaldehyde greeted her from the bolts of materials hanging from chains, which covered the walls in brocades, damasks and linens. Her eyes and nose started to water simultaneously. The reaction was familiar, and her memory scampered back to hours she'd spent in fabric stores with Grandma O'Malley. She'd had the forethought to bring tissues in case the reunion with her father involved tears…of any kind.

She snatched one from her pocket and dabbed, trying not to smear her carefully applied mascara.

Several customers milled about, eyeing the rich

colors in the woven tapestries, running their palms over the nap to change the shading of the velvet. Tara ran her fingertips across a bolt of deep brown fabric—its hue reminded her of Garrett's eyes.

Jerk, she reminded herself.

Soon, an elderly woman with silver hair pulled back into a severe bun turned her attention to Tara. A head-to-foot scan pinched her expression into a condescending sneer. *"Bonjour, mademoiselle."*

"Bonjour, madame." Tara's eyes jerked involuntarily to the door—yes, it was still there—before settling back on the woman. *"Je m'appelle Tara O'Malley. Je cherche Jacques Martin. Est-il ici?"*

A short pause allowed the woman time to exchange her sneer for a knowing smirk. *"Oui. Un instant."*

She disappeared into a back room, giving Tara time to become all-too-aware of the sound of her pulse *swishing* through her ears.

The woman appeared again, followed by a striking, middle-aged man in an impeccably cut gray suit that set off his salt-and-pepper hair, which was combed back and heavily gelled.

His age looked promising, and Tara's breath stopped as she scanned his face for a trace of anything familial and stalled on his mouth. It was wide like hers, and it curved upward into a smile as he approached.

"Bonjour, mademoiselle." His deep voice was

pleasant and welcoming, and she felt her courage bolstered at the sound.

"Bonjour, Monsieur Martin?" He nodded and Tara extended her hand, pumping it a tad too enthusiastically when he took it. *"Je m'appelle* Tara O'Malley. I…uh…" She caught her breath before plunging into the script she had memorized. *"Je viens des États-Unis, et je cherche un ami de ma famille. Il s'appelle Jacques Martin. Il habitait à* Murray, Kentucky." A family friend who had lived in Murray, Kentucky had seemed like the most nonthreatening approach. She watched him closely for a reaction.

The man's gray eyes held a hint of disappointment as his smile thinned. *"Ah, ce n'est pas moi. Je suis désolé."*

Tara swallowed her own disappointment, becoming aware of the way his thumb caressed her hand, which he still held, not even seeming to notice the missing digits. Obviously, they were coming at this conversation from very different angles.

She pulled her hand, but he gripped it tighter and leaned in to whisper something. She didn't understand the words, but his tone took on a smooth and oily quality like his hair. His mouth curved again into a leer that drove the scene past extreme *ick* and into dimensions all its own.

Tara jerked her hand from his, mortified at the turn things had taken. *"Au revoir, monsieur."* She didn't say thank you or try to ask her other memorized questions about whether he knew any other

Jacques Martins she could contact. All she could think about was getting to the door and into fresh air. Once outside, the shudder that passed through her could've rocked a seismic score on the Richter scale as she allowed herself to express it verbally with a loud "eww!"

She took off at a fast walk, not even stopping to get her bearings for a couple of blocks. When she did, she was in front of Rodin's studio and museum—the perfect place to get her mind off of her creepy encounter with Jacques Martin number one.

The garden was especially inviting, quiet and relatively uncrowded compared to the area around the Eiffel Tower. She spent the entire afternoon in the shadow of *Balzac* and *The Thinker,* taking pictures of the statues and attaching them to text messages to family and friends.

Emma called as Tara boarded the metro late in the afternoon to head back home. She reacted with the proper "eww" as Tara related her tale of the first Jacques, and when she heard about Garrett Hughes's request for privacy, she replied with "What a jerk!"

As she had so often in their years together, Tara reminded herself how fortunate she was to have a best friend who viewed the world with a similar enough perspective to her own to make them compatible, yet still different enough to keep their conversations interesting.

Back at her flat, Tara poured a glass of wine and took it and her journal out to the terrace to write about the experiences of her day—another of Emma's suggestions to help her work through the emotion of her search for her birth father.

She'd thought the idea a little silly at first, but as she started to chronicle not only her emotions but her impressions as a first-time visitor to Paris, her hand flew across the pages, filling up one after another. She was especially surprised at the depth of disappointment today's encounter churned up. But plenty more addresses remained to be searched.

"Hi, Tara."

She looked up to see Dylan standing a few feet away, ball and glove in hand.

"Hi, Dylan. How are you today?"

"I'm fine." He stayed awkwardly planted to his spot. "What are you doing?"

She held up the book she'd been writing in. "I went to the Eiffel Tower and the Musée Rodin today, so I've been writing in my journal about those places. Have you ever been to the Musée Rodin?"

"Yeah, lots of times."

She patted the empty seat beside her. "Come tell me what you like best about it."

He hesitated for only a second, then hurried to plop down in the proffered seat. "Dad says I'm not supposed to bother you, but I don't guess I'm bothering you if you invite me. Isn't that right?"

Tara smiled at the child's honesty. "That's right. If I invite you, it means I want some company."

The warmth in Dylan's smile thawed the icy coating that had surrounded Tara's heart as she wrote her review of today's father search.

"What I like best about the Musée Rodin is the ice cream," he answered her original question. "But the statue I like best is *The Burghers of Calais*."

"That was my favorite, too!" Tara was intrigued that she and the six-year-old were both taken by the same piece out of all the choices. "Why do you like that one best?"

"Because my dad told me the story about those guys being heroes. They're not superheroes like Iron Man and Thor, but they saved a lot of people, so I like them."

"Yeah, me, too…for the same reason." Tara made a mental note to include this delightful conversation in her journal. "Is your dad home yet?"

Dylan shook his head. "He has to work late again tonight."

"Well, I wouldn't mind playing a little catch if you'd like."

Dylan shot out of his chair. "Cool! I'll get Dad's glove for you."

They played for almost an hour, but as it neared the time when Garrett had gotten home the night before, Tara thought about what the man had asked of her.

"Whew! I'm getting tired, Dylan." She faked it a little, but not too much. "I think I'd better call it a night and go grab a bite of supper."

"Okay."

She handed the glove back to him and ruffled her

hand through his hair. "Thanks for playing with me. It was fun."

"Maybe we can play again tomorrow," he said and then hurried to add, "if I don't bother you."

"Maybe."

She gathered up her things and went inside as Dylan continued his game by throwing the ball against the wall by his terrace door.

Tara heated some soup and fixed a salad for a light meal. When she sat down at the table, she saw that Garrett had gotten home and was on the terrace playing catch with his indefatigable son.

The guy may be a jerk, but he was obviously doing something right. Dylan seemed well-adjusted and was a delight to be around.

Maybe giving them their private terrace time wasn't such a big deal. She could sacrifice a little.

The Burghers of Calais had been willing to sacrifice everything for the people they loved.

Watching Garrett play with his son—a single dad in a foreign country, a young man who lost his wife—it struck her that Rodin could have immortalized him, as well.

And she'd seen him naked.

Definitely statueworthy.

CHAPTER EIGHT

HENRI'S NOSTRILS FLARED as the coffee cup neared his nose. "Ahh!" He closed his eyes and breathed deeply, a look of something akin to ecstasy relaxing his features. "Is there a more delicious scent in the morning than freshly ground coffee?" He paused, and a wicked gleam lit his eyes. "*Peut-être* a freshly ground woman, *oui?*"

Garrett shrugged. "It's been so long since I've had a woman in the morning, I'm not sure my grinder would even work."

A uniquely French sound came from the back of Henri's throat. It combined humor, dismay and a touch of disdain, and Garrett had never been able to come close to mimicking it, though Dylan already had it perfected. "How are you and your American neighbor getting along?" The Frenchman took his first sip and smiled appreciatively. "You have not mentioned the wild woman in several days."

Garrett tried to take a sip, but the coffee in his cup was still too hot. "I haven't spoken to her since…" Since the day he'd been abrupt with her about giving him and Dylan their privacy…the day she'd looked so stung by his words. Occasionally, he'd see her wander out onto the terrace, but it was always a glimpse through the window. She never came out if he was outside. "For several days," he finished his answer.

"You share a terrace and, for several days, you do not speak with her?"

Coupled with the guilt he was feeling about the whole Tara matter, the question irritated Garrett more than it should. "I told you before, I don't want her around Dylan."

"But Dylan goes to bed, does he not? There is much time to share a bottle of wine after he is asleep."

His friend knew him all too well. Last night, Garrett had started to do just that. After Dylan was asleep, he'd put on a Miles Davis CD and opened a bottle of an exquisite 2007 cabernet that begged to be shared.

Tara was out on the terrace with her own bottle, and she wasn't reading or writing in that book the way she usually did. She was simply sitting alone with her wine, illumined by the soft lights of the night around her, looking lovely and serene. Garrett had actually taken several steps toward the door before his own words had stopped him. *"There isn't a lot of privacy around here, so we'll try to respect yours as much as possible while you're here."*

Approaching her during her private time would be opening a can of worms, and would, of course, require an apology for his previous rudeness to her. Probably best to leave well enough alone.

But she'd been tempting.

Garrett raised his chin as a warning that he was tired of talking about this. "My wine and I did just fine all by ourselves. So, what do you have for me this morning?" He glided into another subject before Henri could make him feel worse. "Have the numbers stabilized enough for me to order my Ferrari?"

Henri handed him the morning's report. "No Ferraris yet, but someday soon, *peut-être.*"

While Garrett was certainly interested in the entire report, he couldn't keep his eyes from searching out the bottom of the right-hand column first. When he did, his heart skipped a beat, and he felt like skipping along with it. An 8 percent jump in sales in twenty-four hours.

Convincing the higher powers that the marginal analysis leaned toward a successful flighting strategy had been a bitch, but worth every penny they'd spent.

Of course, it was too soon to tell how deeply Soulard had penetrated the beer market, but the GPRs were promising. "Do you have the disaggregations yet?"

Henri's sigh implied that answering that question was beneath him. "They are printing now. Go drink your coffee—which is now too cold to be palatable, but your American tongue will probably not notice— and I will bring them to you."

Garrett went back to his office to wait for his friend, but he was too anxious to sit. He paced back and forth, allowing the numbers on the paper to absorb into his brain. Such detail so quickly was beyond his comprehension. He'd worked with plenty of IT specialists, but Henri Poulin was by far the best of the best. The man was a virtual magician with a computer, and he had a sixth sense for anticipating what information would be needed. More often than not, he and his staff had reports generated before they were even called for.

The man would be an asset to any company. Soulard Beer had simply managed to land him first.

As promised, Henri appeared within a few minutes, report in one hand, fresh coffee in the other. "*Voilà*. The market profile is much as you anticipated…with a pleasant surprise in the over-fifty range, *oui?*"

Garrett shook his head in astonishment at the number his right thumb hovered beside. A fluke mention of Soulard—thanks to a friend of a friend of one of the owners—during a television show watched mainly by an older crowd had sent sales soaring, though whether it was truly a penetrated market or a one-time thing only time would tell. But Garrett was hopeful.

"We're out there, Henri. We're really out there."

His friend nodded in agreement. "So tonight, instead of the wine, which you did not share, you share the champagne with your American neighbor, *oui?*"

The mention of Tara brought another surge of guilt and frustration, heightened by Garrett's already overstimulated emotional state this morning. "Damn it, would you let that subject go?"

Tsk. Tsk. Henri clicked his tongue. "I hear you whine often that you miss your home. And yet, when the opportunity arises for you to enjoy the company of a young woman who is not only from your home but is also your nearest neighbor, you do not extend friendship to her."

The arch of his eyebrow made Garrett doubt that *friendship* was Henri's first choice of what he should extend in Tara's direction. But his friend's words hit their intended mark. "Just one more reason I don't need to be around her," he grumbled. "She'll only make me more homesick."

Henri found his reflection in the window glass and adjusted his tie. "The Americans always refer to the French as 'stuffy,' and yet you snub someone for no good reason and act like it is nothing." He shifted his gaze to bore directly into Garrett's. "You are the stuffy one."

Garrett held his tongue and grabbed his coffee cup instead. He took a giant swig, and a thought hit his chest simultaneously with the brew.

He and the coffee had a lot in common.

Both were cold and bitter.

TARA POISED HER pen above the name. Instead of the dark red line that crossed off six Jacques Martins from her list, beside number seven she drew a red star.

He hadn't been her birth father, but he was one she wanted to remember, nonetheless.

Four days, seven prospects and no results that had moved her any closer to her goal. She knew it wasn't going to be easy, but she didn't know it was going to be this hard. Ringing doorbells, walking into shops, trying to converse with strangers in a language she had no grasp of. She was exhausted, and if her search took her all the way to the final name and she would have to go through this thirty-six more times, she wasn't sure her heart could take the battering.

The crowds at Paris's popular sites sometimes made her feel as though the air was being pressed from her lungs, so today she'd opted to get out of the city. Number seven lived in Giverny. She'd always wanted to see Monet's house and garden, so, although she'd much rather have been on a motorcycle with the wind whipping her hair, she'd caught the train to Vernon instead. A three-mile walk from there to the village of Giverny had brought her to the small, quaint cottage of number seven, and her breath had stuttered with hope at the sight.

A neighbor out in the yard next door had called to her—an old woman with kind eyes who spoke no English. But she knew the name Jacques Martin, and her eyes had filled with tears. She took Tara's half hand, caressing it gently while cooing words with sympathetic, grandmotherly sounds, and led her to the small cemetery at the end of the lane.

She pointed out a new grave—not fresh, but newer than those surrounding it—and left Tara with a parting pat on her back.

According to his tombstone, the birthdate of Giverny's Jacques Martin was May 27, 1942, which made him too old to be the man her mother had slept with. But Tara's heart squeezed just the same for the loss of this man she never knew. A plethora of bouquets said he was much loved, and fresher ones—even recent ones—said he was still missed.

She'd felt compelled to leave some of her own, so after touring Monet's gardens and house, she'd sought out a flower shop, and bought two small bouquets of daisies. One she'd left on the grave of Jacques Martin number seven, and one she'd left with his kind old neighbor who'd cried a tearful thanks.

Now, sitting on her terrace, chronicling the day's events in her journal, she felt mired up in melancholy. She needed some fun.

Dylan was throwing a ball against the wall beside their door. True to his word, he'd waved when he came out, but he hadn't come over, hadn't bothered her in the least.

"Hey, Dylan." She closed her journal and put away her pens. "Want a glass of Orangina?"

The boy's grin lifted her spirits faster than the shopping spree she'd been considering—and was definitely cheaper.

"Sure!" He sprinted over to her, dropping his ball and glove into a chair. "It's hot today." He wiped his sweaty face on his sleeve.

"Yeah," she agreed. "Almost too hot to play ball."

The boy answered with a vigorous shake of his head. "It's never too hot to play ball."

"Well, you sit here and catch your breath, and I'll go fix us a cool drink."

She left him at the table, but when she returned a couple of minutes later with the drinks, he was standing in the middle of the terrace with his babysitter, who was on the phone, crying and obviously frantic.

Tara's first thought was of Garrett. Had something happened to him? She rushed to Dylan's side. "What is it? What's wrong?"

Dylan's look was one of concern but he wasn't distraught, and Tara's heart slowed a tad as he took one of the lidded cups from her. "Thanks." He took a deep draw on the straw.

Keeping an ear to the conversation, he translated the blur of words for Tara. "Something's wrong with Monique's father. They've taken him to the hospital. That's her mom on the phone. She wants her to come to the hospital right now, but Monique doesn't want to take me."

"Tell her to go. You can stay with me until your dad gets home."

Dylan grabbed Monique's arm to get her attention and pointed to Tara. His words were too fast for Tara to pick up anything, but Monique's look of surprise and relief told her the message had been received. The babysitter nodded and spoke into the phone again briefly before hanging up and turning her attention to Tara. "Monsieur Hughes—"

"Garrett won't mind, I'm sure," Tara said. "Dylan will be fine with me, won't you, Dylan?"

Dylan spoke in French to Monique first. "I told her we're good friends," he said to Tara.

Tara wasn't sure if Monique understood English, so she shifted her gaze from the young woman to Dylan as she spoke. "I'll tell Garrett what happened. You just go on and be with your father."

"Thank you. Thank you very much." Monique's English was perfect. "I will call Monsieur Hughes later when I know more of my father's condition. My mother does not handle the crisis very well."

She ran to the door, stopping for a last look. "Oh, and Monsieur Hughes has an important meeting and will not be home until around nine-thirty. The dinner for Dylan is in the refrigerator. His bedtime is nine o'clock." She gave a quick wave before disappearing.

Tara checked her watch. It was only six-twenty, so she and her new charge had a few hours to fill. "Want to play some catch after all?"

"Can we go to the park instead? Monique and I go there a lot. It's close. Just down the street."

Tara wasn't sure which park he was referring to. There were several nearby. "Are you sure that would be okay with your dad?"

His eyes grew big, opening a window to his soul as he nodded. The look was too cute to be anything but honest. "It's okay as long as I have an adult with me."

Tara caved quickly. "Well, okay, then. But you'll

have to lead the way because I still don't know my way around the neighborhood very well."

"I know how to get there. We go there all the time. It's easy." The child slipped his hand into hers, catching her two fingers in his grip. His brow buckled with concern. "Does that hurt?"

"Nope. Just don't squeeze hard," she warned him.

His grasp was firm, but easy, as he led the way through their apartment. "Your hand feels weird. It's little. My dad's hands are great big."

Tara remembered Garrett's big hands. More than once during her nap after their first encounter, she'd fantasized about how big and warm those hands might feel on her naked back. But that was before he'd been a jerk. Since then, she'd banished such thoughts…or, at least, most of them.

Dylan guided her easily through the labyrinth of corridors to the ancient wooden door at the back of their building.

Le Parc Royal was just at the end of the block. As soon as they arrived, some children called Dylan by name, and he dropped Tara's hand to go join them in their game of what appeared to be freeze tag.

Tara found a spot on a bench close by and watched, fascinated. Dylan seemed to be popular and well accepted by the group. He had an obvious kind streak—staying close to the younger or slower children so they didn't have to stay frozen out of the game long.

His poor mother…missing out on all this. What

a privilege it was to be able to sit here and watch him. An emotion stirred deep in Tara's chest that hit several vulnerable areas at once. Being a mother someday was her highest hope. Kids were one of the greatest treasures of life. But to have that treasure and then lose it? Her hand trembled as she pushed a curl out of her eye. Did Jacques Martin feel the same way? Would he be sorry he'd missed out on her childhood?

She shook away the melancholy that threatened for the second time that day and glanced at her hand, her constant reminder of the blessing of life.

"Boo!"

She jumped and let out a little squeal, which brought a hoot from Dylan, who'd sneaked up beside her.

"Are you hungry?"

She took his hint. "I *am* hungry. Shall we go eat supper?"

He cocked his head. "Is that another word for dinner?"

"Sort of. Supper's a light meal at night, like lunch is a light meal during the day," she explained. "Dinner's a big meal either time."

He thought about that for a moment. "I think I want dinner."

"Dinner it is."

He took the hand she extended without question, and they strolled home at a leisurely pace. Dylan must have decided it was time for her to learn the

French language properly because, for the rest of the evening—through eating the shish kebabs Garrett had left to be grilled until she tucked him into bed—he pointed to things and drilled her on the correct word, insisting on proper pronunciation. By the time he fell asleep, she figured her French vocabulary had doubled.

Barely a week past the summer solstice, a hint of sun still lit the evening sky even though the clock read 9:33 p.m. Tara had just stepped out onto the terrace to enjoy the last remnants of sunset when she heard the *snick* of Garrett's key in the lock. She hurried back in to greet him.

He had a broad smile when he stepped through the door, which vanished the instant he saw her. "Tara? What are you doing here?"

The panic in his voice spurred her to the important matter first. "Dylan's fine. He's already asleep. Have you spoken with Monique?"

"No. I just got out of a long meeting." Panic had been replaced by disapproval. He dropped his keys and briefcase on the desk. "What's going on?"

Tara's hackles rose at his tone. She clipped out her response as if she were answering a police interrogation. "She got a call from her mom that her dad had been rushed to the hospital, and she needed to get there right away. She was upset and crying, so I told her to go on, and I stayed with Dylan."

"He's okay?" He stepped lightly over to his son's door and peeped in.

"He's fine." Her voice dropped to a normal level as her neck muscles loosened. "We went to the park, and he played really hard. Then we came back and grilled the shish kebabs you had fixed, and I threw a salad together. It was a lovely meal, which we topped off by sharing one of your bold cabernets. Dylan chose it," she taunted, keeping a straight face.

Garrett's eyes widened just like she'd seen Dylan's do so many times. "You let Dylan—" He stopped when her grin broke, and he gave her the first real smile she'd ever received from him. Her toes curled in reaction. "You're kidding, right?"

"Yeah. I had my own cabernet, and he had Orangina."

"You could've opened one of mine. I wouldn't have—" He was interrupted by his cell phone. *"Allô? C'est Garrett."* He paused. *"Oui, Monique..."*

Tara watched the easy manner they'd briefly reached a few moments before dissolve as Garrett spoke to the babysitter. His voice held sympathy, but Tara could also see a milder form of the panic settle into the crease between his brows. It may have been her imagination, but the scar that cut into his lip seemed to have deepened by the time the call ended.

"How's Monique's father?" she asked.

Garrett rubbed his brow. "Not well. It's his heart. They're talking about open-heart surgery, but they're trying to decide if he's strong enough to take it."

"Oh, the poor girl. She said her mom didn't handle crisis well, so she's got her hands full." Thinking about her dad, Sawyer, in the same situation caused her chest to tighten. "I assume Monique's going to need some time off? I sure would."

Garrett nodded absently. "At least a week, probably."

"What will you do with Dylan?"

"There's an after-school program until six. He hates staying for it, but we have to use it occasionally."

"But you haven't been getting home until later than that," she reminded him, immediately regretting doing so when he squeezed the bridge of his nose in frustration.

"Yes, well, normally, I could be off by then, but we've got this media blitz for another three days, so we're having to keep late hours."

"I'll keep him for you." The words came out before her brain fully processed the ramifications of what she was suggesting.

Garrett's head jerked toward her, and she got the feeling he'd forgotten she was there. "No. I couldn't ask you to do that."

"You didn't ask. I volunteered."

His hands went to his hips, and she saw his fingers tighten their hold. "I really appreciate what you did tonight, stepping in and taking care of him. I'm grateful. Really. But I don't think it's a good idea for you to be around Dylan too much."

That comment pushed her too far. Just what in the hell was he implying? "Look, Garrett, I don't know what your problem is with me." She realized her voice had risen. She lowered it to a whisper as she moved away from the child's door, and continued to spit out the words. "I'm a schoolteacher. Kids are my life. I love them, and I'm very good with them. Now, you can stick Dylan in that after-school program, which he hates, if you think that would be better than spending the time with me. But Dylan and I get along well. We genuinely *like* each other. So if you come to your senses and change your mind, you know where to find me."

She charged onto the terrace and crossed to her flat without looking back. Once at her place, she headed straight for the shower, where she could stand in the steam and let the hot spray beat away the day's frustration.

When she got out and dried off, she felt better—more relaxed—but still too wired to go to bed. She left her hair up in the clip and slipped into some loose cargo pants and a camisole, intending to plot out her Jacques Martin search for tomorrow.

She'd just gotten settled on the couch when she was startled by a soft knock on the sliding door that led to the terrace.

It could only be one of two people, and Dylan had been asleep for over an hour.

She looked out. Sure enough, it was Garrett. She slid the door open, but before she could speak, he held up a bottle of champagne and two glasses.

"I'm sorry. I've been rude to you and have been

a terrible neighbor. I'd like to start over." He tilted his head toward the table on his side of the terrace. "Will you forgive me and join me for a drink? I just realized I have a lot to celebrate tonight."

CHAPTER NINE

"DOES THIS MEAN you've changed your mind about my keeping Dylan?" With her arms crossed firmly across her chest, Tara's green-eyed stare bored into Garrett, steady and unflinching—the quintessential teacher look.

Hell, he might as well confess everything. Her look had him convinced she'd find out anyway. "Yeah. I…um…I called Josh Essex after you left. He says you're a great teacher. Honest. Trustworthy. Always concerned about what's best for the kids."

His confession didn't relax her stance even the slightest. Her eyes tightened at the corners, and she tilted her head in question. "What else did he say?"

He gave a sheepish grin. "He said you have a lot of energy, and everybody wants you on their committees because you're willing to do most of the work."

She dropped her arms and her protective wall at last, answering his grin with one of her own and stepping out on the terrace to join him. "Okay, then. I get to babysit Dylan, so I have something to celebrate, as well."

Garrett pointed across the way, where he already had some candles lit on his table to drive away mos-

quitoes. "Is it okay with you if we sit over there…
in case he wakes up?" He hoped the candles didn't
look too presumptuous…or romantic.

"Sure." She nodded and turned to slide her door
closed. A gentle night breeze caught some of the curls
that had worked loose from the clip in the back of her
hair. They stirred around her face, and his fingers
twitched with an unsettling urge to brush them back
and linger for a moment in their softness.

He shifted his gaze from the enticing curls, only
to have it land on the tattoo below her ear. It looked
different in the moonlight, like an exotic jewel em-
bedded into her long, elegant neck at one of the tenderest areas. He imagined following the intricate
design with the tip of his tongue…her warm breath
quickening in response against his naked shoulder.

"Are we…waiting for something?"

Her question slapped him out of his inappropriate reverie. "No. I, uh, was just noticing the…" He
wiggled his finger toward the area that had held him
spellbound. "The, uh, tattoo on your neck. It must've
hurt like hell."

"Not really." She held up her hand. "Compared to
losing two fingers, it was a picnic."

"I'm sure. Well…" He gestured toward his table.
"Après vous."

"So, what are you celebrating?" She gave him a
sidelong glance as they crossed the imaginary line
to his section of the common space. "Other than the
fact that you came to your senses, I mean."

Josh had warned him the woman was known for not mincing words. He set the bottle and the glasses on the table and pulled the chair out for her to sit down, then began removing the foil from around the cork. "I think I told you before that I'm the head of marketing for Soulard Beer?" She nodded. "Well, we're in the middle of a media campaign. I don't want to jinx anything by talking too much about it, but suffice it to say that it appears the campaign has passed all our expectations." A small *pop* punctuated his words.

Tara rose to her feet again in overstated ceremony. He filled the two glasses she held out, then he took one and, continuing the drama, held it aloft. "Here's to Soulard Beer and the venture of your choice. May our successes continue to grow in direct correlation to our friendship."

"To Soulard, new friendships and successful ventures," she answered.

They clicked their glasses together and sipped. The candlelight heightened the color of the liquid to amber and cast a golden glow across Tara's face that was quite bewitching. Pleasant warmth from the shared toast and the fine drink bloomed in his chest making him happy he'd invited her to join him.

They sat, and Tara held her glass out again. "Here's to Dylan, one of the cutest, sweetest, most lovable kids I've had the pleasure of knowing."

Her words caused the muscles in Garrett's throat to constrict, making it difficult for the second sip of champagne to pass. "Tara…" Getting too personal would be a mistake, but she deserved to know where he was coming from in regards his son. "I need to explain my concerns about Dylan, so you don't think I'm a total asswipe."

"*Jerk* was my epithet of choice."

He let that mull in his mind as he swirled his glass, causing a tempest of bubbles to rise to the top. "Okay." He took another sip. "We'll go with jerk."

Tara settled back in her chair, stretching her long legs out in front of her as if preparing to hear a lengthy story.

He took a deep breath. Where to start? "It wasn't so much you personally, as much as…well, how certain things about you remind me of my wife."

"Oh…really?" Tara straightened, brows knitting in concern. "Is there a resemblance? Is that why Dylan took so quickly to me?"

"No, no, it's not like that. Angela was short, black haired, dark complexioned." Garrett wiped his hand down his face. Hell, he needed to just say it. He took another sip, hoping the bubbles would lighten the weight in his chest. "She was bipolar."

Tara's brows shot up. "Oh."

"When she took her medication, she was fine." He continued. "The problem was that she didn't like to take the medication. She said it repressed who she really was. During her pregnancy and then after Dylan was born, she went without it more and more often, and her mood swings flitted from one extreme to another. She could go from the most manic high to the most depressed low in a matter of hours. When I came home from work, I never knew if the woman who met me would be the same one who was there when I left or someone totally different."

Tara sat her glass down gently and leaned forward to clasp her hands on the table. "And what exactly is it about me that reminds you of her? I mean, you really don't even know me."

"I know. But when Angie would get on one of her highs, she would do things on the spur of the moment. She'd come home with a piercing or a tattoo." He waved his hand in her direction. "She had lots of them...said the pain made her feel real and alive."

While he talked, Tara had been listening intently, brushing a finger lightly up and down on her lips. She now used that finger to make figures in the air as if she were adding up some kind of imaginary math problem. "So, since that first day, it's been in your head that I might be mentally unstable because I have a few tattoos and a couple of piercings?"

"Well..." When she put it that way, his logic did sound a little weak. "You also admitted to the motorcycle wreck that cost you part of your hand...and your gorgeous red hair has blue streaks in it. Angie would do wild things like that to her hair, too."

Tara started like he'd pinched her, and Garrett grunted in frustration. He wasn't explaining himself very well and was probably pissing her off, beating around the bush with his dance of avoidance. "Oh, hell." He downed the remainder of his glass. Grabbing the bottle, he topped off Tara's glass and refilled his own. "I know I'm silly. I know that not everyone who has piercings and tattoos and blue hair is crazy like Angie. I know you're not crazy. And if I thought you were, Josh pretty well squelched that."

The side of Tara's mouth lifted in a half smile. "I grew up in a small town as the preacher's kid, and I was always held to a higher standard. I followed the rules and never got into trouble. But as an adult, I realized I'd never learned to express myself. I have a reason for all of these." She gestured to the ring in her eyebrow and the tattoo under her ear. "Play nice and maybe someday I'll tell you what they are."

It had to be the champagne because something about her words shot straight to Garrett's groin, causing a stiffness that made him shift uncomfortably in his seat. He shoved the idea of playing nicely with Tara from his mind. "I guess we all have our reasons for doing the things we do. And my objections to your being around Dylan go back to Angie. He lost his mom when he was three, and he has a definite soft spot for women." He was in too deep to turn around now, so he laid it all out. "I got involved with my French tutor when we first moved here. Big mistake. Dylan latched on to her, and it was really tough on the little guy when we broke up. Ever since, I've been trying like hell to protect him from getting too attached to someone who's only going to vanish from his life."

"Oh, Garrett." Tara dropped against the back of her chair, throwing her arms into the air. "I understand now. You're afraid Dylan will see me every day for a month, and then I'll be gone." Her finger settled on her lip again, brushing back and forth.

Garrett shifted in his seat again, wishing she'd stop calling attention to her luscious lips. "Exactly." His voice was hoarse, and he cleared his throat.

"But there have to be other women in Dylan's life that he's attached to. Teachers? Grandmothers? How do you handle other situations?"

"Teachers he'll see occasionally even after he's left their classes. We call my mom and Angie's mom a lot, usually a couple of times a week."

She tipped her glass his direction. "If that works, then we have our answer. Even after I go home, I'll be as close as a phone call. Dylan can call me whenever he wants to, and I'll take his calls as long as he needs to make them. But I have a feeling he won't need them too long. People have a way of forgetting. Out of sight, out of mind, you know?" A shadow crossed her face, and Garrett got the feeling she wasn't just referring to Dylan, but he didn't press her about it. Whatever it was, it was none of his business.

That she understood and was taking his concern for his son so seriously filled him with gratitude. "You seem to know Dylan pretty well. Have you been spending time together I haven't been aware of?"

Tara's smile was gentle...and disarming. "We play catch almost every night before you get home."

"THAT'S TROUBLESOME." A growl of displeasure underscored his voice. "I gave him strict orders not to bother you. It's not like him to disobey. At least, I didn't *think* it was like him to disobey."

Tara hadn't meant to get her little friend in trouble. "Relax, Dad." She leaned across the table, laying a hand of reassurance on Garrett's. "He told me from the beginning that he wasn't supposed to bother me. He only comes over to my section if he's invited. And playing catch is usually my idea."

Garrett chuckled and turned his hand over to grasp hers. "So you're telling me you and my son have been having clandestine meetings for...?"

"About a week now." She filled in the blank.

He laughed and shook his head. "And here I thought I was keeping him safely out of your clutches."

He gave her fingers a light squeeze. It felt nice, and she squeezed back before letting go. "I'm the one caught in the clutches, I'm afraid. Dylan's a heart stealer."

Pride bloomed on his face. "Yeah, he's pretty special."

The second glass of champagne was making them bold, adding warmth to the conversation, convincing her she could get away with more than what would normally be proper. "Garrett, if you don't mind my asking—and you don't have to talk about it if you don't want to…"

"Suicide," he answered.

Tara recoiled at the word spoken so matter-of-factly, though the tense set of Garrett's jaw and the shadow that veiled his eyes belied a deep pain within.

His response hadn't been what she expected. *Cancer. A horrible accident.* Those she'd been prepared for. But suicide? How did one respond to that? "I'm—I'm sorry," she faltered. "I shouldn't have brought it up."

"It's okay." Garrett downed the remainder of his champagne in one gulp. He reached for the bottle. His hand hovered near it momentarily before he drew it back. "The coroner declared it an accident. She was texting and smashed her car into a tree. But there were no skid marks. No sign of any braking at all." His eyes found a faraway point to focus on—one from three years ago, if she were guessing. "The text was for me. It said, 'I hate you.'"

The icy words sent a shiver down Tara's spine despite the lingering heat of the evening. "That's horrible." Garrett's Adam's apple bobbed in agreement. "No," she corrected herself. "It's cruel. No one should have to live with something like that hanging over his head."

His gaze jerked back, crashing headlong into hers, and this time the pain wasn't hidden. It oozed from him like a sore that had lost its protective scab. "We don't get a choice in the matter, do we?"

"No. No, we don't." Emma had used those same words when they'd talked about the bizarre twist of Sawyer not being Tara's birth father. Her brain spun in circles, searching for a topic she could switch to. Anything that would shift them from this sad conversation. But how could she do that tactfully and without seeming callous?

"She got it in her head I was having an affair."

He didn't wait for any prompting, so obviously he wanted—maybe needed—to talk about this. Tara took a large gulp of champagne to dull her senses.

"I worried about leaving Dylan at home alone with her, but I had to work, so I hired a woman— a housekeeper to clean and cook, but mostly just to be there to keep an eye on things. I never even gave her a second look, but Angie was convinced we had a thing for each other." His hand mopped his face again, and he blew out a long breath. "The night she died, she flew into a rage because I'd given Sally a Christmas bonus that Angie thought was too much. The truth was, Sally was threatening to quit at the first of the year because Angie was getting so hard to deal with, so I'd hoped the extra money would be an incentive to stay on."

He paused and Tara stayed quiet, willing to let him have the floor as long as he wanted it.

"Sally left," he continued, "and I went to Dylan's room to check on him. Angie grabbed the keys and took off before I could stop her. I called the police. They said she hadn't committed a crime, but they'd keep an eye out. Thirty minutes later, I got the text and then a few minutes after that, I got the call from the police. She died on impact." He shrugged slowly as if a heavy barbell lay across his shoulders, or maybe the weight of the world. "End of story."

Tara rolled her shoulders forward and back to loosen the muscles, which had tightened considerably during his tale. She waited to see if he had anything else he wanted to add. When he didn't, she eased the subject in a different direction. "You and Dylan have been through a lot…and you've done a wonderful job of raising him alone."

The compliment brought a tender smile to Garrett's lips. "Thanks, but I can't take all the credit. Dylan probably learned early on to adapt to any situation. He's one of those kids who's easy to be with."

"I couldn't agree more. He's a very kind little boy." She filled him in on the details of Dylan's actions, which she'd observed at the park. As she'd seen so many times during parent-teacher conferences, Garrett's whole demeanor changed when she told him complimentary things about his child. Even parents who came in loaded for bear about a bad grade would calm down and leave with a smile when she told them what a great kid they had. The best part was that she didn't have to fake it. All of them were great kids to her. She didn't always like how they acted, but she always liked *them*.

She shared how touched she was by Dylan's actions toward her. "He doesn't mind holding my hand, but he's cautious and doesn't want to hurt it."

"I didn't mind holding your hand a few minutes ago, either." Garrett's mouth twisted up at the corner. "Fact is, it felt pretty nice."

So the man *was* capable of flirting after all! The heat started in her back and worked its way into her neck and face. She held up her half hand. "It used to feel twice as nice."

Garrett laughed at that. Reaching for the bottle once again, he filled her glass, then emptied the bottle into his own. "This evening took much too serious a turn. Weren't we supposed to be celebrating?"

"Yes, we were. And you also need to fill me in on Dylan's schedule so I'll know what time to be where."

He stood up. "Be right back."

He was gone for a couple of minutes. When he returned, he handed her a sheet of paper. "Dylan's schedule. My friend Henri designed a spreadsheet for me."

She glanced down the entries, which included not only Dylan's school schedule but also his Wednesday schedule, Garrett's numbers and an array of other numbers. The man was nothing if not efficient— and so was his friend. "We haven't discussed it, but I'd like to keep Dylan until Monique is able to come back. Not just tomorrow. If that's all right with you."

Garrett gave his head an emphatic shake. "That's too long, Tara. You're only here for a month. I can't take an entire week of your time. And this is the last week of school. Next week, he'll be around all day."

At that moment, being with Dylan seemed more important than finding Jacques Martin, and she wasn't sure exactly why. It had to do with the privilege of being with him that she'd felt that afternoon while watching him play. Now that she knew the story of his mother's death, she had a fierce instinct to let him know he was worth every second of her time. And Jacques Martin wouldn't be going anywhere other than where he'd been for twenty-eight years. She could pick up the search for him when Monique got back, even if it wasn't for a couple weeks.

She tilted her glass in Garrett's direction. "Even all day will be fine. I've got lots of sightseeing to do. If it's okay with you, he can be my tour guide. I'm going to spend a day at the Louvre, and one at the Musée d'Orsay. And I also want to go to Notre-Dame and Sainte-Chapelle."

"He loves all those places." Garrett grew quiet for a moment, and when he spoke, his voice was steeped in gratitude—and sexy as all get-out. "You're sure you don't mind?"

"I'm sure. I told him I'd take him geocaching if you were okay with it. We can do that while we're exploring the city."

Garrett's heavy brows gathered in question, so she delved into more detail about the pastime. He leaned toward her, hanging on her every word just like Dylan had done when she explained it to him.

"Hell!" He slapped the table lightly. "That even sounds like fun to me!"

Was he asking for an invitation? She ventured out to test the waters. "Then, maybe some evening we can all search for a cache together."

"I'd like that. I'd like that very much." A look came into his dark eyes that was part fun but part something else entirely, and a tingle that couldn't be attributed to the champagne zinged through her. Their gazes locked for a few seconds, charging the air between them with electricity.

They teetered at the edge of something momentarily before Garrett backed off. "So...tell me about the town you grew up in."

"You want to hear stories about Taylor's Grove?"

He grinned. "Actually, I just like to hear you talk."

"Well, if talking's what you want, I'm the girl for the job. When I go to talking, my mouth runs like the clatter bone of a goose's ass."

Garrett's laugh was deep and mellow, bringing a certain heat to the air around her that made her want to hear it again.

For the next half hour, Tara enthralled him with stories about life in her corner of small-town America. She told only the comedies, the things that would keep them laughing, staying away from the dramas that infused life in Taylor's Grove as surely as they did everywhere else—of which her own family was solid proof.

The champagne and camaraderie had finally

worked its magic. Her muscles, which had been so tight before, were loose and relaxed, and she tried ineffectually to stifle a yawn that popped out unbidden. "Oh, wow, I'm getting sleepy."

Garrett looked at his watch. "Yeah, it's way past my bedtime, too. And I've got another long day tomorrow."

They stood up slowly...and reluctantly on Tara's part.

"I hate for nights like this to end." Garrett echoed her thoughts.

"Me, too. But we can pick up where we left off tomorrow night."

"I'd like that." Garrett's tone was husky again. He paused as if he was on the verge of saying something else, but then he picked up the glasses and the bottle. "Thanks for sharing my celebration and volunteering to keep Dylan."

"It's my pleasure." She started toward her flat, feeling Garrett's eyes on her, following her progress across the space they shared. When she got to her door, she turned to look back.

Sure enough, he hadn't moved. "Good night," he called.

She blew an impetuous, giddy kiss in response.

CHAPTER TEN

GARRETT FELT HIMSELF crashing. If the Soulard big-wigs didn't finish their speeches and toasts soon, he was going to fall face-first into the remains of his chocolate soufflé. The rich meal and the magnums of champagne made it impossible to comprehend all that was being said, and he was exhausted enough not to give a damn.

He wanted to be home with Dylan, and…okay, yes, with Tara. The two of them had barely scratched the surface the other night getting to know each other, and there was so much more he wanted to know. But for the third night in a row, he wasn't going to make it home before midnight—too late for any real inter-action, which was probably just as well. The more he was around Tara, the more he liked her, and lik-ing her too much would be dangerous territory for him and Dylan.

He took a sip of water to clear the fog from his brain. Thank God tonight was the end of the cam-paign and the outrageous hours.

Things weren't supposed to have been this hec-tic, but he could hardly complain. The day after his and Tara's celebration, one of the television programs—sort of a French version of *Entertainment Tonight*—had requested an interview with the company's owners, so the marketing department had been thrown into extra-double duty to write fresh, snazzy new lines that would make the owners look cool and hip for the young audience.

The interview had been taped this evening and then the entire company had gone to Le Pample-mousse for an exquisite celebratory seven-course meal that had gone on for five hours and twenty-two minutes, but was almost over.

Tara had been so understanding about all of this, though how he would ever repay her was still up in the air. She acted miffed every time he brought up the subject of money.

The speaker's words faded as his imagination took over with some totally inappropriate things he could offer to make her stay in Paris more enjoyable for them both.

That his mind shouldn't drive on that side of the road was a no-brainer. His life was complicated enough without adding a fling with a neighbor into the mix. But the woman had wormed her way into his consciousness and parked her fine ass there—*not* thinking about her was impossible. An instant, full-blown erection made him shift in his seat, which woke him up just in time to stand and join in the cheer of what he could only hope was the final damn toast.

It was. Everyone around him hugged and said their

adieus and made their French-equivalent promises to show up for work Monday *bright eyed and bushy tailed.* It was a good thing the weekend lay before them because they were going to have one hell of a collective hangover.

"Garrett!" Henri hurried from his table, and they clasped in a hug of camaraderie. *"C'est fini."*

"Oui, c'est fini, Henri." Garrett wasn't sure if they were discussing the campaign or the dinner, but he was thrilled both were done.

They hadn't chatted in days. Not since he and Tara had made their peace. A power outage Wednesday had sent Henri and his staff into panic mode and put them behind with the all-important reports everyone was expecting. And then Garrett and the marketing crew had gotten slammed. His friend was still unaware that Tara was watching Dylan, but tonight wasn't the time to bring it up. Henri would demand all the details.

"Veronique and Jean Luc will come to my house tomorrow." Henri's tired eyes brightened when he spoke of his youngest sister and her son. "Would you enjoy to come to dinner, also? The boys can play, and Dylan can stay the night, *peut-être?*"

Dylan would want to go. He and Jean Luc always had a great time together. But Garrett had really been looking forward to a dinner with Tara, and tomorrow night was the night he'd earmarked.

"Um, actually…you remember my American neighbor, Tara?"

Henri's chuckle was a low growl. *"Mais oui."*

"Well, Monique's father is in the hospital, and Tara has been keeping Dylan for me. I'd sort of promised her we'd make dinner for her tomorrow night. I owe it to her after all she's done this week."

Henri's face split into a wide grin. *"C'est parfait, Garrett. Prépare le dîner pour Tara.* Dylan will come to my house and stay for the night, and you will have the time alone."

Alone time with Tara, and Dylan nowhere around? Garrett's mouth went dry. Even the mention of it filled his head with all kinds of possibilities—dangerous thoughts involving the two of them naked and a treasure hunt where he would search her body for hidden tattoos. His head spun as all the blood in his torso headed southward.

Guilt took a swipe at him. "I've been away from Dylan a lot the past two weeks."

"Oui." Henri was always Dylan's champion. "But you will have the complete day together tomorrow. And Dylan will not want to miss the chance to have a sleepover with Jean Luc."

"That's true," Garrett admitted. But the chance for a sleepover with Tara was what he needed to get out of his mind. Maybe it would be better to go out to dinner? Give her a real night on the town to repay her for her help…and avoid the risks that an intimate dinner on the terrace might lead to.

He clapped his friend on the back. "You're right,

Henri. It's perfect. Dylan will be so excited. What time would you like him at your house?"

"I do not care, *mon ami*. But, if I were you, I would bring him as early as possible, *oui*? And allow him to stay late the next day, so you can *sleep*—" Henri half smiled and half leered at the young woman bussing the table "—for as long as you desire."

Garrett sucked a breath deep into his lungs. What he *desired* and what he *allowed* were two altogether different things.

He wouldn't even think of this as a date. This would be a nighttime sightseeing excursion with a friend.

And that was all.

FAITH COULDN'T STAND the pressure anymore.

What she was about to do would be a life-changing event for her and Sawyer, the kids, the church… maybe the whole town. But she couldn't bear one more second in this tortured hell of a life she'd been living for the past month.

This change was necessary. She'd tried suffering in silence. Remaining stoic. Facing the world with a calm demeanor and pretending everything was fine.

But everything wasn't fine, and her serene facade was crumbling. People were noticing her weight loss. Friends were whispering, speculating on illness. Cancer had been mentioned…and leukemia. Her mom had died of heart disease, so some people were betting on heredity.

If people were talking anyway, why not give them the truth to talk about?

She'd let a lie exist between her and Sawyer for twenty-eight years, and that lie had ended and come to light at long last. She refused to let another one take its place—at least, not for any longer.

All the lying ended today.

She grabbed a luggage handle with each hand and hauled the two pieces from the bedroom.

The door to Sawyer's study was closed. He always used Saturday morning to fine-tune his sermons.

The pot of coffee she'd heard him making a half hour before had barely a cup gone, and the paper sack of Ivadawn's cinnamon-glazed yeast doughnuts still bulged with its contents, a big grease mark soaking through the side.

The sights. The smells. Everything was as it had always been—and yet nothing was the same.

No doubt, Sawyer waited on the other side of the door for her knock—her bidding him to stop his studies a little while and share a cup of coffee and a doughnut.

Faith blinked, expecting tears, but she had none. She'd cried them all. Maybe that's where the weight had gone.

She pulled the luggage across the kitchen floor, the wheels making a racket on the tile. They beat out a *thunk-thunk* rhythm, squealing like piglets who'd been pushed off the hog's teat. She ignored their protest. She'd thought this through for days and had come to the conclusion that only a separation would give her any peace.

Being within touching distance of the man she loved yet not being allowed to touch him was a torture she could bear no longer.

She jockeyed the luggage through the door to the garage and popped the trunk with the button on the key fob. There were already a few items in there boxed up—just a few sentimental things from the kids that she wanted with her...homemade birthday cards and valentines...a few pictures.

She wasn't taking much.

She shuddered at the finality in the sound of the trunk slamming, closing her eyes and allowing the vibration to move through her and out.

"Faith?"

Her eyes flew open to find Sawyer standing in the doorway, his coffee cup poised chest high, a look of bewilderment on his face as if he'd forgotten where his mouth was.

"What are you doing?"

She stepped around the car to face him with nothing between them. "I'm leaving, Sawyer. I can't stand this. I was going to come back in—I wouldn't have left without saying goodbye."

"You're leaving?" His tone was the same one she'd heard when they got the call from the police about Tara's accident. "Where are you going?"

"To your mom's."

It was just across town—a few blocks away. The

house was still fully furnished. They hadn't gotten rid of anything since Lacy died. It wasn't an ideal location. She'd still be smack-dab in the middle of the talk and the meddling. But it would give her a quiet space that wasn't a forced quiet, and it wouldn't cost their tight budget anything extra.

Sawyer's other hand came up to grip the coffee cup like he didn't trust the finger through the handle to hold the weight. "Faith, don't do this. Please don't do this." His normally calm voice shook with emotion. "I've counseled enough couples to know that people don't separate to work things out. People separate to start the process of living away from each other permanently."

She placed a trembling hand to her throat, feeling the steady pulse. Somehow she was living through this. "I don't know what I'm starting. I only know what I'm ending. The lie. I've had all I can take of the pussyfooting around town like everything's fine… pussyfooting around each other, trying to act like we're one thing when we both know we're something else entirely now. I don't know what that something else is, but I'm not getting any answers here. I need some alone time to sort things out for myself."

"I love you, Faith." His words sucked the air from her lungs. "I'm just having a hard time right now." He stepped into the garage, watching her closely like he did the deer in the backyard, afraid the wrong movement might send her scurrying.

She squared her shoulders to show him her leaving

wasn't a fear-induced reaction. She'd thought it over for days and hadn't come to the decision lightly. "I know you are, Sawyer. And I'm so, so sorry for putting you through this. But what's done is done, and I can't take it back. But I also can't continue living in what feels like a perpetual state of punishment."

He leaned against his workbench, pushing some tools out of the way to clear a place for his cup. "I'm sorry. I don't mean to make you feel that way. I'm not trying to punish you." His hands thrust deeply into his pockets. "This isn't even about you. It's about me, and the lie I perpetuate week after week. Every Sunday I preach about love. How love is the answer to everything." He shrugged. "*I* love. And yet, my love isn't enough. I'm trying to figure out why." His hand came out of his pocket, balled into a fist that he rapped against his chest, punctuating his words. "I could understand if it had just been you. But it isn't enough for Tara, either. What am I missing? What do I need to change my message to? How do I lead people to the answer when *I* don't have the answer?"

Seeing him like this made her sick to her stomach. Sawyer—the rock…battered and broken into pebbles. "I don't have the answer, either. But this—" she wagged her finger between them "—isn't the way to find it. So I'm ready to try something else." She jerked the car door open.

Sawyer was there in two steps, holding the door to keep it open. "The whole town will know ten minutes after you get to Mom's. Maybe not even *that* long with Sue as your next-door neighbor."

The woman's name sent a surge through her. "You don't get it, Sawyer. I. Don't. Care. I *want* people to know. I'm tired of living a lie. I am who I am, and you and the town can try to pretend I'm someone else, but that doesn't make it so." She pressed the button on the key fob, and the garage door started grinding open.

"Then, let *me* go." Sawyer's eyes glistened with unshed tears. "You shouldn't have to be the one to leave when I'm the one with the problem."

Dear Lord! She was finally beginning to understand the depth of Sawyer's misery…and the mindset behind the impotence. She had to get out of there before the man broke completely. "I've thought this over, Sawyer. Stay. Leave. Do whatever you want. Just find your answers so we can start getting our lives back together."

"What about Tara? This will ruin her trip if she finds out."

"I thought about that, too." The past few nights, all she'd done was think, her mind wandering aimlessly, shifting directions like a rabbit being chased by a fox. But her focus always came back to Tara. "She's got enough on her plate over there. She doesn't need to be worrying about us, too. When I call Thea and Trent, I'll ask them not to say anything when they talk to her. I'll call Emma, too."

Faith climbed into the driver's seat and started the

ignition. A small tug pulled the door from Sawyer's grasp, and he stepped out of the way.

She backed out of the driveway, leaving him standing there, a lost look on his face. With a push of the button, she lowered the garage door.

CHAPTER ELEVEN

THE EIFFEL TOWER was even more beautiful at night—an image in lacy, gold filigree, more stunning than any photo could possibly capture.

Tara just wanted to stand and drink it in.

"It's even better from over there. The Trocadéro." Garrett pointed to a crowded pavilion across the way. His hand found the small of her back, sending a delicious shiver up her spine. "But we'll have to hurry."

"Why? It doesn't appear to be going anywhere."

Garrett laughed and gave her a wink. "You'll see."

The wine served during the cruise had apparently worked some magic because Garrett had loosened up, at last. When he'd first picked her up, he'd been stiff and distant, treating this more like a guided tour than a date. Up until this moment, it was as if they'd reverted back to square one with the flirtation of the other night forgotten—at least, on his part. She, on the other hand, had been giving it all she had. That he'd finally touched her was encouraging.

The cruise had been beyond delightful. The views of Paris from the Seine with each movement of the boat bringing more opulence into view…the running commentary of fascinating tidbits told in the tour guide's sexy French-infused English…the undivided attention of the ruggedly handsome man sitting at her side. *Ooh-la-la!*

Now, walking toward the Trocadéro, she kept turning around, eyes constantly drawn back to the Eiffel Tower, half afraid it actually *might* disappear, the other half unwilling to miss a second of the view.

Garrett took her hand, causing the endorphins in her brain to break into a happy dance. Keeping her in tow, he threaded through the crowd, his urgency evident. She paused the questions and comments, keeping pace with his jog up the steps to the crowded top level of the pavilion, where they found an open space and fell against each other laughing and gasping.

"Whew!" Garrett checked his watch, then flung his arm around her shoulder and whirled around to face the landmark. A few seconds later, the Eiffel Tower erupted into a twinkling mass of brilliant white lights, diamonds encrusting the gold filigree— a royal brooch worn by the Queen of Cities.

"Oh, my gosh!" Tara squealed as the crowd shouted and broke into applause. Caught up in the excitement, she intertwined her fingers with the ones on her shoulder and tilted her head against the side of Garrett's face. "You're right. This *is* better." A blissful sigh accompanied her next breath.

"Told you."

She swiveled her head and watched the side of Garrett's mouth rise slowly in a lazy smile that oozed sexy. Her insides coiled with heat. "Don't give me that Mona Lisa smile, Garrett Hughes. I can't stand here gawking at you when I've got tourist business to take care of."

The twinkle in his eyes when he laughed made her even more reluctant to let go of his hand, but a video of the glistening tower to post on her Facebook page couldn't wait. Her heart skipped a beat, though, when she put her phone away, and his hand found hers again.

"C'mon." He bobbed his head in the direction of the landmark. "More good stuff awaits."

They wove their way through the crowd and back across the Seine via the Pont d'Iena, but the slower pace did nothing to calm her breathing. Garrett's sudden decision to stay in constant physical contact by holding her hand or resting an arm around her shoulders kept causing her breath to hitch. By the time they stood on the top level of the Eiffel Tower, she was dizzy with excitement and the effects of looking down from the thousand-foot height at the exquisite city below.

She closed her eyes for a moment and tried to recapture some calm. "I still can't believe I'm here, standing at the pinnacle of worldly sophistication. If Taylor's Grove could see me now…" She massaged her face, which ached from the smile she'd been wearing all night. When she opened her eyes, a lustrous golden dome caught her attention. "Ooh. What's that over yonder?"

"Yonder?" Garrett's deep laugh brought a flush of embarrassment to her face.

"Guess I haven't stood at the pinnacle long enough to absorb much of that sophistication, huh?"

"I wasn't making fun. That laugh was pure enjoyment. Hearing you say things like that brings home a lot closer." He pulled her around to face him, brushing a finger down her heated cheek. "I'd like to find a quiet place where I could close my eyes and just listen to you talk."

Oh, Lord! Heat moved through her again, having nothing to do with embarrassment. Were all guys in Paris hot? Or was it just something about being in this city? "Thanks," she murmured. "That was a nice thing to say." Over his shoulder, she could see the couple behind them locked in a kiss of romance novel quality.

So maybe it *was* the city.

Garrett leaned in so close she could feel his breath against her cheek. Was he about to kiss her? Her own breathing came to an abrupt halt.

Instead, he pointed. "The gold dome 'over yonder' is Hôtel des Invalides, Napoleon's tomb." His boyish grin, so much like Dylan's, said he was obviously pleased with the reference to their personal joke.

"Hôtel des Invalides." She repeated the words, using her best French accent. Being short of breath made it sound even better. "Only the French language could make a tomb and a military museum sound so divine."

"It's pretty interesting, really." His eyes lit up. "We could go there tomorrow, if you'd like. Dylan loves it, and there's a tradition about touching the foot of the Mansart statue in the garden."

"I went one day last week although I think I missed the Mansart statue." Tara drooped her lip in a pretend pout and watched as Garrett's gaze moved to her mouth then back up slowly to tangle with her eyes. There was enough electricity in that look to keep the City of Lights in business for a while, but if he didn't kiss her soon, she was going to blow a breaker.

His eyes darkened. "Well, if you missed Mansart, we can't take any chances. There's another tradition we need to take advantage of right now." With a tilt of his head, he directed her gaze to the couple next to her, who were also enjoying a sensuous moment, oblivious to everyone around them. "Tradition says if you kiss on top of the Eiffel Tower, romance will forever spread out around you like the city below." He leaned toward her again, hesitating as if asking permission.

Tara answered him by meeting him halfway. Their lips touched, and she expected something short and chaste, but once her mouth settled on his, it felt so nice, she was in no hurry for it to end. Her hands found his waist and his hands found her back, and they relaxed against each other, warm and comfortable, yet pleasantly enticing. The kiss lasted much longer than she thought possible with no tongues involved.

She leaned back a little, meeting his gaze, but kept her hands where they were. Likewise, his stayed put. "I like this tradition," she said.

"Well, there's another one, too, you know."

She quirked an eyebrow. "You're making these up, aren't you?"

"Yeah." The side of his mouth rose in that yummy lopsided grin.

"Well, tell me anyway."

Garrett cleared his throat. "If you kiss a second time, it means you'll come back."

"That's the Trevi Fountain in Rome. Surely you can be more imaginative than that."

"Okay, how about if you kiss a second time, your love will shine more brilliantly than the tower itself."

She pursed her lips, pretending to ponder it, and finally nodded. "Works for me."

His mouth covered hers again, but remained gentle even when she opened and met his tongue. There was no hurry…no urgency…just a long, languid kiss that left her knees weak and her lungs devoid of breath.

"You don't kiss like a girl from Taylor's Grove," Garrett whispered.

"Actually, I kiss *exactly* like a girl from Taylor's Grove," she whispered back. "We didn't have any movies, or teenage hangouts. The only thing to do was park by Kentucky Lake and make out until we got it down pat."

Garrett chuckled. "You did more than get it down pat. You perfected it."

Tara batted her eyes playfully at him. "I had more practice than everybody else. I was a virgin until I was twenty-three, so kissing was my forte."

A serious look settled on Garrett's face as he stepped back and took her hands. "That's a tidbit I never would've guessed. What other things am I going to learn about you that will surprise me?"

Her own recent surprise—the one that gave her a reason for being there—pricked her heart. "I'm still in the discovery stage myself." His brows buckled in question at her cryptic response, but she didn't give him a chance to ask whatever it was he was thinking. She was having too glorious a time at the moment to get into the subject of Jacques Martin. Instead, she pointed at the famous avenue in the distance with the arch at the end. "Champs-élysées and Arc de Triomphe."

"Oui. L'avenue des Champs-élysées et l'Arc de Triomphe," Garrett repeated in what sounded like perfect French to her no matter what Dylan said about his father's pronunciation.

She sighed. "You can take the girl out of Taylor's Grove, but you can't take Taylor's Grove out of the girl."

Garrett caught her chin with a finger and gently turned it toward him. "Don't *ever* lose the Taylor's Grove. It's pure gold." He touched his lips to hers again in the tenderest of kisses, and she gripped the railing tighter as her knees went weak.

Garrett pointed to the other side of the viewing deck. "Now, let's take a look over 'yonder.'"

They headed in the direction he'd indicated, not quite making it to the other side before Tara's cell phone rang. Her mom's name came up on the caller ID. "I need to take this. Do you mind?"

"You ask this of a single father?" He ran a finger down her arm. "Of course not."

Saturday night was an odd time for her mom to be calling. But then, it *was* two in the afternoon at home. She swiped the button to answer. "Hi, Mama."

"Hey, sweetpea. Just wanted to see what you're doing." Her mom's voice sounded tired. She'd probably been picking tomatoes from the garden. Or maybe canning, which was a job she hated.

"Actually, I'm having dinner with my neighbor Garrett."

"That's Dylan's father, isn't it?" The voice on the other end perked up a bit.

Tara winked at Garrett, who'd moved far enough away so as not to hear the conversation. "That's right. Dylan's spending the night with a friend, so Garrett's treating me to a night on the town. We've been on a Seine river cruise, and we watched the Eiffel Tower light up, which is the most gorgeous sight ever. I'm actually talking to you from the top of the tower right now."

"Oh! I'm sorry, sweetie. I—I didn't mean to interrupt your date. I'll, um, I'll let you go."

Tara's senses went on alert. Something wasn't right. She could hear it in the way her mom's voice strained and tightened all of a sudden—like she was trying to sound okay when she really wasn't. "What's wrong?"

There was a pause on the other end. "Nothing. I just haven't talked to you in a few days, and I wanted to see how you were doing."

Okay, so her mom was probably just worried about the Jacques Martin search. Tara didn't want to get into that. It might put a damper on what was turning out to be a fabulous night. "Well, I'm doing great." She threw an extra load of exuberance into her voice. "I've got lots to tell you, but it'll have to hold until sometime when I don't have somebody waiting for me. We're just about to head to dinner."

"Yes, I understand. I should let you go then."

Her mom's tone slipped into sad, and Tara's gut twisted. "Are you sure you're okay?"

"I'm fine. I'll talk to you tomorrow...or sometime soon."

Something unspoken niggled at Tara. "Wait, um, how's Dad?"

"He's...okay."

"Which means not great."

"He's still upset."

"But he sounded better when I talked to him yesterday." The last call from her dad had made her hopeful that everything at home was finally getting back to normal. At least, he talked about everyday things—the first tomatoes, the doe with triplets still in spots that had come into the backyard.

"It's me he's upset with. Not you." The voice on the other end of the line cracked. "I'm sorry. I'm calling from Grandma O'Malley's house, and it's just making me overly sentimental."

Ah! There it was. Mama was calling from Grandma's. She was finally going through things, deciding what to get rid of and what to keep. "Well, don't stay too long. No sense in working up a case of melancholy. All that stuff will still be there tomorrow and the next day and the day after that."

"Yeah, I don't know how long I'll be here..." Her mom's voice faded. "But, I'll let you go now. Enjoy your dinner."

Tara walked to where Garrett stood. "I will. Talk to you later."

"Bye, sweetpea. Love you."

"Love you, too. Bye." Tara blew out a long breath as she touched the button to end the call.

Garrett was watching her, concern hooding his deep-set eyes. "Is everything okay?"

She cocked her head and gave her brows and her shoulders a simultaneous shrug. "I wish I could say yes to that, but I'm not certain it'd be the truth."

"Why? What's going on?"

Tara chewed her lip, wondering how much to tell him. He'd been very forthcoming about his wife.

And with Emma thousands of miles away, it would be nice to have someone to talk to. "I'll tell you all about it," she promised. "But not until after dinner."

"NOTRE-DAME IS GORGEOUS in the moonlight. So majestic." Tara's voice was full of wonder and awe—a pleasant, almost childlike quality that Garrett had noticed throughout their night out, beginning with the cruise. It had shifted his focus completely away from the platonic sightseeing tour he'd originally planned.

Attentive, appreciative and enthusiastic about everything he suggested, Tara had been the perfect date. It had been a long time since he'd spent time with a woman who had such a zeal for life, and it felt good. Damn good.

He'd gotten caught up in her enthusiasm, and somewhere between her dreamy sigh as the boat passed under Pont Neuf and her squeal as the Eiffel Tower shimmered to life, he'd thrown caution to the wind and allowed himself to think of this night as a date.

Now, with her back to him and his arms around her waist, she was snuggled against him with the breeze whipping her hair to the side, the moonlight glinting on that tattoo below her ear. This *all* felt pretty damn good.

"I was thinking the same thing about you," he answered, and she reached up and caressed his cheek in a gesture that, at that moment, seemed more intimate than a kiss.

He wasn't sure where the night was going to end, but it wouldn't be here on Pont Notre-Dame. Suddenly, he was anxious to get home. "You ready?" he murmured into her ear.

She nodded, breathing another of those dreamy sighs that made his breath catch, and slipped out of his arms, but only long enough to catch his hand. "Ready."

She was in such a good mood now, he hated to bring it up, but they still had the rest of the stroll home, and he was curious to know what had bothered her so much during the phone conversation at the Eiffel Tower. "When your mom called earlier, you seemed worried. Want to talk about it while we walk?"

"I suppose." She gave him a small smile. "Nothing could seem too bad when it's filtered by Paris in the early morning moonlight, right?"

Tara told her story with the same enthusiasm that infused everything she did, captivating him with her tale of a family torn apart by a secret over twenty-five-years old. Garrett could almost hear Grandma O'Malley's dishes breaking right along with the hearts of her family members.

His own parents were still devoted to each other after thirty-seven years together, so putting himself in Tara's shoes made his gut twist. "This whole experience must be a nightmare for you." He pulled her against his side as they approached their building. "So how many of these Jacques Martins have you checked out so far?"

"Fourteen," she said dully, and the lack of inflection told Garrett just how much that answer bothered her.

"And you're just making cold house calls?"

She nodded. "My telephone French is even worse than my in-person French."

That made Garrett smile, but then an image of Tara walking naively into a seedy neighborhood popped into his mind and his grip on her shoulder tightened. "I don't want you doing that anymore. Paris is relatively safe to walk around in, but it's a city, and there are places you shouldn't be going—especially alone."

She shrugged. "I don't know how else to do it. I mean, if I do find him, and he doesn't want anything to do with me, at least I'll know what he looks like. I'll have that to—" her voice broke "—to keep with me."

Garrett glanced down and saw the hope glistening in her eyes. Tara was easy to read. She might be talking in terms of Jacques Martin not wanting anything to do with her, but her dreams lay in a different direction entirely.

She looked up at him, and her smile trembled. Beneath all that zest for life lay a fragile soul. Garrett was filled with several kinds of desire, but the most prominent at the moment was to protect her. He pulled her into his arms, kissing the top of her head. She melted against him, and he felt the warmth deep in his heart.

When he spoke his voice was huskier than he meant it to sound. "When we get to your flat, I want to see this list."

"ONE LAST GLASS of wine on the terrace?"

Tara kicked off her shoes as soon as they walked through her door.

Garrett's arms came around her from behind, and he kissed her neck. All of the touching tonight had put her senses on high alert, and this caress sent a shiver into all the right places.

"I was thinking champagne might be more appropriate," he answered.

She frowned. That did sound like the perfect ending to this date—or perhaps the second most perfect ending. "Sadly I don't have any champagne."

"I do, and my place is just a few yards away. I'll get it and some glasses. You get your list of addresses."

They met on the terrace a few minutes later, Garrett with an already-opened bottle of bubbly and two glasses, and Tara bearing her list of possible fathers.

Garrett held her chair for her and then pulled the other one close enough that their thighs touched when he sat. He lifted his glass. "To tonight." He gave her that half smile that made her toes curl.

"To tonight," she agreed, and took a sip. The bubbles tickled her nose, and left an effervescent trail from the tip of her tongue down the back of her throat and into her chest.

Garrett scooted her list over in front of him, and began talking to her about the addresses and making notes on where she would be safe to go alone and where she wouldn't.

"I won't be working so late this week, and I might even be able to take off a little early and go with you to these places." He'd put Xs by the four that were located in neighborhoods he didn't trust. "These two—" he pointed to one on rue Racine and one on rue de Condé "—are near the Luxembourg Gardens. Have you been there?"

She shook her head. "Not yet."

"The Sorbonne is in that area, and the Pantheon. That's where Foucault's pendulum is, which is really cool—Dylan loves it." He looked up from his list and peered closely at her. "You haven't been taking Dylan." It wasn't a question.

"No. I didn't think I should. What if there was a scene with one of the men?"

"But you've lost a lot of time this week, staying with him. Time you could've been using looking for your father."

"I've been able to get in about one place a day. And, if Monique gets back by Wednesday, I'll still have almost two weeks. I hope I don't have to go through all forty-three," she added.

Garrett pushed back in his chair with a disgusted

sigh. "You should've said something earlier, Tara. You've made a huge sacrifice of your time."

"Being with Dylan isn't a sacrifice. Dylan's real and precious. Jacques Martin may not even still exist." The honesty in her words hit her hard, and she felt a tear slide down her cheek. "I may be looking for someone who has already passed away or somebody who won't want me even if I find him." A sob swelled in her throat, and she took a sip of champagne to wash it down. She would *not* allow this beautiful night to be marred by an emotional meltdown of any sort.

Garrett's hand cupped her chin, and he turned her face toward him. "I can't imagine anyone who has met you not wanting you."

He pressed his lips to hers gently, but it was like he'd touched her with a branding iron. She'd never experienced sizzle from a kiss like she did in that moment.

Her hand crept to the back of his neck and she pressed him closer, opening her mouth to the exploration of his tongue. She heard the subtle groan in the back of his throat as he breathed more fire into the embrace.

His arm slid around her waist, and he stood, pulling her with him and against him until the only separation of their bodies lay in the thin fabric of their clothing. She could feel his desire, and she rubbed her palms against his back to fan the flame higher. All the while he kept possession of her mouth in a kiss that made all the others of her life seem like child's play.

She knew without a doubt what she wanted, and she pulled her mouth away long enough to make her feelings known.

"Make love to me, Garrett."

She didn't have to ask twice.

In an instant, he'd bent down to brace an arm under her knees, and he lifted her as easily as he might lift a child. "Grab the list. Just leave the bottle and the glasses," he instructed, leaning her near enough to the table for her to grab her papers.

"Do you have condoms?" he asked, and she shook her head in response.

He inclined his head toward his flat. "Then my place it is."

He strode across the terrace with her in his arms, and she could almost understand what made ladies of yesteryear swoon. If she'd ever played out a scene that was swoon-worthy, this was it. Her heart was beating a strong cadence against her chest, making her wonder if he could feel it.

Between the two of them, they managed to maneuver the doorways without too much distraction, and soon he was laying her on his bed and placing the list on the bedside table.

He sat, his weight pressing the mattress down and rolling her to her side. "Now, it's *my* turn." The back of his fingers brushed lightly across the fabric cover-

ing her breast, bringing immediate heat to the area…
and others, as well.

She made an effort to give her voice full volume,
but it came out as a whisper, heavy with desire. "To
do what?"

His eyes held that mischievous twinkle, and he
grinned. "To finally see *you* naked."

CHAPTER TWELVE

IT HAD BEEN a while since he'd undressed a woman—even longer since the woman had been as tall and lean as Tara—and Garrett wanted to prolong the experience as much as desire would allow.

He stretched out beside her on the bed, and immediately her hands began to unbutton his shirt. He grasped them gently and shook his head. "I'm glad you're eager, but I've fantasized about exploring your body and its tattoos for days. Can I have a little fun before we get to the serious stuff?"

"Ooh." Tara's eyes lit up. "You want to do some body geocaching?"

"Exactly. How many, um, caches, can I expect to find?"

She held up her left hand, fingers spread. "Five."

He took her hand and brushed his tongue across the tips of her fingers. "This will be my cache finder. Now, you have to lie still, and you can't give me any hints. Understood?"

She nodded and lay back against his pillow, arms at her side and eyes closed. Her hair spread out like a flower in bloom around her. Even the blue tips, which he'd found so strange in the beginning, now enhanced the effect, adding depth to the overall appeal of the woman.

He brushed back a lock that curled around her neck and bent his head to the mark below her ear that had kept him mesmerized for long periods of time in his daydreams. With the tip of his tongue, he traced the pattern, feeling her responsive shiver at his touch.

The tattoo was an intricate triple spiral that he'd seen before but had never thought much about. "What does this one mean?" His tongue flicked lightly around one of the loops.

"It's the Celtic symbol for life, death and rebirth. Oh! That feels really nice." She wriggled beneath him. "I got it after my grandmother died. Ironically, she turned out not to be my biological grandmother, and I'm not even Irish—"

He cut off her speech with a kiss. "Shh."

She grinned, and he went back to tracing the tattoo slowly with his finger and then his tongue.

He allowed his tongue to wander to her earlobe, nibbling there for a while before moving on to the rim of her ear and the delicate skin behind it. She threaded her fingers through his hair and pressed him closer, her breath coming in pants with an occasional moan of pleasure. The erotic sounds urged him to hurry, but he reined his body in.

Her breath caught as he fingered the first button on the front of her pale blue dress and slid it through the hole. A small V appeared in the square neckline of the dress and deepened as each button gave way, each punctuated by a small gasp.

The third button confirmed what he'd already suspected—she wore no bra—and deep within the area between her breasts, a delicate green stem appeared. Two more buttons and he was able to lay the bodice open. He stopped for a moment to take in the sight.

Her breasts were small, but beautifully shaped with perky nipples, drawn tight with excitement. Below the right breast was a small daisy with a bright yellow center and white petals. Its stem wound across her torso from one side of her rib cage to the other.

"Number two." Garrett bent his head to trace the flower with his tongue, but the nipple was too enticing. He sucked it quickly into his mouth, and was rewarded with an appreciative squeal that lowered into a moan as Tara's back arched off the bed. He flicked his tongue on the very tip, then made a wet path to the daisy and around its many petals. "What's this one mean?" he asked, as he started across the stem.

"My deflowering. Giving up…my virginity at…at…oh!" Her words came in spurts, and Garrett watched her fist the sheet into her half hand. "Twenty-three…petals. Ah!"

As his tongue continued its journey, Garrett opened three more buttons to reveal a lace thong that matched the color of the dress. The vision shot directly to his groin and he hurried to undo the final buttons and lay the dress completely open.

Tara's pale body speckled with freckles against the

blue material...with the delicate daisy and the wisp of blue lace...was worthy of the Louvre. A few small scars that he guessed were from her spleen removal were still visible, but they added an element of danger that spoke of her genuineness. When he sat back to look at her, she propped herself up on her elbows, arched her back in a languid pose and let her head drop back. The straps of the dress slid down her arms in slow motion, and Garrett's heartbeat accelerated.

To hell with the tattoo hunt. He wanted her. Now.

He hooked a thumb into the lace and tugged as she lifted her hips. The lace slid down her legs, exposing a small pink heart on her flat stomach, two inches above the top of her left thigh.

She gave him a coquettish grin. "That one's just for fun. Sort of a reward for getting this far, you know?"

"I think I'm ready to capture the prize." He stood up and pulled his shirt over his head.

"You're giving up mighty quickly." She punctuated the challenge in her voice with a raised eyebrow.

Garrett unfastened his belt and trousers, shucking them, his briefs and his socks in one fluid movement. "I'm not giving up. I just think it may be time to probe deeper into this mystery." He climbed into the bed, sheathing himself as quickly as his eager fingers would allow.

Tara reached out and brushed the back of her finger across his lips. "Will you use the same instrument you've been using?"

"I'll start with that one." He tried to sound official, but he couldn't hold back the grin that twitched his mouth. "But then I'll probably have to switch to something larger and more sensitive."

She gave a delighted laugh and opened her arms wide to greet him.

He met her embrace, rolling on top of her, covering her neck and shoulders with kisses, then sliding down to torture her time after time until she was wild with need.

She responded in kind, placing kisses, nips and licks on any part of his body that ventured near her mouth. Her touch burned through him like a set fuse. At last, she wrapped her legs around him, locking him into position, and if he'd had any thoughts of lingering, they were lost in a haze of lust.

He slid into her exquisite tightness, catching her erotic gasp on his tongue. Her fingernails scraped along his back as she met his thrusts, curving into him as her back arched higher.

He reached the edge but backed off, refusing to make the plunge without her.

"No!" She ground out the words through clenched teeth. "Don't…slow…oh! Oh, Garrett!" Her legs, her arms, her hands—it was as though every muscle in her body tightened its hold on him, taking control, throwing him over the precipice to join her in the free fall.

Time stopped, and they floated in midair, riding

the currents up and down until they once again touched solid ground.

He collapsed on top of her but worried that his weight might be too much, so he rolled off, gathering her to him.

They each took a deep breath, and the single syllable exploded from both of their mouths simultaneously.

"Wow!"

TARA WOKE TO the bright morning sun warming her front and Garrett's warm body spooning her from behind. His arm snuggled around her waist, holding her close and secure. She closed her eyes and listened to his slow, deep breathing, reliving the night before.

Garrett Hughes was the stuff of dreams. That he'd planned the perfect date for her spoke volumes, but nothing could compare to his lovemaking. It was as if he could read her mind, recognize all the subtleties and nuances of her movements and breaths. Time after time he'd brought her to climax, and even when he'd finally driven home, he'd held back until he was sure she would make it one last time with him.

She'd never had anyone like him, and—a lump formed in her throat—after she returned home, she might never again.

But she had last night…and hopefully there would be several more repeat performances before she returned to the States.

She sighed and an involuntary tremble of emotion shook her. Garrett's arm tightened around her, pulling her closer. "You cold?" His breath caught the back of her ear, making her shiver again.

"No. It's just my body's reaction to the nearness of you." She turned a little, so that her head rested against his cheek.

"Mmm. That's nice." She sensed his smile although she couldn't see his mouth. "Last night was pretty special."

A contented sigh escaped from her lungs as she nodded. "Yeah. It was."

Garrett raised himself up on an elbow, and the loss of his embrace rolled her onto her back. He caught her gaze and held it, brought her hand to his lips and placed a tender kiss to the palm. "I don't think I've ever enjoyed myself so much with anyone else. It was…fun…and hot…and—"

"Ooh-la-la?"

He chuckled. "Your French has certainly improved."

She cupped his cheek with her hand, brushing the thick growth of stubble with her thumb, then moved it over to brush the scar that cut through the top of his lip. "Did you get spiked here, too?" She hoped not. His tale of his thigh getting ripped open by a kid sliding into third base with metal spikes made her cringe, but she didn't even want to think about that happening to something as sweet as his lips.

He shook his head. "A memento from Angie. We were walking in our neighborhood late one night, and she ran over and climbed on our neighbor's trampoline and started jumping really high. I was sure she was going to break her neck, so I climbed on to get her off, and when I got hold of her, she head-butted me." He pointed to his front tooth and ran his finger along the next one beside it. "Lost two teeth, as well."

Little by little, Tara was piecing together the nightmare his life with Angie must've been, and it made her admire his strength and resilience all the more. "I'll kiss the boo-boo." She softly pressed her lips to the spot.

Garrett's hand traveled to the small of her back and caressed the site of her largest tattoo. "Tolkien's initials, eh? I knew something was there. I just couldn't make it out through that wet dress you had on when we first met."

She squeezed her eyes closed, feeling the heat creep into her face. "What a way to meet! I was soaked and frustrated, and you're standing there naked—"

"Trying to figure out if I could subdue you by throwing my towel over your head."

They laughed together, and then they laughed harder as the memory of the ludicrous situation loomed larger in their minds. She collapsed on top of him, and he rolled her onto her back and started kissing—and laughing—his way down to the tattoo of the small chain that circled her ankle—"a reminder to not be chained down by other people's ideas of who I should be," she had explained.

His finger and thumb encircled her ankle, adding a third dimension to the tattoo, and he gave a tug, parting her legs slightly. His lips began a steamy line of kisses that traveled up her calf.

"Oh, yeah." She wiggled her butt deeper into the bedclothes.

"I think I know the real meaning behind this tattoo." He tightened his grip on her ankle, and gave her that lopsided grin that made her insides melt.

"And what would that be?"

"I think…" He continued the line of kisses up the inside of her thigh. "I think you are…a slave…to your desires."

The next set of kisses continued upward, convincing her he was probably right.

CHAPTER THIRTEEN

GARRETT GAVE TARA a small tour as they hurried toward Henri's, pointing out some of the more interesting sites in this part of the city.

After surprising her with breakfast in bed—complete with chocolate croissants, an omelet extraordinaire, sausages and pureed strawberries mixed with champagne—Garrett had surprised her, and himself, even more by suggesting she go with him to pick up Dylan. One of her Jacques Martin addresses wasn't too far from Henri's house, and on the way home, they could go by another Jacques Martin address on île Saint-Louis.

He didn't want his time with her to end yet—and she didn't seem in a hurry to leave.

Though she'd confessed that meeting his best friend coupled with the prospect of meeting her birth father made her slightly queasy, not even that double whammy caused her to back down.

She'd returned to his apartment in the now-infamous yellow sundress, which was smart on her, and Garrett was proud to have her on his arm. So proud, in fact, that they'd gotten a later start than he'd hoped because he'd had an overwhelming desire to remove it.

Once they reached their destination, he guided her up the sidewalk to Henri's door, which flew open while he was still in the process of knocking.

"Hi, Dad." Dylan's eyes widened along with his grin. "Tara!" He rushed out to greet the surprise visitor with a hug, and Garrett's heart was divided. His son was thrilled to see Tara, and she him, but the affection they already shared wasn't going to make her goodbye easy for any of them.

Garrett shoved the thought from his mind. One bridge at a time. The one he'd crossed last night had landed him in Wonderland, and he would stay there as long as possible.

"Garrett? Entre, entre!" Henri's voice came from somewhere deeper inside the house.

Jean Luc and Veronique showed up close on Dylan's heels, both of them excited to see Garrett again, so he wasn't quite through the introductions when Henri entered the room.

His friend took one look at Tara—not a quick look, but a bold, head-to-toe-and-back ogle that made Garrett want to punch him in his handsome face— and immediately transformed into the sexy, suave Frenchman women flung themselves at. He stepped toward her, hand extended. *"Bonjour, Tara. Bienvenue chez moi."*

Garrett's hand instinctively went to the small of her back to stake his claim, but he reminded himself that he didn't have a claim on this woman—she was a free spirit who would be going away soon, disappearing out of their lives as suddenly as she'd popped in. He dropped his arm back to his side.

Tara gave Henri's hand a brisk shake. "Thank you, Henri. It's nice to meet you." As soon as she pulled her hand free, she caught Garrett's arm and latched on to the crook of his elbow.

Henri's eyes followed the movement, and his smile softened into a look of genuine affection. Then he shifted his gaze to Garrett and gave him a brotherly pat on the shoulder. "Can you stay? The boys help Veronique plant the lettuce."

"Please, Dad?" Dylan was always reluctant to leave any place where he was having fun.

Garrett was aware how anxious Tara was to check out the two addresses they had, but he wanted Henri to spend a little time with her, too. "Okay." He nodded. "But only for a few minutes."

"It will only take a few minutes, and I will try to keep him clean," Veronique assured them with a smile as she followed the two boys outside.

Henri led Garrett and Tara into his living room with its low-slung, ultramodern furniture, which Garrett detested. The Italian leather in white and gray tones reminded him of a lounge that might be frequented by the storm troopers from *Star Wars*.

Their host indicated they were assigned to the love seat, throwing a wink Garrett's way while Tara was getting settled. It was a small piece with abrupt ends and no arm rests, and two people sitting on it made for cozy conditions.

Garrett started to protest, but they weren't staying long…and Tara's thigh pressed tightly against his was nice.

"Do you enjoy Paris, Tara?" Henri asked.

"Yes. Very much." She shot Garrett a grin that would've seemed innocent if she could've controlled the blush that crept into her cheeks. "It's a beautiful city. Photos can't do it justice."

"What sights have you seen?" Henri settled into his favorite chair that looked to Garrett like a giant check mark.

Tara started naming off the places she'd visited, and Garrett watched Henri's face tighten with concentration.

"You have the beautiful accent, but I am sorry that I do not understand all you say."

Tara laughed. "I've been encountering the same thing for two weeks now."

Garrett could tell that Henri hadn't picked up all of that, either, but it didn't seem to matter. His friend liked Tara, and he was glad for that. And if Tara felt uncomfortable, she didn't show it. She had a manner about her that put people at ease. Now it seemed silly that he'd gone out of his way to avoid being around her.

"Do you happen to know anyone around here named Jacques Martin?"

Tara's question startled Garrett, and he shifted in

his seat. She turned to him and shrugged. "I figured I could just ask Henri about the address that's close by. It might save us some time."

"Tara is in Paris looking for someone," Garrett explained to the unspoken question in Henri's eyes.

"My birth father," she added. "I just found out about him, and I came to Paris to try to meet him. His name is Jacques Martin."

Garrett translated what Tara said into French, along with an abbreviated version of Tara's story, and how she'd been going to addresses she'd generated from the phone book and the internet.

When he finished, Henri shifted his attention back to Tara. "The world, she is small. *Oui,* I know of the Jacques Martin who lives near. But he is not of the age to be your father." His words were slow and distinct and edged with a tenderness Garrett had heard often when they spoke of Angie…or Dylan. "He is *peut-être* thirty or thirty-five."

Tara's shoulders had visibly stiffened with Henri's declaration that he knew such a man. Now they sank…and slumped…and Garrett's heart sank with them. He saw her lip tremble slightly before she caught it between her teeth, but she gathered her composure quickly. "Well, thank you anyway, Henri." She looked at Garrett and let out a deep breath. "Another one bites the dust, huh?"

Reflexively, his arm looped around her shoulder and gave it a squeeze. "That will just give us more time to spend looking for the right one."

She nodded and gave a tight smile that he sensed covered a flood of disappointment. She was strong, this one. And though she didn't need his arm anymore for physical or moral support, he left it around her anyway.

TARA AND GARRETT rounded a corner and emerged from the cool shadow of a building into the bright sunlight. Dylan had been walking between them, holding both of their hands, but now he ran ahead to look into the window of a shop with a kite hanging outside. Despite the heat, Garrett tucked Tara's hand under his arm as they walked, bringing her right side into a contact that felt much more intimate than he probably meant it to. She realized with a smile that her body was still stuck on some kind of thrill mode from last night.

She'd had an adequate six hours of sleep, dozing off around four, a full hour after Garrett's soft snores started. But his kisses had flavored her dreams, and she'd woken to find his desire still raging. Then there had been breakfast and the visit with Henri. Hours had passed, yet she remained suffused with an excitement that made the events of last night seem only moments ago.

Now Garrett's hand casually caressed hers as if it had always been there, and they were heading to rue Dante, an address that housed a map shop owned by a Jacques Martin.

"Have you thought about what you'll say to your

father when we find him?" Garrett shot her a side-long glance as he maneuvered the two of them down the narrow sidewalk, all the while, keeping an eye on his son.

"I've gone over the scene in my head almost non-stop, but it plays out differently each time, depending on his reaction. I'll just play it by ear." Her cell phone rang before he had a chance to respond. "Hello?" she answered.

"Hey, lovebug."

The nickname brought a smile to her lips. "Hi, Dad. This is a surprise."

"Yeah, I haven't talked to you in a few days. Is, uh, everything going okay over there?"

Worry tinged his tone. Was it related to this quest for her birth father, or was something else bothering him?

"Everything's wonderful. I'm having a great time."

"That's good. Thea said your neighbor is showing you the sights?"

So her mom had told Thea, but hadn't said anything to her dad. That meant Mama had figured out it was a bona fide date.

She didn't want her dad to get the wrong idea about Garrett—or maybe the right one—and she felt weird talking about him in front of him. She chose her words carefully. "Yeah, that's right. I'm taking in all the tourist attractions. In fact, my neighbor Garrett and his son and I are on Île Saint-Louis right now. We're going to visit Notre-Dame and Sainte-

Chapelle this afternoon." She didn't mention their first destination on the island.

"Sounds like you have good neighbors."

She could almost hear her dad's inner voice convincing him this guy was just being neighborly. Taking her under his wings, which, of course, in her dad's point-of-view, would have to belong to angels.

"The best," she agreed.

"Well, I just wanted to hear your voice."

"And?" She laughed.

"And you sound like you're having the time of your life."

"I am, Dad."

"I'll let you go then. Love you, lovebug."

"Love you, Dad." She slid the phone into her pocket as Garrett and Dylan stopped in the middle of the block.

Garrett pointed to a small shop across the street. "That's the address."

This could be it. She swallowed and nodded. The sweet phone conversation that had brought home and Dad so close was suddenly replaced by what felt like an unknown, scary universe only a few yards away.

Garrett dropped her arm but held her hand as she stepped into the street, anchoring her to this side of the abyss.

"Are you sure you want to do this, Tara?" He spoke low, like he might give away a secret if he raised his voice. Dylan held his other hand, but the child's attention was farther down the street.

She looked hard into his eyes. "I'm sure."

"Why?"

"Why?"

"You love your dad. I hear it in your voice. And he loves you. What will it do to *him* if you find the man who conceived you?" He leaned in and lowered his voice to a whisper. "And that's all he did, Tara. He merely deposited some sperm."

His last sentence jolted her, considering he'd done the same thing with her a few hours ago. Though, hopefully, the condoms caught all the frisky creatures. But was this his way of reminding her that one-night stands were no big deal?

She jerked her hand from his. "This isn't about my dad." His question was the same one her parents had asked her over and over when she started planning this trip. How many times would she have to explain her actions? "It's about me—about who I am. I need to know my true roots. Is that so difficult to understand?" Maybe it was to someone who'd always known who he was. "I always thought I knew who I was, but there's a half of me I know nothing about. I'm not trying to hurt anybody. I'm simply trying to know myself better."

Garrett gave a resolute nod, grabbed her hand again and tucked her arm under his, close to his side once more. "Then come on. Let's do this."

"Are we going to Berthillon, Dad?" Dylan tugged his father's hand and pointed.

Garrett stooped, not letting go of either hand.

"We'll go a little later. But first, we're going to go in that shop over there. Tara is looking for someone."

"Like a geocache? But with people?" The child held up the plastic ring from the canister they'd located a half hour before.

"Just like that," Garrett agreed, and the thought that she might be on the verge of finding a treasure made Tara's heart race.

The three of them marched across the street to the door beneath the engraved copper sign, which was worn to a weathered green patina.

Garrett opened it and stood back for Tara to enter first.

An elderly gentleman rose to greet them from behind a desk covered with neat stacks of paper weighted down by miscellaneous items that included a jewel-encrusted sword hilt and a marble ashtray in the shape of Italy.

"Bonjour, monsieur. Je cherche Monsieur Jacques Martin." The words she had practiced so often fell from Tara's tongue.

"C'est moi. Je suis Jacques Martin."

Tara understood his answer—she'd heard it several times before—and her heart sank with disappointment. This gentleman had to be in his seventies, or eighties even.

"Parlez-vous anglais?" she asked.

The old man shook his head. *"Non."*

An uncomfortable silence hung in the air between

them as he waited for her to speak, curiosity plain in his eyes…and maybe a hint of fear.

She wasn't sure what to do next. She couldn't just leave. He deserved an explanation that she couldn't give him in French. She turned to Garrett for help.

At just a glance from her, he picked up the conversation, explaining their reason for being there. Tara watched the transformation in the man's face as he gained understanding of their mission.

When Garrett asked if he knew any other Jacques Martins who might fit their criteria, the old man shook his head, turning sympathetic eyes to Tara. *"Je suis désolé, mademoiselle."*

Tara forced a half smile. *"Merci beaucoup."*

The gentleman said something else and Tara looked to Garrett for a translation, but it was Dylan who spoke up. "He said he wishes you were his daughter. It would be very nice to have a beautiful daughter like you." The child's arm went around her leg for a quick hug.

She blinked back the tears that stung her eyes. "Thank you." She ruffled Dylan's hair and nodded to the old gentleman. "That's very kind."

When she found her birth father—and that was the only possibility she was going to consider—she hoped his sentiments would be the same.

As they said their adieus, the old man squeezed her hand and said something.

"He said good luck," Dylan told her.

Back outside the shop, Garrett let go of Dylan's

hand and nodded, and the child took off at a run. Garrett's arm slid around her shoulder with a comforting hug as they followed in his son's wake. "Don't be sad, okay? You still have a lot of Jacques Martins on your list."

"I know." Her breath left her in a huff. "I told myself this wasn't going to be easy, but it's hard to not get my hopes up. Every time I find one, I'm positive it's him."

Garrett leaned into her as they walked. "And I'll be here if it's not," he whispered. "Every time."

His breath caught on the rim of her ear and feathered down her neck, causing an unexpected shiver that slithered down her spine and coiled deep within her belly. A low chuckle confirmed he felt her response and had known what it would be. "I know what you need."

Fueled by the frustration of another false lead, irritation flickered inside Tara at Garrett's words— and the smugness behind them. Men's minds were like boomerangs that always came back to the same thing. "Not everything can be fixed by great sex," she pouted.

His eyes opened wide in surprise and then softened with a playful glint as he nodded toward the storefront they were approaching and where Dylan was already waiting. "I thought maybe something from here would lift your spirits. Berthillon. World's best."

Her eyes followed his nod, her face heating at the

conclusion she'd jumped to. "Ice cream!" She gave an embarrassed laugh. "Sorry."

"Never apologize when you've used *great* to describe it." The corner of his mouth twitched before it broke into one of his dazzling smiles. "But maybe this will cool you off." When he opened the door to the shop, the chilly air from inside did exactly that.

Sweetness hung in that same air as they entered, and Tara could taste the sugar on her tongue just from sniffing. Her mouth watered in anticipation as she looked over the list of flavors *du jour.*

"What would you like?" Garrett asked.

"A cup of strawberry," Dylan announced.

Despite the many choices, Tara's mind stalled on the sixth one down. "One scoop of cappuccino chocolate chip on a cone, please."

"My favorite." Garrett shifted his smile toward the young woman behind the counter, words flowing so smoothly from his lips that Tara could almost imagine them having their own flavor named after them.

The woman's eyes drifted lazily down Garrett as she leaned forward in open flirtation. The woman saw something she liked, and she put her message out there without hesitation.

Thea was like that.

Since birth, Tara's sister had dared the world to try to stick the *preacher's kid* label on her while Tara had tried to live up to the expectation—until she was twenty-three. The irony that Thea was the preacher's kid by blood while *she* was the bastard child squeezed at her again.

If she found her birth father, it would be news she'd want to share. But how would that news go over in Taylor's Grove?

Garrett's low chuckle drew Tara out of her reverie. The woman behind the counter had evidently said something that tickled his fancy.

"She said she likes your tattoo." He handed Tara the cone. "And I said I do, too."

Tara didn't recognize the emotion that had flared briefly as jealousy until his words transformed it into butterflies in her stomach. "Thanks." She tipped the cone in his direction.

He grinned. *"Je t'en prie."*

He paused, and she realized he was waiting for her to take her first bite. When she did, the silky texture spread a burst of coffee flavor across her tongue, and she let out a groan of pure pleasure.

A lazy smile touched his lips. "I like that sound." He took a bite and tilted his head toward the door, calling to his son. "Come on, Dylan. Let's go back down by the river."

Dylan dropped another spoonful of sprinkles into his cup and ran to join them.

As they walked along the Seine, eating their ice cream and enjoying the shade from the hazelnut trees, Notre-Dame came into view—majestic and serene. They approached Pont Saint-Louis, which connected Île de la Cité with the small island they were on, and Tara pulled out her camera.

"Here. Let me get one of you." Garrett took the camera from her and handed her his cone. Using mostly hand gestures, he positioned her with her elbow on the wall of the bridge and Notre-Dame in the background, and took quite a few shots, moving farther away each time. In between, she gave quick licks to the ice cream, which threatened to melt all over her hands. Satisfied at last, Garrett returned to her, laughing as she took a huge swipe with her tongue on both cones. He slipped the camera back into her purse and zipped it closed.

"Dad, can I go over there and watch the puppet show?" Dylan pointed to a knot of children sitting on the lawn of the cathedral in front of a portable puppet stage. Their giggles and claps infused the air with happy sounds.

"Sure, sport. We'll be right here."

Tara and Garrett stepped off the bridge and moved to the side behind the group of kids.

Tara held Garrett's cone out to him, but he dropped his gaze to her mouth and paused. "You have chocolate on your lip."

As her tongue made a quick jaunt around her lips, he leaned down and caught it with his mouth, capturing and muting her startled gasp. Her grip tightened around the cones she still clutched in each hand. She became aware of his erection forming against her front and the stone wall against her back. Whoever made being between a rock and a hard place synonymous with trouble had never been kissed by Garrett in Paris.

The tender kiss made her brain go all fuzzy.

"Did you get it?" she asked.

"Did I get what?"

"The chocolate."

He laughed. "Yep. All gone." He took his cone from her. "Now I have a much sweeter taste in my mouth."

The kiss and the fire she'd felt in Garrett's touch brought heat to her lips. She cooled them by burying them deep in the ice cream and threw a worried glance in Dylan's direction, finding his attention glued to the puppet show. "What if Dylan had seen?"

Garrett took a lick from his cone, seeming to weigh his words. "He's seen me kiss people in the past, and he's never been traumatized by it."

"Well, yeah, of course. But we don't want him to get the wrong idea that this is anything serious…like with you and your tutor."

"Yeah. You're right." He turned away to lean his back against the wall, and she felt the distancing in the move—both mental and physical.

Well, they'd had their night together…and their morning…and their afternoon. Twenty-four hours of romance was more than she'd ever expected on this trip. She should be grateful and satisfied that she had that to remember.

But Garrett's nearness made her feel hot and needy…and anything but satisfied.

When she took her next bite, the ice cream hung on the back of her tongue, making her shiver and causing a moment of excruciating brain freeze.

She remembered the admonishment her dad would give her when she did the same thing as a little girl.

"Don't bite off more than you can handle," he would say.

Now that she'd made love to Garrett, she knew exactly what her dad meant…though this time it had nothing to do with ice cream.

CHAPTER FOURTEEN

IT WAS 9:25 A.M. on Sunday, and Faith was still in her pajamas. She couldn't remember the last time that had happened.

If ever.

Oh, she'd stayed home with the kids when they were sick, but she always gotten dressed, even if that just meant slipping on jeans and a T-shirt. When *she* was sick, getting dressed was a must because *her* being under the weather always brought the women with their casserole dishes. It wouldn't do for them to stop by unexpectedly and catch her in a robe. That would be snickered at in the community for three to five days, depending on what other gossip popped up in the meantime.

Sawyer was at church by now. What was he telling people? No one had paid any attention yesterday that she was at her mother-in-law's. It was commonplace for her or Sawyer or the kids to be running in and out. And she'd gone to their cabin on Kentucky Lake for the better part of the day. That's where she'd called the kids from. The situation didn't seem so dire when she sat on the dock, watching the sunset on the water.

It occurred to her that she should move in there rather than Lacy's, but that would leave Sawyer to face the community alone, and that hardly seemed fair since he was the innocent in all of this.

The Marsdens' house next door was dark when she'd returned. With any luck, they were out of town. But she hadn't heard anything about their being gone, so that was unlikely.

Still she could hope.

She took her coffee cup and wandered aimlessly around the house until she found herself on the screened-in back porch. The forsythia and spirea bushes, tall and gangly and in bad need of pruning, had formed a privacy hedge around the backyard. Lacy had said it amounted to laziness, but Faith always suspected it gave much-needed privacy from her neighbor's eagle eye…and serpent tongue.

Lacy's roses and hydrangeas were in full bloom, a living canvas of color, and the swing was usually the perfect place to enjoy the sight and scents, but she was too restless. She could, however, cut some of the blooms and bring the divine scent indoors. Maybe it would be good aromatherapy.

She pushed the door open and descended the steps, letting the spring slam it back.

Sawyer's beloved bass boat, a treasured inheritance from his dad, sat under the carport, covered and untouched since this ordeal started, despite her husband's passion for the sport. His best sermons usually contained some fishing stories. The day would come—soon, she hoped—when he'd hook the boat up and head for the lake. That would be her sign that healing had begun.

The dewy grass squished between her toes as she padded barefoot to the potting shed. Packets of unopened seeds lay in a pile on the potting bench next to the gloves and a hand trowel, placed there by hands that had expected to come back for them.

Well, hands were back—just not the same ones these items were waiting for.

Faith picked up the seeds and the tools and stalked out of the potting shed with a purpose. She was an action person. And until a better action came to her, this would do.

She dropped to her knees in the dirt, ramming her hand into one of the gloves with determination. Something squished in the tip of one of the fingers, wringing a startled cry from her tight throat.

She jerked the glove off and shook it. A black spider with long, crumpled legs fell out. It was dead, but she was terrified of the creatures and looking at it still raised goose bumps on her arms. Then her eyes caught the red hourglass shape on its back, bringing her to her feet with a squeal of horror. A black widow! "Eww!"

"Who's there?" a sharp voice demanded from the other side of the hedge.

Sue! Another black widow would've been preferable. Faith's flight-or-fight instinct kicked in, and she looked around wildly for a means of escape.

"Who's there, I said? Answer me, whoever you are, or I'm calling the sheriff."

A flush of heat spread through Faith, but with it came an awareness of the cool dirt beneath her feet, which were firmly planted in a yard that belonged to her and her family.

Fight it would be.

"Don't be alarmed, Sue. It's me. A spider scared me."

"Faith?"

She shouldn't have been surprised, considering who she was speaking with. Nevertheless, Faith was startled to see a pair of arms snaking through the middle of the thick bushes, pushing them aside, and leaving her completely exposed to her neighbor's gawk.

"What in the world are you doing here at nine forty-five on Sunday morning…in your pajamas? Why aren't you at Sunday School?"

"Why aren't *you* at Sunday School?" Oh, *that* was sure the perfect, snappy comeback.

"I'm not feeling well." Sue sniffed as if she needed to add evidence. A sneeze followed, which couldn't have been faked.

It ran through Faith's thoughts that she could beg off the same way. She could say she wasn't feeling well, which was actually the truth, and had come to Lacy's house so Sawyer wouldn't catch it. But, any way she tried to spin it would be a lie. And when the news broke, which it might've already done, she'd be caught in her lie—even if the truth was nobody's business.

She'd told Sawyer she didn't care who knew. She was tired of living a lie. No use starting a new one now.

"I'm going to live here for a while, Sue." She didn't have to try to keep emotion out of her voice. It was dull and lifeless with no effort needed.

"Why? Is something wrong with your house?"

"No. Nothing's wrong with the house."

"Well, I don't understand why y'all would move out of your house that's only—what? Twenty years old?—into this place that obviously needs so much work. It'll drive Sawyer crazy. He doesn't have time now to take care of everything at the church that needs doing, much less fix this place up."

"Sawyer isn't moving, Sue. Just me."

"What? Do you mean to tell me…?" Aghast was too light a term to describe the woman's face. "Wait just a minute."

The arms jerked from the shrubs, allowing the stems to shoot back upright into their intended positions. Before Faith could get her wits about her, Sue had made her way to the end of the hedge and was coming through the gate attached to the side of the house.

Faith met her by the Mr. Lincoln tea rose—Lacy's favorite.

"Do you mean to tell me you and Sawyer are separated?" Sue's voice was a hodgepodge of emotion with shades of disbelief, incredulity, curiosity and a tinge of unchecked amusement all balled together.

"That's correct."

"Why?" Sue's eyes narrowed and anger took top billing. "Has he been messing around on you?"

"No." Faith shook her head emphatically, wanting to squelch that rumor before it got wings. "Never. Sawyer's the most loyal, trustworthy husband who ever lived. He would never even *think* about cheating."

Sue crossed her arms, tapping her fingers against her bicep. "What is it then? I mean, why else do couples separate?"

"Couples separate for a lot of reasons, Sue. Sawyer and I have some things we need to straighten out, and I needed space to think. And time alone," she added.

If she picked up on the hint, Sue chose to ignore it. "Well, who all knows? I mean, is he going to make a public announcement this morning at church? The congregation has the right to know if their preacher and his wife are going to get a divorce."

"I didn't say anything about divorce." Faith interlocked her fingers to keep from lashing out at the silly ninny.

"No, of course you didn't. But if y'all are separated, certainly divorce is a possibility. Anybody with any sense knows that."

Faith took a deep breath, her head filling with the scent of Lacy's Mr. Lincolns. Her mother-in-law had lived by Sue for thirty-plus years and was one of the few people who truly cared about the woman. The thought cooled her temper and guided her words. "I pray it won't come to that. And I don't think it will, but whatever the outcome, Sawyer and I need the prayers of the community. And we need privacy."

Irritation flared in Sue's eyes as her mouth clamped shut. At least it had stopped her from saying whatever her next comment was going to be. "Privacy isn't something Taylor's Grove's very good at. We're all family here. We care about each other." She sneezed again, and pulled a tissue from the pocket of her khakis to wipe her nose, which was beginning to look raw.

"As long as people let that care guide their actions, I can't ask for anything more," Faith said.

"Yes, well…" Sue looked at her watch. "I'll leave you alone. Give you some of that privacy you need."

She turned and practically sprinted from the yard, leaving Faith to wonder why Sue had bolted the way she did.

Following a hunch, Faith went back into the house, changed out of her pajamas and took a seat in the living room next to the window.

Just as she suspected, Sue and her husband, Ed, left their house at 10:17 a.m. Their hurried pace gave away that they were trying hard to make the ten-thirty service at Taylor's Grove Church despite Sue's cold and the old people she'd be putting at risk with it.

As to what message they would hear, Faith couldn't

be sure, but somehow Sawyer would manage to bring love into it.

She headed to the kitchen to pour herself another cup of coffee. She would need the caffeine. When church let out, her day was going to get very busy.

"I'M TELLING YOU, Emma, if I'd made a list of things to include in my most perfect day, I could check most of them off. Finding the right Jacques Martin would be the only thing without a mark in front of it."

Emma's dreamy sigh came across clearly. "Mmm. I'm thrilled for you, and jealous down to my star-spangled toenails."

"Oh, that's right! Tuesday's the Fourth of July. It's weird being in a place that doesn't celebrate it." That Garrett had provided her with the best fire-works she'd ever experienced ran through her mind, but she didn't voice it. She'd gushed enough about him already. Any more and Emma would get the wrong idea.

"But you'll be there for Bastille Day, right? That's sort of the same thing, isn't it?"

"Yeah, that'll be my last day here. I fly out the morning of the fifteenth." Her gaze strayed across the terrace to Garrett's flat, where she watched the lights wink out in Dylan's bedroom, and followed Garrett's progression as he appeared in the foyer, headed toward his kitchen. Her stomach knotted and she changed the subject away from her leaving. "Are you going to the cabin for the Fourth?"

"I, uh." Emma coughed loudly into the phone. "Sorry! Something went down the wrong way. Your parents cancelled the picnic this year."

"Cancelled? Why?" The July Fourth picnic at the cabin on the lake had never been cancelled. It was a tradition.

"They're calling for the weather to be bad." Emma's explanation didn't make sense.

"If it rains, we've always just moved the picnic into the cabin."

"But this year, there's a chance of some really nasty weather. You know, tornadoes and stuff."

"Oh." Tara wasn't sure what "and stuff" referred to. Garrett appeared in his living room, sipping a glass of wine. He leaned over and picked something up from his coffee table, and a second later, strains of Miles Davis drifted through Tara's open window. "Garrett is so hot, Emma. I wish you could meet him."

"Well, maybe some time when he's in St. Louis, we'll run up there and do some shopping."

"Yeah, maybe we'll do that." He disappeared into his bedroom, and Tara's mind shifted back to the cancelled picnic. "Tornadoes and stuff, huh?"

"Yeah. Hey, uh, I hate to cut this off, but my cycling group is riding the Tunnel Hill Trail today."

"No problem. Talk to you soon."

"Hope tomorrow's even better than today for you! Bye!"

"Bye."

Tara stared at the phone for a minute. Something was up about the picnic. There was an edge to Emma's voice.

Mama had said Dad was down. Was he so depressed they would cancel the picnic?

She hit Trenton's number.

"Hey, pinky."

She laughed. Garrett and Dylan had been so accepting of her deformity, she'd almost forgotten about it while she'd been there. "Hey, bro. I was just talking to Emma, and she said the picnic was cancelled."

Trenton paused. "Yeah. Yeah, that's right."

"But it's never been cancelled before. If it stormed, we always just moved inside."

"Yeah, well, uh…tell me what you've seen since the last time we talked."

Was he changing the subject? "What is going on?"

"What do you mean?"

"I mean, the last time I told you about my sightseeing, you told me your eyes were glazing over, but tonight, you want to know all about it. What gives, Trent? I feel like I'm getting the run—"

"You're fading out, sis. Hello?"

Tara checked her connection. Five bars. "Quit messing with me, Trenton. Is everyth—"

"Hello? Hello? Sorry, sis. I think I've lost you."

"But you're coming in loud and clear."

Beep. Her phone read Call Ended. She called him back immediately, but it went straight to voice mail.

More angry now than worried, she punched Thea's

number. It rang several times before going to voice mail. Was Thea avoiding her, too?

The air seemed hot suddenly, so she stepped out onto the terrace.

"You're pulling your lip. What's wrong?" Garrett was walking toward her with a glass of wine in each hand.

She held her phone out. "My family."

His chin buckled in concern. "Is somebody sick?"

"No." She ran her thumb and middle finger into the hair at the top of her head, and flipped the sides out of her face. "They've cancelled the July Fourth picnic, which has never happened before, supposedly because of weather."

Garrett's shrug suggested she was overreacting. "That sounds plausible."

"Yeah, I guess." She stuffed her phone into the pocket of her shorts. "I'm probably just being paranoid. You were right about my dad being bothered by my looking for Jacques Martin, though. I think the whole situation's got him depressed."

Garrett held out a glass of wine to her. "Well, you're here, and the die is cast, so just roll with it."

"I hope I don't read 'em and weep."

He grinned. "That's poker, not craps."

"Oh." She took the glass he offered and tipped it in his direction. "Then let the good times roll." She took a sip of the tongue-pleasing, full-bodied wine. Garrett's wines were always superb. Or maybe it was the presence of the man who flavored the drink.

"Speaking of which, I thought we decided it wouldn't be smart to spend the evening together."

After the afternoon's excursion, they'd returned to their respective flats, not wanting Dylan to get ideas about their time together. She'd stayed tucked away out of sight while they played their nightly game of catch and grilled their hot dogs.

"He's asleep. He won't see us together." Garrett's lips on hers made acquiescence much easier. With a hand at the small of her back, he guided her to the bench beside his door.

She helped him clear away the balls and gloves that littered the seat. "What if he wakes up?"

"He won't. He never does. The kid's always been a sound sleeper."

As soon as they sat, Garrett's arm went around her shoulder and pulled her close. She relaxed against him, his solidness and the wine making whatever was going on at home seem very far away. "I like Henri."

She felt the vibration of Garrett's chuckle against her shoulder blade. "He likes you, too, but he had a hard time understanding what you were saying."

She laughed. "Nobody's ever had to translate my English into regular English before. My kids at school are going to love this story."

"Henri's been a good friend. He took a liking to me as soon as we met, and he adores Dylan. I'm anxious to hear what he has to say about you tomorrow." He let loose with a growl, and his best Henri imitation. "*Mon Dieu,* Garrett, theese Tara, she has the voice of the angel but the look that ees hot as hell."

Tara giggled and pressed her palm to her hot face. "He's quite the lady's man, huh?"

"If you made that plural, you got it right. Henri can charm the clothes off a woman with the raise of an eyebrow."

She gave him a sidelong glance. "You don't do so bad yourself with that lazy, one-sided grin."

"Is that right?" Garrett sounded genuinely surprised. He leaned forward and looked her in the face. "Like this?" He did an exaggerated lift to the right side of his mouth that left a goofy expression on his face.

Tara tried to stifle her laugh, but it burst out, along with some wine-colored spit that landed on Garrett's nose. "Ack! I'm sorry!" The apology would've been more effective if she'd been able to control her laughter, which she couldn't.

Garrett closed his eyes and wiped his sleeve down his face, and his lips relaxed into a yummy, genuine smile. "It's okay. We've exchanged spit, as I recall. Along with other bodily fluids."

There it was. One side of his mouth dropped, leaving the other raised in that look that made her insides squirm.

His eyes locked with hers and darkened. "It didn't work."

She cocked her head, holding his stare. "What didn't work?"

"Your clothes are still on." He leaned forward, touching his lips to hers. She opened her mouth to him, tasting the wine that seemed to have grown sweeter on his tongue. He followed as she leaned back into the bench. They both found the side table and managed to set their glasses on it without ever breaking contact with their mouths.

The kiss intensified when she ran her hands through his hair, pressing him close, inviting his tongue deeper. His arms encircled her with heat, on her neck, shoulder, breast. Reflexively, the small of her back came off the bench as she arched against him. He wasted no time accepting the offer, running his hand under her T-shirt and her bra, brushing her nipple with his thumb.

She came up for air, reluctantly pulling her mouth away. He continued to kiss the side of her lips, her cheek, her jaw line, and down to her neck, still brushing her nipple, driving her insane with the light touch. She needed more. So much more.

"We have to stop now," she warned, "if we're going to stop at all."

Garrett leaned his head back to look at her. His hand dropped from her breast, but the back of his fingers kept contact along her rib cage and stomach. "Why would we stop?"

"Dylan." The word came out on a gasp as he caught her other nipple between his fingers. "We don't want him to get...oh! To get...the wrong idea."

"He's sound asleep." He kissed her eyelids tenderly. "And we could be, too, in a couple of hours."

Tara raised her lips to his. "Are you asking me to spend the night?"

Garrett kissed her gently, and then backed his face away until they could actually focus on each other. His hand brushed her cheek. "I want you so badly. We can make love in my bed, and go to sleep in each other's arms. I'll set the alarm to wake us up and you can go back to your place before Dylan gets up. He won't even know you stayed the night."

The child would be in her charge all day tomorrow. If she was going to be on her best game, she needed a good rest tonight—and that wasn't going to happen if she and Garrett stopped now. She would spend the rest of the night in turmoil, aching to have him inside her.

"Okay, let's go."

He stopped to check on his son on their way to his bedroom.

She went on ahead and was waiting, naked and more than ready, when he met up with her two minutes later.

"I CAN'T KEEP avoiding her calls, Mama. She's going to figure out something's up."

Faith had known that Thea would have the hardest time with the lie they were perpetrating on Tara. The two girls had always been close, had always shared everything. But she'd thought she could count on

Trenton—Mr. I-can-keep-my-cool-in-all-situations.
Apparently, he'd blown it, too—a fact that Thea had
started their phone conversation with.

"She might suspect, Thea, but she can't know unless somebody tells her. I told her Sawyer was still
having a hard time with things. Can't you just reit-
erate that?" Faith rubbed her throbbing temple, certain that any more pressure in her life would cause
it to rupture. She'd talked to far too many people
today, trying to explain the separation Sawyer had
announced from the pulpit without giving away intimate details. She didn't need things with Tara to
go awry now, too.

Her younger daughter sounded close to tears.
"I can try. But you know how she always finagles
secrets out of me."

Faith knew all too well. Christmas presents. Surprise parties. No secret was safe if Thea got hold of
it. If her oldest child had any inkling something was
up, she could easily get the youngest to sing like a
canary, without even having to bribe her with seed.

"Can't you just be too busy to talk to her?" Faith
suggested.

"And miss all the good stuff about the new guy?"
Incredulity oozed over the line. "Not a chance."

"What new guy?" It was Faith's turn to be incredulous. "Has Tara met somebody in Paris?"

"Um…no. Of course not. I mean, they're just
neighbors."

Faith knew that once Thea started crawdadding,

you were mere seconds away from getting the low-down. She pressed in quickly, overwhelming her younger daughter with questions. "Tara's involved with her neighbor? Dylan's father? What's his name? How do you know?"

"His name's Garrett, and, for one thing, *you* told me they went out."

Okay, she had her on that one. But Faith wasn't about to let this go. Tara was her firstborn, and it sounded as if she was going to need some direction from Mama. "But, I thought it was just an innocent date. That he was showing her the sights. Is there more to it than that?"

"No, no, of course not. All they did was visit some historic sites." Thea would be twirling her hair around her finger about now. She claimed it helped her concentrate, but it mostly let her family know she was withholding information.

"I thought they went to dinner, too."

"Well, yeah. That's what I meant. All they did was see sights and go to dinner. Emma just said that she really liked him."

Faith's head spun with that news. If Understate-ment Emma said "really liked," that meant Tara might be shopping for an engagement ring as they spoke. "Really likes him as in doing things she shouldn't even be thinking about doing because she doesn't know him well enough to be doing those things? Or thinking about them?"

"Uhh, geez, Mama, I've got to go. I totally forgot

that I told my friend, uh, Melody that I'd help her, uh, move some furniture around today. I'd better get over there. Love you. Bye!"

Faith closed her eyes and groaned. Tara was sleeping with some Garrett guy in Paris. Her baby. Involved with somebody she hadn't known long enough to barely be friends with, much less lovers. Getting serious with someone she had no chance at a relationship with because everybody knew that long-distance relationships didn't work. Surely, she knew by now that "absence makes the heart grow fonder" was a fallacy. "Out of sight, out of mind" was the truth.

Or maybe Tara wasn't getting serious. Maybe this was just a fun fling. A month of sex and then head home without a backward glance. That was even worse.

Faith twirled her wedding band, which had grown loose on her finger. She and Sawyer had tried to instill a belief in their children that physical intimacy was the highest means of showing love, and sex was not something to be taken lightly.

Like I did.

Her past hadn't just come back to haunt her, it was claiming squatters rights smack-dab in the center of her life.

Well, she may not have been the perfect role model, but that wouldn't keep her from being the best mother she knew how to be. "But I did it" was an excuse parents used way too often. She'd done a lot of things she didn't want her kids to do, and she hoped they learned from her mistakes.

She picked up her phone and touched Tara's number.

Her daughter answered immediately. "Mama?"

Faith saw no use easing into this. Tara's frankness came straight from her own gene pool. "Thea tells me you're sleeping with your neighbor."

"She *what?*"

Anger and horror, but no denial. "Okay, she didn't come right out and tell me, but you know how she loses her composure and can't think of what to say? Well, she just did that, and we were talking about you and your neighbor, so I'm pretty sure I've jumped to the right conclusion."

"I don't think this is something I want to talk about."

"Of course you don't. I knew you wouldn't. So don't talk. Just listen. You need to think about the consequences of what you're doing. You're setting yourself up for heartbreak because you're going to lose either way."

A noisy sigh came from the other end of the line, but Faith wouldn't relinquish the floor. At least Tara hadn't hung up on her. "If you fall in love with him, you're going to be leaving in two weeks, and everybody knows long-distance relationships don't work. And, if you're not in love and just doing this for fun, then you're following in my footsteps. And look where they led me."

"Mama…"

"I just don't want you to make the same mistakes I made, and I'll go to any lengths to keep that from happening."

"Like calling me in the middle of the night?"

Faith looked at her watch. Six-twenty. Which meant it was after one in the morning in Paris. The tide turned, and guilt swept over her. She'd disturbed her daughter's sleep and probably scared the wadding out of her, too. "Oh, sweetpea, I'm so sorry. I didn't even consider the time difference! Go back to sleep. I hope you're alone. I love you."

"Love you, too. Bye."

Faith dropped the phone on the table and picked up the photo that sat on one of Lacy's hand-crocheted doilies. Her family smiled back at her—her family as it used to be a couple of years ago. The family she wanted back. Smiling. Hugging. United.

With the first utterance of Jacques Martin's name, that family had vanished, and Tara had started looking for something to hold on to to keep her world upright.

Maybe that's what she was doing with this Garrett person. Perhaps he was giving her something in Paris to hold on to while the world shifted beneath her feet.

But, if Tara found her father, she might not need the other man to hold on to.

A flash of inspiration lifted Faith's spirit.

All this time, she'd been hoping Tara wouldn't find

Jacques Martin. She'd been afraid of what it would do to Sawyer and the family.

But fear of the unknown was a crippling kind of fear. The kind that held you back when destiny was calling your name. It took *faith* to step out into the darkness, as her mama always told her. That's why she named Faith what she did.

Tomorrow, she would start with calls to Murray State University. Somewhere, someone would know something about Jacques Martin.

If Tara was determined to find her birth father, and if finding him would fill the void and keep her from making a huge mistake, then her mother would help her find him.

Faith would lead the way.

"Sorry about that." Tara shot Garrett an apologetic look and set the phone back on the bedside table.

He gave her a sleepy grin and reached up to brush her hair from her face. "It's okay. My mom does weird things like that, too."

Tara covered her eyes, hoping by some feat of magic the gesture would make her invisible. "No chance you didn't hear what she was saying, is there?"

It didn't work because Garrett found her hand with no trouble and pulled it away from her face. He faked a sorrowful expression, but the twinkle in his eye gave him away. "Nope."

She groaned her exasperation, sinking back down into the pillow.

He sat up enough to lean on an elbow. "But maybe she's right."

His voice was quiet, and it made Tara's heart thud in her chest. "You mean, you think we're making a mistake by having sex?"

His expression became somber, and the mirth left his eyes. But heat replaced it, along with a look the depth of which thrilled her and terrified her at the same time. "I mean, I think we're making a mistake if we believe we can walk away from this in thirteen days and treat it as if it meant nothing."

Thirteen days. He'd used the exact number rather than the more arbitrary two weeks. He was counting them, just like she was. A knot formed in her stomach, hearing him verbalize the same agitation she'd dealt with all afternoon. "What do we do about it, though?"

"I think the first thing to do is to be honest about what's really going on, so we know where we actually stand without any pretense. I'll go first." He rubbed his hand up and down her arm a few times, and she sensed he was trying to work up his courage. "I'm falling for you, Tara." She watched his Adam's apple bob as he swallowed hard. "My connection with you has been so swift and hard, it scares me. I've wanted to ignore it. Act like it wasn't there. But you've been on my mind for two weeks now, and, after that first touch Saturday night, I don't want to think about *not* touching you. I already *know* you. I think I've *always* known you. I've just been waiting for you to show up in my life. Does that make sense?"

She placed her hand against his chest, could feel his heart pounding at the sincerity of his words. "You said it prettier than I could, but I feel the same way. It depresses me to think about going home and leaving you and Dylan. I know that's crazy—I *have* to go home. But…" Emotion clogged her voice, and she cleared her throat. "What if the reason I'm here isn't to find my birth father? What if I'm here to find you and Dylan?"

He brushed a tear from her face that she hadn't realized was there. "I love that idea, and I love that it's in your mind. It tells me this isn't one-sided on my part."

She shook her head. "It's not one-sided on your part."

He touched his lips to hers. "But don't give up on finding your father yet. He may still be out there."

She felt her chin quiver, and she pressed her lips together to hold it still. "I'm not giving up, but I get my hopes up a little higher each time, and that makes me fall harder when it doesn't pan out."

"I wish I could snap my fingers and deliver the right Jacques Martin to you."

Garrett lay back and pulled her close against him in a hold that made her feel protected from any hurt the outside world might throw at her.

"So what do we do now?" she whispered.

"About Jacques Martin?"

"About us."

He kissed her forehead and her eyelids. "We handle it the same as the search for your father. We keep our hearts open to any possibility, and we believe that, if we're meant to be together, love will find a way."

Tara raised herself up this time, needing to see his eyes. "Love?"

He shrugged. "We can break out all the moves to dance around it, or we can call it what it is."

She cocked her head and smiled at his straightforwardness. "Love." She laughed. "Mama would be so horrified if she knew."

He gave her a tender smile. "You have good parents. Weird, but good."

"I know." She lay down, her head on his chest listening to his heart. It was a sweet sound, a gentle sound that would lull her to sleep very quickly. "If I were smart, I'd get up and go home right now so the alarm wouldn't have to wake us up so early."

"Mmm," he answered and she couldn't tell if the sound was affirmative or negative.

"But I've never been accused of being a brainiac."

"You couldn't be too smart, or you wouldn't have stayed a virgin until you were twenty-something. What a waste of talent."

She smiled and continued smiling until his breath slowed to the deep sounds of slumber.

CHAPTER FIFTEEN

"TARA, SHE IS LOVELY, Garrett."

Waiting in Garrett's office for him when he arrived, Henri was obviously anxious to talk. He had his cup of espresso in hand and one for Garrett, covered to keep it hot.

"*Bon matin, Henri.* It's good to see you, too." He gave his friend a smile. "I knew you'd like her."

"Her hair is very wild and crazy." Henri's hands flew above his head, gesticulating to make his point. "*Mais, ils sont fabuleux!*"

Henri never had a hair out of place, so it was interesting that he'd find Tara's wild curls fabulous.

"And her poor hand! *Mon Dieu!* Does it cause her pain?"

"She never complains about it, but she warns Dylan and me not to squeeze it too hard. She sustained some major injuries in that motorcycle wreck. It's amazing she's even here." A lump swelled in Garrett's throat at that thought. He tried to get rid of it by swallowing his espresso in one gulp, which garnered him a disapproving eye roll from his friend. "But, I'm thrilled she is." Even that felt like an understatement.

"*Oui, c'est évident.*" Henri paused, weighing what

was coming next. "Can you share with me the circumstances of her father, this Jacques Martin? Did she recently learn of him, or has she known of him throughout her life and has only now the means or desire to search for him?"

Garrett didn't think Tara would mind, so he brought his friend up to speed on the circumstances surrounding Tara's conception.

"Très interéssant." Henri thrust his bottom lip out and made a French sound that meant he was mulling something over. "And you say she found names and addresses in the telephone book and on the internet?"

"That's correct."

Henri shook his head. "Such lists would not be complete. He might be not listed. He has the cell phone, *probablement. Oui?*"

"Yeah. She knows that." He and Tara had already talked about her archaic means of searching. "But she's doing it the only way she knows how."

"Did she consider to hire a private detective?" His shrug suggested it was so obvious he shouldn't even have to mention it.

Garrett leaned back in his seat to get comfortable. He appreciated Henri's interest in Tara's predicament. Had his friend already figured out how very special she was to him?

"I suggested that, but she said she didn't know anyone in Paris who could recommend one, and she was afraid, if she hired someone blind, he'd turn out to be a shyster."

Henri's nose wrinkled like he smelled something unpleasant. "*Qu'est-ce que ça veut dire*—'shyster'?"

"A crook." Garrett explained. "Someone who cheats people out of their money."

"Ah!" Henri nodded. "*Je comprends*. But what if she finds this Jacques Martin, and *he* is the shyster?" His eyebrow lifted to make his point.

"We've discussed that, and she's aware that she'll have to be careful and trust her instincts," Garrett agreed. "She's a pretty good judge of character. She told me that if you'd looked her up and down one more time, she was going to ask you to leave a *few* clothes on her because she didn't want to catch a cold."

Henri had a good laugh at that. "It was the test for you, *mon ami*. Not Tara. And it worked. Your hand made the fist very quickly."

Garrett recalled the flare of jealousy that had shot through him, and he had no doubt Henri was speaking the truth.

"But do not worry." Henri gave a dismissive wave of his hand. "I will allow you to keep Tara for yourself."

That pulled a laugh from Garrett. He'd never encountered a woman who would choose him over Henri—until Tara. But she left him no doubt as to who her choice would be, and it felt damn good to be the winner for once. Good enough that he had to rub it in a bit. "This is one you have no chance with. Did you see the way she latched on to my arm after you ogled her? She wasn't the least bit affected by your debonair French ways."

Henri's warm smile lit up his face. "The woman was blind. I have heard that the climaxes may cause that condition."

Garrett's face warmed at the truth in Henri's folklore, but he wouldn't cheapen what he had with Tara with locker-room talk. "Back to Jacques Martin." He made his point by switching to their former subject. "It doesn't look promising that she'll find him. It's like looking for a needle in a haystack."

Henri's nostrils flared. "What is this needle in the haystack I always hear of? American idioms do not make sense. Why would someone put a needle in a haystack? Would he be sewing in a hay field? Why would it not be like finding a needle in the pin cushion?" He crossed his arms imperiously, making Garrett certain Napoleon Bonaparte's blood ran in his friend's veins.

"I don't know, Henri. Make it a needle in a pin cushion if you want, but, either way, finding him is difficult and not likely to get any easier."

Henri drummed his fingers on the desk, staring at them for a minute. Then he slid his eyes up slowly to meet Garrett's. "You are falling in love with her. I see this in your eyes when you speak her name."

"Yeah, I, um…" The serious turn in the conversation was far removed from their usual banter. "I believe I am."

"Dylan is very fond of her. He brought her into

most conversations during his visit." A hint of worry edged Henri's voice. "You had a fear this would happen."

The strong coffee…or something…made the muscles around Garrett's heart tighten. "But love's a process that takes time, Henri, and if the right woman comes along, I have to open myself up to the process. Unfortunately, that means opening Dylan up to it, too."

"And you think Tara could be the right one?"

Garrett took a deep breath, and the tightening loosened a smidgen. "Let's just say it feels right at this time."

Henri broke eye contact, brushing at something on the desk. "And when will she leave?"

"The fifteenth." The reality of the time they had left closed off Garrett's throat and made breathing impossible for a few seconds.

"If she found her birth father, would that change her plans? Would she stay longer, *peut-être?*"

Garrett hadn't considered that, but it was certainly a possibility. Extending her stay to get to know her father would make perfect sense. "I don't know. I guess that could change things. She has the summer off, so she wouldn't *have* to be back until the middle of August." His heart beat faster at the thought.

Henri pushed out of his chair. "Well, I must begin the work, *oui?*"

"What's your hurry?" His friend's swift change

in manner was out of character. With the campaign over, Garrett had expected him to take it easy today.

"I have important things to do." Henri pointed his finger dramatically upward as he hurried from the room.

Garrett rolled his eyes at his friend's theatrics. "Frenchmen." He chuckled. "Probably headed to the restroom."

"Do you see it yet, Dylan?"

Tara glanced up anxiously into the sprawling tree where Dylan was searching.

"Not yet." The child caught the branch above his head and used it to make his way to the other side of the trunk.

Tara checked the cache finder again. The treasure had to be up in the tree. "I'll give you a couple more minutes, then we'll have to give up on this one." Her eyes darted around the park. No security guard in sight.

"I don't want to give—wait! I see something!" Dylan swung his arm over a branch and ducked under it. "There's a hole! And it's got something in it!"

The giddy excitement in his voice was infectious. Tara held her breath as he slid his hand in to retrieve what he'd found.

"Got it!" He held up a small plastic container in triumph.

"Drop it to me, so you have both hands to climb

down." Tara held her arms out, and her partner did as he was instructed.

Following the tradition to keep geocaches secret, they strolled leisurely with the treasure to the closest bench and pretended they were merely opening a mundane plastic box.

Dylan's bottom lip drooped in disappointment when he ripped the lid off and peered inside. "There aren't many items. Not like the one we found yesterday."

Tara gave him a pat. "Yeah, but that makes this one even better."

"Why?" He gave her one of those skeptical looks kids save for when they know adults aren't being completely truthful.

She flipped open the log. "This cache was hidden on March 3, 2011, and it's only been found…" She counted the entries. "Nine times. That means it's a really difficult cache to locate, and *you* found it!"

The grin that broke across his face was a duplicate of his dad's, making Tara's breath hitch. "Wow! That means we're good at this, aren't we?"

"We're better than good. We're freakin' awesome!" She held up her hand, but then thought better of allowing him to hit the one that had been injured. She switched to the other. "I want an official high-five for that. A high-three just won't do."

Dylan giggled and slapped his palm against hers. Then he dug in their Crown Royal pouch, which had been donated to the cause by Garrett, pulling out one of the special tokens he and Tara had made that morning, and traded it for a gold medallion with a fleur-de-lis embossed on it.

Then he shimmied up the tree and placed the cache back in the hole where he'd found it.

Tara was absorbed in watching Dylan and didn't hear the police officer approach. When the man spoke, she wheeled around to find him giving her a look that was none too friendly.

He shook a finger at Dylan, then at her, his voice stern and unyielding. She couldn't understand a word he said.

"I'm sorry." She had no idea how much a tree-climbing fine might run, but she didn't want to find out. "I don't understand what you're saying."

Dylan was making his way back down. "I un—"

"Be quiet, Dylan." She shot a silencing look his way.

The policeman's facial features lost their hard edge. *"Madame."* He spoke slowly and precisely. "To climb trees is not allowed. We warn of the danger." He pointed at the sign in front of their tree.

Tara willed her face to flush, and she touched her hand to the base of her throat for added drama. "Oh, I'm so sorry. My French isn't very good, so I didn't realize that's what it said. I should've checked my phrase book."

Dylan dropped from the bottom branch to land beside her. "But you said you wouldn't need that book as long as I—"

She pulled him to her, clamping her hand lightly over his mouth. "Shh, Dylan. Don't interrupt the adults." Then she turned her attention back to the police officer, smiling sweetly while thickening her Southern accent. "The visitor's guide said that the Luxembourg Gardens were a wonderful place to bring children." She played the sympathy move by wiping her face with her injured hand.

Just as she'd hoped, the policeman grimaced at the sight, caught himself and then gave her an overly cheery grin. "It is of no great importance, *madame*. Your son is safe."

Dylan nudged her leg at the policeman's error.

She ruffled his hair with her good hand and placed her other index finger to her lips. "Shh. Let the nice man finish what he's saying."

The policeman leaned toward Dylan and wagged his finger. "You may not climb these trees. And when you climb the trees at your home, you must always be very careful. Do you understand?"

Dylan nodded. "Yes, but I don't have any trees at my house."

"That is unfortunate." The man's chin buckled in a look of sympathy. "Perhaps someday you will." He turned his attention back to Tara. "*Au revoir, madame.* I hope you will enjoy your stay in Paris."

"You're very kind. Thank you." Tara gave a small wave as she guided Dylan toward the walkway.

"You sort of told that policeman some fibs." Dylan threw an accusing frown her way.

"Yes, I did," she admitted.

One corner of Dylan's mouth curved into a half smile that was identical to, and just as charming as, his father's. "You let him think we didn't know what that sign said."

"Yeah. I probably shouldn't have done that, but I didn't want him to fine me—fine means paying money as a punishment for breaking a law."

"I know what it means. It makes Dad mad when people park on the sidewalk. He says he's glad they got a fine."

She chuckled at the child's honesty.

"You let him think I was your son, too."

His half smile burst into a full-blown grin that Tara answered with her own. "I didn't think that one would hurt anyone. It wasn't something he could fine me for. I mean, you'd look pretty weird with one of those yellow tickets stuck to your head."

His childish giggle filled her ears and warmed her heart at the same time.

"I wish you *were* my mom." He took her hand. "You're fun."

The air whooshed out of her lungs, but she managed a choked "Thanks, Dylan. You're fun, too."

Backed by the swiftness of a six-year-old's attention span, his face lost its smile. "Yesterday, Dad said you were trying to find your father. How'd you lose him?"

Oh, wow! This one was going to require the most finely honed of her teacher talents. "Well, your dad has told me that you lost your mother when you were three. That kind of lost means—"

"That she died, and now she's up in heaven."

"That's right. But I didn't lose my father that way. I think he lives here in Paris." Dylan's knitting brows said the explanation wasn't enough. "He moved away before I was born." She tried again. "So we've never gotten to meet. But I came to Paris to look for him."

"Do you have a mom?"

"Yes, I have a mom *and* a dad." She anticipated his next question. "A man named Sawyer married my mom. He loves me very much, and he's my dad just like *your* dad."

"Did they have sleepovers?"

Tara swallowed her startled gasp. If she'd learned anything from teaching, it was that sometimes a kid's wording could be wonky. "What do you mean?"

"My friend Michelle has a new dad. He used to eat with them a lot. And then he and her mom started having sleepovers, and they got married. Now she's going to get a new baby sister."

"Sometimes it happens that way," Tara agreed.

Dylan pinned her with that wide-eyed look that was so easy to read, and she braced for what was coming.

"You want to have a sleepover at our house to-night?"

"Thank you for asking, but that's probably not a good idea." She could read the disappointment in the child's dangling lower lip.

"Well, if you wanted to have sleepovers, that would be okay. Maybe you and my dad could get married and you could be my mom."

His suggestion was so innocent…and so earnest… it filled her heart to the point of breaking. "Let's sit a minute, okay?" She sat down on a nearby bench and pulled him into her lap. "You planted seeds with Veronique yesterday, didn't you?"

He nodded. "Veronique said they would grow into a salad."

"Well, see all these trees and flowers?" She motioned to the artfully landscaped area around them, and his eyes followed her gesture. "Each of these plants started from a seed, and each of them grew into something special. Now, I like you and your dad very much, and that's like planting a seed of friendship. Sometimes friendship grows like a flower. It's very beautiful, but it stays small. And sometimes friendship grows into something much bigger and stronger like a tree. That's the kind of friendship that becomes love. The thing is, both kinds of friendships, whether they're the *like* kind or the *love* kind, both need time to grow."

She paused, but for once the little boy didn't have any questions. "So, like I said, you and your dad and I have planted the seed—" She drew his attention to a green sprout just popping from the ground. "But we don't know yet what it's going to grow into. We'll just have to wait and see." She pressed on, determined to keep her message upbeat. "I'll have to go back to my real home soon, but even after I leave Paris, our seed is going to continue to grow into something."

"You could stay with us."

"If I did, my mom and dad would *really* miss me, just like I'm going to miss you and your dad when I leave. But he and I have already decided that we'll talk on the phone a lot—talking is sort of like sunshine to a seed—and you're going to call me whenever you feel like it—like you do with your grandmas and grandpas. And after a few months, let's say like after Christmas, if it looks like we're going to grow into a tree, we'll make plans for me to come back for another visit...or for you to come visit me. Deal?"

He smiled and nodded. "Deal."

With no forewarning, he threw his arms around her neck. He was soft and warm, and the summer sweetness of the tree he'd climbed earlier still clung to him.

Just as suddenly, the tears that had been hovering close to the surface since the start of this conversation burst from Tara's eyes like a spring shower.

Dylan loosened his hold and sat back, gaping at her. "Are you crying?"

Tara sniffed. "We can't expect our seed to grow with just sunshine, can we?"

He shook his head.

She swiped at the tears, and flung the excess water from her fingers. "Then I'll water it, too."

He grinned and she pulled him into another quick

hug. Her words had been playful and light—the exact opposite of the weight she carried in her heart.

Garrett's worst fear had come true. Dylan had imprinted onto her like a newly hatched duckling. Problem was, she felt the same way about him and his dad.

Oh, she talked a good game. Give the seeds time to grow and all that. But when the time came for her to leave and these hugs were the goodbye kind, how would she ever be able to let go?

CHAPTER SIXTEEN

FAITH PUSHED THE box out of the way with her calf and pulled out the last one from the depths of the hall closet. She'd set a goal to work through a closet each day, throwing away what was of no use or sentimental value, boxing up the items the family might want to keep, and filling trash bags with things that could be donated to charity.

The job occupied a good part of her brain but didn't require too much concentration, and left plenty of room for wandering thoughts. The call to Murray State had proven futile this morning. The offices were closed until Wednesday due to the July Fourth holiday weekend. And the call to Sawyer had been just as futile.

He'd expressed no interest in helping sort through things when she'd let him know what she was up to. His voice sounded dull and listless, and she suspected he'd had another sleepless night. He'd told her to do whatever she saw fit with his mom's stuff. He trusted her to make the right decision. There had been no emotion in his tone.

What else could she expect? He'd been through

the wringer yesterday, by all accounts—all seventeen accounts if she included both visitors and phone calls. She'd suggested that he take the boat out for a day of fishing and relaxation today, but he hadn't taken the bait.

Her heart fell at the sound of a knock on the front door. She stood motionless. Maybe if she didn't move, whoever it was would think she was out and would go away. She was tired of visitors and tired of talking.

Another knock, more persistent this time.

Snatching a washcloth from a box of linens, she wiped her sweaty face and headed to greet the unwelcome guest.

Ollie Perkins stood on the front porch, clutching his violin case in one hand and his red bandanna in the other.

"Hi, Ollie." Faith edged the screen door open slowly, giving him time to move out of its arching path.

"Morning, Faith." He raised the case in explanation of his visit. "Thought maybe your soul might be hankering for a little music to soothe it."

Faith choked at his words. When Lacy had lain too sick to get out of the bed, she would ask for Ollie to come soothe her soul with his music. He always obliged.

"Come in. My soul needs soothing for sure." She held the door wide. Once inside, Ollie stopped and glanced around the living room slowly, as if he were taking inventory of the furnishings.

"Wanted to make sure you hadn't moved anything." He grinned. "I'd hate to bang into one of Lacy's beloved lamps."

Faith reached to take his arm, but he moved toward a chair with a meaningful shuffle, so she let him do it on his own.

"How's your mom this morning, Ollie?"

"Fair to middlin'." He made short work of settling his case on the floor at his feet, and getting it open. "Tara doing okay over yonder in Paris?"

Faith nodded and then realized he couldn't see her. "She's enjoying herself. I talked to her last night." Heat crept into her face as she remembered the impulsive call she'd made and the conversation that had precipitated it. At least Ollie couldn't see her embarrassment.

"What d'ya need this morning? Hymns? Jigs? Reels? Any particular requests?"

Faith sat on the arm of the recliner. "I'm not sure what I need, Ollie. Just something pretty."

"How 'bout this?" The haunting melody of "Theme from *A Summer Place*" glided from his strings, and Faith slid from the arm of the chair onto the seat. The tune had been one of her mom's favorites.

She closed her eyes, letting the beautiful strains carry away some of the tension. As the last note died, she took a deep breath, and felt it plunge to a space long neglected at the bottom of her lungs.

"That was beautiful." She sighed. "I didn't realize you played that kind of music."

"I don't play it nearly often enough. Here's another."

Faith smiled as "Moon River" filled her ears. She could almost feel herself being pulled along by the current, peaceful and calm, not caring what lay "waiting 'round the bend."

On and on, Ollie played. One song after another with barely a pause in-between. Mostly romantic songs from movies, his choices revealed a side of him she'd never known.

An amiable silence fell between them, as if words were unnecessary and inadequate. Once, her phone rang and he'd stopped to let her answer. But the caller ID identified that it was Nell Bradley from the Ladies' Prayer Group. She let it go to voice mail.

"This one's my favorite. It's called 'Today.' A folk group called The New Christy Minstrels made it popular back in the '60s. The words are really pretty."

"Can you sing it?" Faith had never heard the old man sing, even at church, but there was such openness about him at the moment, he might be persuaded.

Her question drug a laugh from his belly. "My screeching would not be soothing to your soul. Look the words up sometime, though. You'll appreciate them."

The song, like all the others, was beautiful, and

Faith was sorry when it ended…and intrigued. "What makes that one your favorite?"

Her visitor leaned over and put his violin back to rest in its case before he answered her. He also mopped his face, and wiped his eyes, which had grown misty.

"I was in love once. That was our song."

Faith had never thought about Ollie in that way… as someone who would fall in love. He'd been devoted to his mom, had lived with her his entire life in the house he grew up in until she went to the nursing home. That another woman had ever been in his life seemed impossible. Who could it have been?

"I never knew that, Ollie."

"No one did." He leaned forward to rest his elbows on his knees, and somehow pinned her with his dead-on gaze. "He was married."

His words sent a shockwave through Faith's system. Her fingers reflexively tightened on the chair arms.

"Yes, sweet Faith, you heard me right. Have I shocked you?" His voice was quiet and smooth, holding no hint that he was asking for sympathy…or anything from her, for that matter.

"Yes," she answered. "I had no idea…"

"No one ever has, that I know of." He paused, but his rheumy gaze didn't waver. "You see, Faith, everybody's got something. There's not a person in Taylor's Grove hadn't been through an ordeal. That's what life is. How you come through it's the key." He leaned back, seeming more comfortable now with the conversation he'd dropped her into. "Loving is never wrong."

"But I didn't love him, Ollie. He was a one-night stand, and I haven't seen him since." Her mouth was moving, telling this old man her story, and she wasn't sure why. But it felt cathartic, and she didn't want to stop. "Tara was the result. That's why she's gone to Paris. To find him."

"You never told…anyone."

"Not until Memorial Day. The whole family found out at the same time. Sawyer included. Now he's questioning our relationship." She leaned forward, pressing the matter. "But that one incident doesn't define us, does it?"

"Only if you let it."

It was hard to believe that, with all the women in town Faith could've turned to, it was a seventy-seven-year-old man she was confiding in. But it felt right somehow. Ollie understood. And now she understood the passion always present in his music.

"What do I do now? I've apologized so many times, I can't say those words anymore with any feeling. But Sawyer can't get past my betrayal. I knew I was pregnant when we got married. I made him believe Tara was his."

"You accept the situation for what it is. And what it is is over and done with. We can't go back and change the past. Do you want me to talk to Sawyer?"

"No." She shook her head. "He has to decide on his own who to turn to."

Ollie closed the lid of the violin case and latched it. "Your secret's safe with me, Faith."

"And yours with me."

"I knew that before you told me. But as for Tara's lineage, I think that's Tara's choice to tell or not. People are making all kinds of speculations as to what this separation stems from. Nobody's focusing on the past. Everybody thinks y'all have been through a recent trauma. An affair or maybe a near-affair. I'll tell you though, some in our midst are out for blood and they don't care what the cause is or who's to blame."

"I...we anticipated that."

"I'm sure you've thought through everything. In the middle of the night when you shoulda been sleeping would be my guess." He picked up his case to leave.

Faith stood up to show him out. "Ollie? Whatever happened to the man you loved?"

"Died too young."

She hugged him like she would have one of her children. "I'm sorry things couldn't have been different for you two."

The old man sniffed and wiped his eyes on his bandanna. "'The universe is unfolding as it should.'"

How desperately she wanted to believe that... wanted to believe that somehow all of this was going to turn out okay. "Thank you for coming by." She gave his back a pat in parting. "You gave me an hour of sheer joy."

"No better compliment than that. Keep your chin up. This'll pass."

She watched him stroll down the steps and all the way to the sidewalk that ran along Main Street.

"Bless your heart, Ollie," she whispered as she closed the door. "If you can endure this town, so can I."

"I'M GLAD MONIQUE'S father is doing well enough for her to come back, but I'm going to miss my time with Dylan. I talked to him about my leaving, by the way."

The subject dampened Tara's spirits even more than the rain that was keeping them from the terrace this evening. She'd fought tears all afternoon—weepiness wasn't usually in her nature.

"How did he take that news?" Garrett closed the terrace door against what was now a downpour as a streak of lightning lit the sky.

Tara secured her hair into a ponytail. The humidity was making it feel like a bush had sprouted on her head. "He didn't like it much." She reached for the bottle and divided the remainder of the wine between their two glasses.

Garrett flipped the air conditioner on. "I don't like it much, either."

An accompanying rumble of thunder added drama to his words, and jarred a renegade tear from Tara's eye. She brushed it away while Garrett's back was to her, determined not to spoil one of the precious few nights they had left.

"I guess it's back to the search for dear old Dad tomorrow." She cringed at the subject she'd changed to. Her futile search for Jacques Martin was the second most depressing thing on her mind.

Garrett sat down on the couch and patted the cushion next to him. "Maybe tomorrow will be the day."

"Maybe." She forced a smile she didn't feel as she handed him his glass and sat down.

Garrett stretched his legs out and put his arm across her shoulders, its weight a comfort, an anchor in this stormy emotional sea she was currently tossed about on. His fingertips brushed her temple, and she leaned against him. "What's the matter, love? You seem down tonight." His concern was edged with caution. He'd practiced those same words on Angie time after time, no doubt. Tara wanted no resemblance between her actions and those of his deceased wife.

"I'm just more emotional about this Jacques Martin stuff than I want to admit." She settled on the half truth, leaving out the part about him and Dylan, gnawing her bottom lip when it quivered.

"Don't give up hope." His fingertips brushed her forehead and her hair. "There's still time."

She nodded, but her mind was shaking its head. Time with him and Dylan was growing much too short. Another tear eased from her eye, catching on Garrett's finger as it brushed her cheek.

He leaned forward and looked directly into her face. "Oh, baby, don't cry," he said, and, of course, the gentleness in his manner opened her water works to full force. He took her glass from her, and set both of them on the coffee table.

"I'm s—sorry." She swiped at her eyes and tried to control the sobs, but the words came out on snubbed breaths. "I'm…usually…not the…crying…kind."

"I know." He kissed each of her eyelids. "I can tell."

"You…can?" Her breathing stuttered in her chest.

Garrett nodded. "You're the bravest woman I know. Facing the things you've gone through." He kissed her injured hand. "Coming here alone in search of a man you've never met." His labored sigh filled the space between them. "I've acted like such a coward at times. You put me to shame."

He leaned in and pressed his lips to hers. His touch was calm and warm. It stilled her…and excited her. "You should never feel that way because you have nothing to be ashamed of," she said. "You lived through hell and carried Dylan safely through it all."

A fleeting grimace touched his mouth and then it was gone, replaced by a small pucker that deepened the scar on his upper lip. "You know, maybe we haven't been making the most of the manpower available." He shifted to face her. "Why don't we split up the remainder of the names on your list? Between the two of us, we could get all of the Jacques Martins covered. You'd have to take the ones farther away, but I could cover the ones closer to the office and on my way home."

"You'd do that for me?"

He cupped her face in his hands, tilting it so she was looking directly into his. "I would do anything for you, Tara." His eyes took on a darker hue, and he kissed her with more fervor than before.

Her body stirred with longing, and she pressed closer. "Well, I'd like to do something for you…to repay your kindness." She gave him a soft smile. "Think Dylan's asleep?"

"Long ago."

She stood and held out her hand. "We can talk when he's awake. Let's make better use of our time alone."

She led the way to his bedroom.

Barely inside the door, he kissed her, long and hard, and the stirring intensified. The way this man affected her with just a kiss! Heat surged through her, every fiber sizzling.

They broke contact only briefly while she pulled his T-shirt over his head and threw it on the bed. Then her eager palms sought the taut planes of his stomach muscles. His hands lost no time reciprocating, ridding her of her clothes. He grasped her rear and pressed her front against him.

With a little hop, her legs were around his waist, and he backed over to his bed, pausing only long enough to grab a condom from the drawer. He lay down, keeping her on top.

Astride him and in the driver's seat, she shifted into high gear and stomped on the gas.

Their lovemaking was fast and furious and wild like the storm that battered the window, leaving them sweaty and gasping for air.

But soon, and with what turned out to be fortuitous timing, a burst of lightning struck, followed immediately by a rolling concussion of thunder. It sent a chill through Tara and had her grabbing for Garrett's cast-off tee. She slipped into it just as the bedroom door flew open, and a terrified Dylan streaked into the room.

"Dad, the thunder's too loud!"

He drew up short at the side of the bed, the terror in his eyes giving way to confusion. "Tara?" His face broke into the wide grin she adored. "You decided to sleep over!" he crowed. "Why didn't you tell me?"

"Well." She looked to Garrett for help, but he answered her with an I've-got-nothing shrug. She glanced at the clock that read 12:43 a.m. "We just remembered that it's July Fourth, which is a holiday in the States. Why don't we make a tent and pretend we're camping out?"

"Cool! I'll go get my pillow!" The child ran from the room on a mission, and Tara and Garrett lost no time jumping from under the covers to don their shorts.

"Seriously? Sleeping on the floor?" Garrett speared her with a disgruntled look. "I've got to work tomorrow."

"Oh, shut up." She laughed and pulled the blanket from the bed. "And go find me some rope."

Garrett's frown dissolved into the same enthusiastic smile Dylan displayed. "Now you're talking."

He sprinted from the room, as well.

"For the tent!" she called after him.

CHAPTER SEVENTEEN

THE FIRST RAYS OF SUN caught the prism Lacy had always kept hanging in the side window of her bedroom, coloring the opposite wall with a rainbow that required no rain.

Faith was awake and had been for some time. As she watched the hues deepen, she was reminded of the story of Noah and his ark. If only her rainbow could be a sign like his had been—a promise that the storm was over...or maybe would be soon.

It was going to be a beautiful Fourth of July. Maybe she would call the kids and Emma and have a picnic at the cabin after all. Then they could stop lying to Tara.

An unexpected noise drew her from the bed to the front window. She cracked the blinds to find Sawyer hooking the bass boat onto his truck. Another good sign! If he felt like going fishing, it surely meant he was getting back to normal.

She held her breath, hoping he would knock on the door and invite her to go along. But when he got back in the truck and slammed the door, she let the breath out slowly, waving goodbye to him with an unseen hand.

They'd only spoken briefly since the conversation in the garage Saturday. Three days ago—though it seemed like three years.

She picked up the novel she'd been reading and wandered to the kitchen. Bacon and eggs sounded good for breakfast. Or an omelet perhaps. Her stomach had been so upset, food seemed like the enemy. But since Ollie's visit yesterday, she'd managed to eat lunch and supper, and breakfast was on her agenda for this morning.

She arranged some slices of bacon on the tray, and put them in the microwave to cook.

If the dear old man could go through what he had and never complain to anyone about the unfairness of things, she could certainly bear this. He had nothing except memories, but she'd actually been blessed.

She had Tara.

She picked up her phone and touched her precious daughter's number.

Tara answered on the first ring. "Hi, Mama."

Uh-oh. She sounded breathless. Oh, surely not. It was midafternoon over there.

"Hey, sweetpea. Have I caught you at a bad time?"

"No, a good time, actually. I could use some cheering up."

Faith assessed the situation quickly. Tara wasn't distraught. Just down. Man trouble? Had she seen the folly of her ways? "Why?" She used her sympathetic mom voice. "What's wrong?"

A long sigh whispered over the line. "I just located another wrong Jacques Martin."

"Oh, that's got to be hard. I know you had your hopes up."

"I've been thinking about this whole thing...my snap decision to try to come find him."

"Yeah," Faith agreed. "It was a bit hurried."

"Well, you know how you and Dad always taught us that everything happens for a reason? I'm thinking that the reason I'm here may not be to find Jacques Martin. Maybe I came here to meet Garrett and Dylan."

Emotion gripped Faith's heart and squeezed. "Oh my, Tara. That sounds way too serious."

"I am serious, Mama. I'm falling in love with him. Them."

"Honey." Faith switched to her let's-be-reasonable tone. "It's too soon to be thinking about that."

"And yet, here I am thinking about it. That's what makes me think it's real."

Arguing would do no good. Tara had Sawyer's stubborn streak, blood-relation or no. When either of their minds got set a certain way, they held on to the belief like a snapping turtle holds a stick...and they wouldn't let go till it thundered. "I don't know what to say."

"You don't have to say anything, Mama. Just be happy for me."

"I'm always happy for you, sweetpea. Happy for you in my life."

Tara's laugh sounded relieved. "Love you."

"Love you, too."

"By the way." Tara's tone changed. "Emma said the picnic was cancelled because of weather." It was a statement, but the question was evident.

"Well, it's turned out pretty after all, so I'm thinking we might throw one together." The microwave dinged, reminding Faith of the breakfast she'd started. "Your dad's already headed to the lake, in fact," she added for authenticity.

"Good. It sounds like things are back to normal."

Faith wouldn't answer that with a lie. "My bacon's ready, so I need to go, sweetpea. You be careful, now. You hear?"

"I hear. See ya."

"See ya."

Faith opened the microwave and set the bacon on the counter. Despite its mouth-watering aroma, her appetite had fled once again.

So Tara believed her reason for being in Paris was to meet Garrett.

"The universe is unfolding as it should." Ollie's words from yesterday scampered across Faith's brain, causing the hair to rise on the back of her neck.

Only one thing would change Tara's mind back to her original intent…and shake her loose from the stick she was clamped on to.

Faith sent up a prayer for thunder in Paris…in the form of an address for the elusive Jacques Martin.

GARRETT ENDED THE call and gestured Henri to come in.

The Frenchman held a paper fisted in one hand and a mysterious expression on his face. He stepped in and closed the door behind him.

"What's up? You been watching those old Pink Panther movies again?" Garrett chuckled at the joke that his friend obviously didn't understand. "I was just talking to Marc Fornier. He's agreed to add Soulard to the beer flight dinners at le Verrou."

"C'est formidable!" As was his custom, Henri chose the armless chair at the north end of Garrett's desk. He perched on the edge, resembling a bird on a wire.

"Yeah, wonderful news for us."

Henri nodded. Garrett hadn't seen so much excitement in his eyes since they'd test-driven that Ferrari last year. "And I may have wonderful news for Tara." Henri pushed the paper he held across the desk.

Garrett scanned the document, a spreadsheet, much like the one Henri made for Dylan's activities, but this one held a list of names—well, actually the names were all Jacques Martin. Most had two columns of addresses, work and home, and a slew of other columns, some filled out and others empty.

Three names had been circled in red.

Garrett pulled his copy of Tara's list from his pocket and compared the two. They were totally different. He dropped the new one on the desk and spread his hands in question. "What is this?"

"*Ce sont les Jacques Martins* who are not in the telephone book or found easily over the internet." Henri's rigid posture hardly matched the nonchalant tone he affected.

His friend's manner, so different from his normally perfect composure, sent a chill up Garrett's spine. "Where did you get this information?"

"If I tell you, *mon ami,* I will have to kill you." His grin dissolved as quickly as it appeared. "*Vraiment,* Garrett, no one must know that I have done this."

"What did you do?" Garrett fought to control the panic in his voice. "Hack into a government website or something?"

"*Oui.*" Henri shrugged one shoulder. "Or something."

"Damn it! You could get arrested."

"*Oui,* and go to the prison for a very long time. *Mais seulement* if it becomes known. This is why you must tell no one." He wagged his finger. "Not Tara. Not anyone." The wagging finger dropped to point at the circled names. "But I am certain one of these is the correct man. The three are of the correct age to be the father, and all were in the U.S. during the right time."

Garrett's hands were sweating. He clenched and unclenched them, not sure if he should kiss Henri or kick his ass for pulling such a stunt. "How did you get your hands on all this?"

"Much information is available, *mon ami*. One only needs to know where to look." He gave a sly grin. "And how."

Garrett became aware of how fast his heart was racing when a drop of sweat ran into his eye. He wiped it off, then reached for his phone. "Tara could be meet—"

Henri snatched the phone from his hand. "Tread carefully, Garrett. These are men of means. They are not found easily *pour une raison.*"

Garrett jerked his hand back. "You mean they're crooks? They might be dangerous?"

"Non." Henri's bottom lip drooped as he pondered the question, then he pinned Garrett with a meaningful stare. "But there is some reason they—how do you put it?—'fly below the radar.'"

"Shit!" Garrett wiped his hand down his face.

Henri answered with a low chuckle. *"Oui,* and very deep. And, *s'il te plaît,* you must burn the document when you finish with it."

Garrett studied the names and addresses circled in red. If he made first contact with Tara's father, he could assess the situation and arrange for their meeting—and prepare them for each other.

He grabbed a pen and made the notes he needed, then returned the paper to his friend. "Do whatever you want with it, Henri. I have what I need."

Henri's perfect posture slumped in relief, but only slightly. *"Peut-être* Tara will stay in Paris a little longer *maintenant.* To know her father, *oui?"*

That Henri had gone to such measures to gain him and Dylan more time with Tara was staggering, and Garrett was overwhelmed with emotion. Loosening his tie did nothing to ease the tension in his neck and jaws. He leaned forward to capture Henri's gaze. "I'm speechless…that you would go to this extreme. You're a devoted friend, Henri, and Dylan and I are so blessed to have you in our lives."

Henri's Adam's apple bobbed, and for a split second, Garrett thought he saw mistiness in the Frenchman's eyes. "We are more than friends, Garrett. *Nous sommes frères.*"

Garrett stood and walked around the desk, pulling Henri to his feet and into a hug. "Brothers. I like that."

They slapped each other's backs extra hard to keep things on a mature male level, and then Garrett checked his watch. "If I leave now, I can go by the Kléber address on the way home."

He gathered the papers he'd been working on and stuffed them into his briefcase in the improbable event that he'd feel like looking at them once he got home. His gut told him tonight was going to be an exciting one with Tara.

Hell, every night was exciting with Tara.

Henri held the office door open for him to pass. "*Bonne chance,* Garrett." He added another hardy clap on Garrett's back.

"Thanks." Garrett headed toward the elevator,

walking backward for one last acknowledgment to his friend. "I owe you," he called as the doors opened.

Henri's hands were in his pockets and he gave a shrug. *"Oui."*

Less than a half hour later, Garrett stood in the massive corridor of an ancient but elegant building that looked as if it had once housed a large corporation, but had now been divided into small, though impressive, suites.

The door his hand rested on had a thick, leaded glass window trimmed in rich mahogany. The etching on it read simply: *Jacques Martin, le concessionnaire.*

So this Jacques Martin was a distributor of goods although no hint was given as to the kind of goods distributed. But the location of his business spoke of his success.

Garrett pushed the door open to a small waiting room. Stepping inside was like hopping from one century to another. While just as elegant as its exterior, the office interior was very contemporary decked out in blue-gray walls with low, Italian leather sofas in the hue that he called purple but Henri insisted was *l'aubergine*—eggplant.

A young woman who looked as though she had been supplied by the Chanel School for Receptionists sat at a desk of sorts. Made either of glass or clear acrylic, it had no drawers and no real legs—except for the model-worthy ones that belonged to the receptionist. The workspace was nearly bare, holding only a small appointment book, an equally small pad, a pen, a cell phone and the elbows of the receptionist, though not her weight, as she sat very straight.

"Bonjour, monsieur." She greeted him with a tight smile. *"Comment puis-je vous aider?"*

"Bonjour, madame. Je m'appelle Garrett Hughes." He concentrated to keep the question out of his voice. *"Je voudrais parler avec Monsieur Martin, s'il vous plaît."*

A question lit her eyes, gone as quickly as it appeared. She glanced at the appointment book. *"Avez-vous pris rendezvous?"*

Was he expected? Hell, no. Nor was the news he was bearing, if this turned out to be the right guy.

"Non. Je suis ici pour—" he chose his wording carefully *"—une affaire personnelle."* It didn't get much more personal than this.

A flare of color bloomed in the young woman's cheeks, but her manner remained cool and poised as she stood. *"Un moment."*

The tight, black dress clung to every curve of her body as she swayed to a door at the end of a long, narrow hallway. He watched her movements, imagining what the dress might look like on Tara, and found himself grinning at the image despite the nervousness that was causing his heart to beat a staccato rhythm.

The young woman rapped twice and stepped inside the office, though Garrett couldn't hear an invitation.

He stood waiting for two of the longest minutes of his life, and then the door opened again, and the young woman swayed out, followed by a middle-aged man with deep-set eyes and jet-black hair, combed back much like Henri's coif.

"Monsieur Hughes?" The man questioned, and Garrett's mouth went dry.

The lips. The mouth. It was the same one he had kissed a thousand times over the past week.

And it belonged to a man who, without a doubt, had to be Tara's father.

CHAPTER EIGHTEEN

GARRETT HAD BEEN led into a false sense of security by Jacques Martin's easy, though cautious, manner.

The preliminaries had gone smoothly with the two men sitting across the desk from each other in Martin's office. Yes, he was Jacques Martin. Yes, he attended a year of college at Murray State University. His English was flawless, and he had shifted to it almost immediately.

The trouble started when Garrett asked if he remembered Faith Franklin.

A flash of recognition lit Martin's eyes at the mention of her name, or perhaps it was the sudden understanding of where this conversation was leading. His face drew in, as if he was concentrating hard. "No, I remember no person of that name."

Garrett had thought that might be the answer. He plunged ahead with the details of the story, assuring Jacques Martin that his memory was of no concern. "You and Ms. Franklin—Faith—celebrated together on graduation night. She admits that you both had too much to drink and ended up in bed together. A few weeks later, she found out she was pregnant from that encounter."

The Frenchman's face blanched. "That is impossible."

"But true." Garrett used the understating technique Henri was so fond of.

"Faith and I…" Jacques paused. "Had no relationship."

His use of the woman's given name convinced Garrett she was indeed remembered and hope flickered in his chest. "Perhaps not, but you slept together, and a daughter was conceived. She's twenty-eight years old now."

Martin's white pallor seeped away, replaced by a red that had a purplish quality—though not quite *l'aubergine*. "And I suppose this person hired you to find me?" Resting on the desktop, his hand clenched and unclenched repeatedly.

"No." Garrett thought it best not to shift the focus to him and Tara. "She's a friend of mine, and she's come to Paris to find you."

"Surely with her hand out expecting part of my fortune."

The acid in his tone burned Garrett's insides as an image of Tara's injured hand flashed through his mind. "Tara's not like that. That's her name, by the way. Tara O'Malley. And she's not a…a gold digger. She's a wonderful person." Reminding himself to remain calm, he loosened his fingers from their tight grip and spread them wide to show he had nothing to hide—and neither did Tara. "She only wants to meet you. Nothing else."

Jacques snorted derisively, and then shrugged as if he were turning down a piece of chocolate. "I have no desire to meet her."

Garrett noticed his fingertips were leaving perspiration marks on Jacques Martin's antique cherry-wood desk. He shifted farther back in his chair. "She's come a long way just hoping for a chance to meet you. She's a daughter you should be proud of."

Jacques's head tilted. "Is she?" He arched an eyebrow. "So are my other two children who were born to me by women other than my wife. My very jealous wife."

"But Tara is from a relationship twenty-eight years ag—"

Jacques Martin's fist slammed on the desk, but his voice was almost a whisper. "There was no relationship!"

Nothing good would come of engaging this man in a heated confrontation. Garrett backed off and tried for an offhand, man-to-man approach. "Surely, your wife wouldn't be threatened by anything that long ago, Monsieur Martin." He forced his lips up at the corners. "We all bear the sins of our youth."

The Frenchman leaned on his forearms, his tone conspiratorial and quiet. "My wife is young and beautiful—you met her when you arrived—and she is jealous of everything, even things that happened two years before she was born."

The new information slid into place, and the puzzle began to form a clearer picture in Garrett's mind. The young woman in the waiting room was a jealous trophy wife with a philandering husband who had two known children from outside his marriage. Now there was a third. Jacques Martin's character solidified, and if Garrett didn't care for him before, he disliked the man intensely now. He motioned with his head toward the door. "Your wife?"

"Yes, and my receptionist. Yvette is quite spoiled, and she detests sharing my fortune with the two other bastard children who surfaced. She threatens divorce *if*—" he placed meaningful weight on the word "—she learns of any further indiscretions. I have no desire to pay more alimony or look for a fourth wife yet, though I suspect I shall someday. Perhaps *then* I will arrange to meet your friend."

The statement was wrong on so many levels. Garrett had a strong desire to punch the Frenchman right in his arrogant pout. Believing Tara could have come from the loins of this asshole took a stretch of the imagination.

The two men eyed each other for a long moment, then Jacques Martin stood. "Now, Monsieur Hughes, I have work to do. If you will excuse me." He gestured toward the door.

Garrett stood and straightened to his full height, playing the intimidation card just for the hell of it. "I'll tell Tara you don't wish to see her, but I don't think that will keep her from coming anyway."

"If you do not want your friend hurt by rejection, I suggest you keep her away. If she comes here, I will refuse to see her." The man spoke as if he were referring to a cocktail mixed incorrectly.

Garrett's words pressed through gritted teeth. "Tara is a person. A beautiful, precious daughter." He paused, shifting his stance to throw one last curveball. "She looks like you, you know."

Interest flickered in Martin's eyes along with the hint of a smile. "Yes?" Obviously, that touched a nerve with the conceited bastard. But the moment passed quickly, and the near-smile glided into an oily sneer. "Then my imagination will have to serve me well. *Au revoir,* Mr. Hughes."

Garrett's imagination churned up an idea. If Martin could just see Tara's smile, hear her laugh. Could anyone who knew her not want her in his life?

Especially the only person in the world who could have created her?

If his plan didn't work, he had nothing to lose, whereas Tara and Jacques Martin had everything to gain if it did.

"I think it would be only natural to want to know what your father or daughter looked like, especially if you were aware of a strong family resemblance."

Jacques Martin pursed his lips.

"Like that." Garrett pointed to the man's mouth and smiled. "She looks just like you when you do that," he lied.

Martin's mouth flattened into a near-smile.

Garrett took that as progress and pressed ahead. "I understand why you don't want your wife to know about Tara," he lied again. "But that shouldn't stop you from meeting her."

"Non." Martin shook his head. "That will only open a door that should remain closed. I cannot chance that she might begin making the demands to see me."

Garrett pushed on, fully aware he was treading on dangerous ground. "What if it's done in such a way that she doesn't suspect who you are?"

He'd reached the point-of-no-return, and suddenly it felt as if the air in Garrett's lungs wasn't enough to sustain speech. He dropped his arms and shifted to give his chest room to expand, astounded to see Martin follow his lead. The man was invested in the conversation! A jolt shot through him. Was it possible this might actually work?

Martin's head tilted in question. "And how would you suggest that should be accomplished, Monsieur Hughes?"

Garrett held the breath steady as it left his lungs. "Perhaps we could arrange for a chance meeting. Somewhere you might easily go alone without raising your wife's suspicion."

Martin's eyes narrowed. "Go on. I am listening."

"Saturday morning, we could be at Place des Vosges at…let's say eleven o'clock?" Paris's oldest square was close to home and one of Garrett's favorite places. "You could be there and engage us in conversation. Perhaps share a bench with us."

"And you believe this Tara O'Malley will charm me, win my affection, and I will choose to inform her of my identity." There was no question in the tone.

If he looked very closely, Garrett could see a hardness that he didn't want to notice tightening the edges of Martin's mouth. He shifted his gaze to look directly in his host's eyes. "Yes, sir. I believe exactly that."

"And if I am not won over, what then?"

The twist in Garrett's stomach caught his heart as it sank, far too aware he was offering up Tara, the woman he loved, as a dispensable pawn in this risky game.

"I promise not to tell her who you are." Garrett jerked a business card from his pocket. He jotted Tara's number on the back and threw it on the desk in front of the man. "That's her number. I'll leave it up to you to contact her when you feel it's appropriate." That probably wouldn't be until Mrs. Jacques Martin number three was out of the picture, but Garrett felt reasonably sure it would happen someday. Maybe sooner than later.

A wall of silence fell between them and remained for what seemed like an eternity. Finally, Martin picked up the card. He turned it over to Garrett's information. "Soulard? Ah, the new beer I have been hearing about, yes?"

Garrett's ears perked up at the friendliness in the tone. Maybe they were getting somewhere. "Yes, that's right. We're a fledgling company, but we're doing very well."

The tips of Martin's fingers turned white as he gripped the corner of the card, and he shot Garrett a menacing look. "I have many friends in positions of power, Garrett Hughes. If this woman…this Tara… attempts to make any contact with me, it could be very, very bad for your 'fledgling company.'"

The ice in his voice sent a chill up Garrett's spine, but he kept his gaze locked with Jacques Martin's. Soulard. Everything he'd worked so hard for. And Henri…*damn! Damn! Damn!* He held out a hand that he willed not to tremble. "And I give you my word that will not happen."

Martin studied him for a moment longer then grasped his hand with a firm shake, turning them so that his was on top, in the position of control. "I trust you are as honest and intelligent as you seem. I will be at Place des Vosges Saturday morning."

Garrett turned and made his way out the door on legs that were stiff and wooden, breathing deeply to battle the nausea churning up his insides.

"Au revoir, madame." He nodded to Jacques Martin's third wife as he passed.

"Au revoir, monsieur," she answered, her cheeks blazing with color.

How much had she heard…or suspected?

No doubt, Jacques Martin was already rehearsing

the lie he would use to calm her down. It would be interesting to see what happened when the Frenchman's icy manner clashed with his wife's heated one, but Garrett had no desire to stick around for that collision.

It was the Fourth of July.

Paris might have a fireworks display after all.

Garrett prayed that Henri and Soulard didn't get burned by the fallout of the explosion.

"YOU CAN'T GET 'em like this in Paducah, and certainly not in Taylor's Grove." Tara studied the meaty olive before popping it into her mouth. She rolled it around, like Garrett had taught her, appreciating the silky texture and allowing the subtle flavor of the oil to prepare her tongue for the burst of flavor. When she bit into it, the briny tang brought her taste buds to full attention. She held the plate out to Garrett, who declined the offer.

"You seem preoccupied." She pointed to the Scotch he'd chosen tonight over his usual wine. "Is everything okay?"

"Sorry. Hard day at work." He smiled and tilted Tara's face up with a finger under her chin. "Let me get my mind back where it belongs."

The kiss with a Scotch chaser brought a yummy warmth to her lips and a smile to accompany it. "That makes my two Jacques Martin strikeouts today bearable."

Garrett's smile wavered. "No luck, huh?" She shook her head as he pulled a pen and his copy of her list from his pocket. He drew a line through the top name. "This one isn't him, either."

"Thanks for checking, though." She got comfortable again with her head against his shoulder. It was too hot to sit so close on the terrace, but she couldn't resist the opportunity to relax in his arms and pretend that their time together wasn't waning.

Garrett didn't seem to mind. He'd chosen the bench over the separate chairs and pulled her close when they sat down.

He cleared his throat, and the way his body stiffened against her side told her he was about to say something that made him uncomfortable.

"I know we've talked about it a little, but what will you do, really, if you locate your birth father and he won't meet you? I mean, he could refuse to even see you."

Bless his heart. Garrett was so concerned about how this ordeal would affect her. "I won't take no for an answer. I've come too far for that." She kept her head on his shoulder, but laid her hand against his chest. "You've still got a lot to learn about me, and my stubbornness is one of those faults you're going to run into."

His heartbeat quickened under her palm. "What if he threatens you? Or—" He stopped abruptly, and the concern in his voice pulled her around to face him. The worry she'd heard was etched in his face.

"If he throws me out?" She shrugged. "I'll still have accomplished what I came for. I'll have *seen* him."

Garrett took a deep swallow of his Scotch and a grimace followed. "But if *I* find him, he could threaten me. Or Dylan. Or Soulard."

Anger flashed through her at the thought. "He wouldn't dare. I'd get the law involved. I assume there are laws here to protect the innocent? And why would he threaten you or Dylan? Or Soulard...?"

Garrett didn't answer. Just stared mutely at her flat across the way. His silence jolted a question from her mind.

"What's with the worry all of a sudden?" She leaned in front of him to capture his attention. "Did something happen today?"

He glanced at her, then away, and shook his head. "No, of course not. I was just imagining scenarios."

She hadn't realized how seriously he was taking all this. Coming off the huge media blitz, his head was obviously wrapped around the future of the company. And he was always superprotective of Dylan.

Taking him up on his offer to help her search for her father had been a mistake. He didn't need another responsibility or anything else to worry about.

"Tell you what." She interlaced her fingers with his. "Forget about looking for Jacques Martin. If it's meant for me to find him, I'll do it on my own. And if I don't find him, so be it." The worry lines on his forehead relaxed a bit, but they didn't disappear completely.

She pressed on. "Come straight home after work from now on. That will give you more time with Dylan." She shrugged her eyebrows playfully. "And if you play more catch with him, he might tire out faster and go to bed earlier, which will give you more time with me…" She moved to straddle his lap. "To explore my very…naughty…stubborn side."

His eyes met hers and the worry wrinkles deepened again. His glance shifted to her eyebrow ring and seemed to fixate there. "I wish we had more time." He touched the piercing with a fingertip. "I need to know…want to know…everything about you."

She captured his attention by placing his palm against her breast. "You want to know how I'm going to react when I'm placed in, shall we say…different positions?"

She rocked forward and pressed her mouth to his for the most erotic kiss she knew how to give. When she pulled away, she met his dark gaze and lowered her voice. "Take me inside and you can find out."

Without so much as a grunt, he stood up.

She wrapped her legs around his waist and let him carry her to his bedroom, and, once there, she took control of the situation, making good on her promise.

But, try as she might to get him to relax, intuition told her at least one of his brains was focused somewhere else.

FAITH WAS WORRIED TO the point of being almost frantic. Sawyer usually didn't stay out fishing this late.

It was nearly dark, and most of Taylor's Grove's population had vacated the town to watch the fireworks display at Kentucky Dam.

The day with the kids at the cabin had been pleasant although it wasn't the same with Tara and Sawyer absent. But Thea, Trenton and Emma, who claimed to be "the nearest thing to a daughter without all the pain involved," had kept her laughing for a good chunk of the time.

Any mention of Tara had usually involved something funny. But Sawyer's name had come up with a forced infrequency that dampened her spirit as much as the fake rain they'd lied to Tara about.

Just before nine o'clock, after a wait that had seemed a lifetime but was actually only a little over three hours, Faith heard the truck in the driveway and said a word of thanks that her husband hadn't fallen overboard and hit his head on the boat and drowned.

He probably wouldn't make the effort to see her, so she went outside.

"Hey." She spoke quietly as she approached and watched him flinch at the sound of her voice.

"Hey, Faith." He glanced up as he cranked the boat

trailer loose from the hitch. "Trent called. He said y'all went to the cabin. Did you have a good day?"

The gentleness in his tone made her breath quiver in her chest. "It was nice." She hesitated. "Not like when we're all together, though."

He nodded and it felt like agreement whether he meant it as such or not. He picked up the tongue of the trailer and guided it back a few feet to its regular spot under the carport. The muscles in his arms and back bulged under the exertion, and the sight caused a flutter in her belly.

She closed her eyes, not wanting to need him, not needing to want him, so desperately. When she opened them, he was rubbing some grease off his palms onto his jeans, which was a little better, but still reminded her he was all man. She moved even closer to where he stood.

She glanced around nervously for a conversation starter. The boat was already covered, and she didn't see a cooler anywhere. "Did you catch any?"

"A few. Couple of pretty nice ones, but I let them go. Didn't really feel like messing with cleaning them." He pulled a rag from his back pocket, and lovingly rubbed away the dab of grease he'd gotten on the hull. Satisfied, he rammed the rag back where he got it. He leaned his back against the boat and hooked his thumbs in his front pocket. "Could we, uh…talk for a little while?"

"Sure!" She cleared her throat to subdue the eagerness in her tone. "Do…do you want to come in?

I have some strawberry lemonade made. And rhubarb pie."

Rhubarb was his favorite, so passing it up would send her a distinct message. Her breath stopped as she waited for his answer.

Darkness had fallen while he put the boat to bed, but she saw his eyes flash in the moonlight. "Sounds good." He nodded, and her heart answered by picking up the quick rhythm.

She waited for him to fall into step beside her. "I've been going through your mom's stuff, making piles to keep, throw away and give away."

When he opened the door for her, his hand touched the small of her back. It was probably a reflexive move, but she pretended it was on purpose and relished the burst of warmth it sent through her.

While she cut the pie and poured the lemonade, they made small talk about the family treasures she'd discovered in the back of closets. They moved to the table on the back porch and the conversation moved with them to the kids. Even the talk about Tara stayed amiable.

"She thinks she's in love?" Sawyer chewed a bite of pie slowly. "That's a little impetuous, even for Tara. Don't you think?"

"I agree. But she's just like—" *you* was on her tongue, but she bit it back "—an old mule about things. She'll have to figure it out on her own." The first sip of tart lemonade made Faith's mouth pucker, and the flutter started again when Sawyer grinned. "A little heavy on the lemon," she warned, and shifted her focus back to Tara. "She'll be home in a couple of weeks. Once she's away from him, he'll lose his appeal."

Sawyer laid his fork down. "Unless it's really love. Then being away from each other's going to make them miserable."

The question in his eyes was unmistakable. And, if he'd only asked, she'd have gladly told him how utterly miserable she was without him. But he didn't ask. And he didn't say he forgave her. And he didn't ask her to come back home. She waited, but the words didn't come.

Instead, he went back to his pie, and she pretended the drift in conversation hadn't happened. "Trent was surprised you didn't ask him to go fishing with you today." Actually, Trenton had been peeved when he found out he'd been left behind. Fishing with Dad had always been part of his Fourth of July.

"I had things I needed to think about. It was best for me to be alone." Sawyer wiped his mouth with his napkin and laid it beside his plate. "The pie was delicious. Thanks."

"You're welcome."

He began to rub his lip with the tip of his finger and her senses went on alert. "I need to tell you something, Faith. I want you to hear it from me first. Not out in town."

Her fork rattled against the plate, and she let it slide from her grip. "What is it?"

"Arlo came to see me yesterday."

The president of the Board of Fellowship's name made the air rush from her lungs. "Already?" Her voice was a hushed whisper with no force behind it. She and Sawyer had just separated Saturday, and this was only Tuesday. Surely no one would be pushing them yet.

"He said the board's meeting next week." Sawyer's eyes dropped to his hands folded in front of him on the table.

Faith's breathing came faster, and her head swam from the excess of oxygen.

"He's got some obvious concerns." Sawyer's eyes rose to lock with hers. The support was what she needed, and her breathing slowed as he continued. "And Sue's raising a big stink about our separation— just like we knew she would. Her argument's that we're being so secretive, it has to be something earth-shattering."

Faith's mind flipped back and forth as she considered Ollie's advice yesterday. "I told you I didn't care who knew, Sawyer, and I don't, but I've been thinking..." Scrunching her fingers to make quotation marks in the air she said "'The secret' is more Tara's than ours to share. I was going to leave it up to her."

He nodded. "That's what I want, too. I'm glad we're in agreement about it."

Faith voiced her thoughts. "Sue's going to keep worrying the snot out of everybody until she gets some answers."

"She may get them. She may not." Sawyer leaned back to rest his elbows on the arm of the chair and spread his hands. "We'll just wait and see."

Faith picked up his plate and stuck it under hers, which still contained half a piece of pie. "Tara won't be home until after the meeting. So, if the board meets next week, what does Arlo think will happen?"

"Oh, he was pretty adamant about that—" Sawyer swallowed hard. "Sue's already got the votes lined up. They're going to call for my resignation."

CHAPTER NINETEEN

"AND I THINK he'll do it, Henri." Garrett pushed his *flammkuchen* aside. "Tara's father may be the most despicable son of a bitch I've ever met."

He'd barely touched his lunch, and, since he'd begun his tale to Henri about yesterday's ordeal with Jacques Martin, his friend hadn't touched his, either, seemingly determined to drink his meal instead. A special section of hell was probably designated for those people who wasted a meal from a Paris brasserie. To have wasted two servings seemed especially heinous.

But Garrett had been badly mistaken when he thought he'd be able to eat after filling Henri in on the details. The looks of horror that kept cracking the Frenchman's perfect facade were shredding Garrett's insides almost as much as the information he was hiding from Tara.

"Several times I started to level with her, but the damn tattoos and piercings kept reminding me of Angie and her wild ways and I'd remember that she has a bit of a wild side, too. I mean, we haven't known each other very long. What if…" The waiter brought Henri's third martini while Garrett declined a second glass of sauvignon blanc. "What if she decides she *has* to see him no matter the consequences?"

"And Tara *does* have the wild hair." Henri pointed a philosophical finger upward as he sipped his drink. "What if you and she break up and she desires to hurt you? The women like the revenge."

"I don't believe Tara would ever stoop that low."

"The blood of the son of a bitch runs in her veins, *oui?*" Henri growled into his glass. "And you did not believe Angie would ever leave Dylan. *C'est vrai?*"

Garrett flinched as the comment pierced the protective area of his psyche. Yes, he'd ignored signs that Angie was spiraling out of control. He'd battered himself for years over that one. But for Henri to bring it up right now was out-of-character.

"That's your last drink, Henri. You're getting drunk and mean, and I'm cutting you off."

Henri sneered. "You would cut me off from the last drink I may get in a very long while? They do not serve the cocktails in prison, *mon ami.*"

"You're not going to prison." Garrett massaged the back of his neck where the muscles were in knots. "No matter what happens, I'm not going to let anyone know—" he lowered his voice to a whisper "—where I got his address. Not Tara. Not anyone. I told you your secret is safe with me, and it is. I promise."

Henri sat the drink on the table, looking more downcast than Garrett could ever imagine. "I am sorry, my dear friend. I say the cruel things in anger. I only wanted to help Tara, and now the sweet soufflé goes *poof!* into my face." He drummed his fingertips on the table.

"If we'd been together longer, I'd feel more comfortable telling her the truth. But right now…" Garrett ran his hand through his hair. "I just can't. And I feel like such a lying sack of shit because I can't."

Henri took another drink, and his mouth pulled into a deeper frown. "Is the sack of shit lying as in telling an untruth? You cannot know what it is because the sack disguises what is inside? Or is the sack of shit lying on the ground doing nothing and is therefore worthless?"

"You can take whichever meaning you want, Henri." A remorseful sigh pushed from Garrett's lungs. "Either one fits me perfectly."

What he'd done hit him with the impact of a sledgehammer to his chest.

If things with Martin worked out, Tara surely would forgive the underhanded means he'd used to obtain the end. If they didn't work out—if Jacques Martin never made contact—Garrett would have to live with his lie, but Tara's exemption from the heartbreak of the rejection would serve as his consolation.

His gut churned the way it used to during a championship baseball game. In his mind's eye, he was once again standing in the batter's box. The pitcher had just given all he had to a well-executed curveball. Garrett had swung and connected, and the ball was hurtling into the stands.

Now he had to wait for his vision to clear to see if he'd hit it foul or if he'd scored the game-winning home run.

"Tara had tuna on her pizza today, Dad." Dylan made a retching sound and squinched his face into a mask of horror. "Doesn't that sound icky?"

"It does sound icky, sport. But let's leave the sound effects off at the dinner table, okay?" Amusement twinkled in Garrett's eyes when he turned back to Tara. "Did you do that on purpose?"

"No." She reached over and gave a gentle tweak to Dylan's nose. "And I shouldn't have even told you, you little twerp."

Dylan giggled around his last forkful of mashed potatoes.

"I was craving pizza, and I couldn't translate the toppings, so I just pointed to one." She squinched her face to match Dylan's. "I chose poorly."

Garrett's laugh heated the already warm night air. She took a sip of the sweet iced tea she'd made to go along with the special Southern dinner she'd prepared of country-fried steak and gravy, mashed potatoes, green beans, fried okra and biscuits.

"You were hungry." She pointed to Garrett's plate, which looked as if it had been licked clean of his second round of helpings.

He nodded. "I didn't eat much lunch. Had too much on my mind." The tight lines around his eyes softened, and his lips relaxed enough for the scar to deepen. "But this meal—whew!" He leaned back and patted his stomach. "Gave me back my appetite."

"You want to talk about whatever's on your mind?" Tara prodded. He seemed better than last night, but something was still eating at him.

He winked and gave her a gentle smile. "Later."

The way he said the word tightened a coil deep inside her. Oh, for heaven sakes! The things this man could do to her with one word.

"Dylan!" A child's voice called from below, and Dylan ran across the terrace to the opening that accessed the courtyard beneath their terrace.

"Sit." She ordered Garrett back into his seat when he started to help her clear the table.

Dylan ran back to the table. "Jules has a new puppy! Can I go see it?"

"Sure." Garrett pointed to the opening. "Yell at me when you get down there and when you start to come back up."

Dylan nodded.

"Be back in a half hour."

"I will," the boy promised.

A little enticement would help him get back on time. "I fixed ambrosia for dessert," Tara informed him.

He cocked his head, giving her a quizzical look that made him a miniversion of Garrett. "Was it broken?"

"What?" It was her turn to be confused.

"You said you fixed it."

Sheesh! Nothing got by the little scamp. "I *pre-pared* ambrosia for dessert," she explained. "We'll have it when you get back."

"Okay." He took off at a full gallop and they heard the front door slam behind him.

Tara shook her head in feigned exasperation. "Guess I thought some Southern cooking would infuse some of the jargon into him."

Garrett stood and stretched. "I haven't had a meal like that since I've been here. You're a good cook."

She grinned. "When I get the hankering."

Garrett chuckled as they moved to the railing to watch for Dylan's appearance in the courtyard below. The little boy with the new puppy held it up proudly to show them, and they praised and cooed at it from one floor up.

In no time, a red-faced Dylan scampered into view, waving at them and then turning his complete attention to the neighborhood's newest member.

Garrett took her hand as they walked back to the table. "I'm up now, so you're going to let me help with these dishes." His stern voice didn't match the smile that teased at his lips.

She held up their locked hands. "Guess we have to let go, first."

He stacked the plates as she took care of the empty serving dishes. Not a scrap of leftovers for tomorrow's lunch. Her mom always said that was a good sign.

"So what did you do today, other than cook…and

order an icky pizza?" He didn't ask about her Jacques Martin quest for the day, so she didn't mention it.

He was obviously aware she'd tell him when she found the right one, so for once, she left her elusive birth father out of the conversation. Besides, last night the subject had made him antsy. She didn't want a repeat performance of that.

"I went to Sacré Coeur." She loaded the dishes into the dishwasher as Garrett put things back into the fridge and cabinets.

"Oh? Did you take the funicular up to it?"

"No, I wanted to walk the hill," she answered. "The basilica was so beautiful, and the view from up there? Spectacular!" She chatted on about the Montmartre area's quaint streets.

"What else did you see?" He wet the dishcloth and wiped the crumbs and drips from the countertops.

"Well, I went to the cemetery and then I roamed around the Moulin Rouge area, but I didn't go in the theater." She paused, studying which button to push. She chose one and gave a satisfied smirk when the sound of water met her ears. "Man, those sex shops around there are sleazy. Not what I expected."

Garrett threw the dishcloth into the sink and pulled her into his arms. "Not a place I want you going without me, either."

His mouth came down on hers hard and insistent in a kiss that left her breathless and quivering. When he straightened and their lips parted, his arms remained locked around her as if he knew she would need the extra support.

And she did.

She leaned back and shook her finger. "You shouldn't kiss me like that so early in the evening. It sends my mind to places it shouldn't be. Gives me a terrible hankering for you."

He grinned, but then his eyes grew dark, his face serious. "I've got something I want to talk to you about." He nodded toward the door. "But we need to go back outside and listen for Dylan."

Her stomach squeezed at the intensity of his tone. "Is everything okay?"

"It will be if I can get you to consider something with an open mind." With a hand on her back, he led her outside to the terrace and the area with the railing.

"You sure are being cryptic." She peered into the courtyard below, but Dylan hadn't reappeared. He still had about ten minutes of his half hour remaining. She leaned an elbow on the wrought-iron barrier, giving Garrett her full attention.

"I don't mean to be." Garrett's voice was husky. "Fact is, I want to lay it all out for you." He faced her, leaning on his elbow. "I love you, Tara. We've said that's crazy to say this soon, but it's how I feel. But…" He paused and took her hand. "I'm not crazy enough to think we know each other as well as we need to in order to make any commitments."

For a minute there, she'd had the crazy idea he was

going to propose, and it had her heart thudding so hard she could feel it from her temples to her toes. His last sentence calmed that quaking some, but she still couldn't trust her voice not to squeak.

Garrett didn't give her time to respond anyway. He plunged ahead with his proposal of a different kind. "I want you to consider staying longer. You've said yourself, you really don't have to be back until August. Stay a few more weeks."

"My ticket…"

"Can be changed. I'll pay the fee. Stay with me and Dylan, Tara." He let go of her hand and slid his fingers into the sides of her hair. "Let's use whatever time we have to explore this thing between us. It feels more right to me than any relationship ever has."

Tara stood speechless for a moment, her brain whirring too fast for her mouth to catch up.

Garrett seemed to understand. He leaned in to capture her mouth with another kiss that was soft and beguiling, packed with emotion.

More time with Garrett and Dylan was exactly what her heart had been yearning for, and it leaped in her chest as she considered his offer. "I would love that."

"Dad?" Dylan's voice broke the moment. He stood in the courtyard below, hands on hips. "I called you three times before you heard me," he chided, but his grin said he really didn't mind.

"Sorry, sport. Didn't hear you."

"Yeah, because you and Tara were kissing. I'm on my way up," he called as he disappeared from view.

Garrett's gaze returned to hers, his hands still in her hair. "That was a yes from you, I think?"

She nodded. "That was an enthusiastic yes from me."

"Good."

His mouth closed down on hers again, and it was his kiss that she felt this time from her temples to her toes.

CHAPTER TWENTY

"AND IT'LL GIVE me more time to look for you-know-who and visit some places I haven't had time for yet."

The verdant, rolling hills of the French countryside came into view as Tara's train pulled out of the station, while images of the opulence of Versailles still spun in her head. Trying to accurately describe the place to Emma had proven futile, and even the photos she'd taken wouldn't do justice to the unfathomable beauty of the palace and its grounds.

"Garrett says we can take a weekend trip to the Loire Valley," she continued. "And we can do a weekend in Brussels, too, which is only four hours away. Isn't that crazy? He can be in Brussels, Belgium, in about the same time it takes us to get to St. Louis."

"What's crazy is my best friend's falling in love with a guy I've never met, who lives across the ocean, and she's pretending that she's extending her trip because she wants to see more of the country."

Tara grinned at the exasperation in Emma's tone. Ms. Counselor could take anything a troubled teen threw at her with calm patience, but Tara's quirky manner could send her into a dither faster than a bluegill on a cricket.

"I can't help it, Emma." Soul-lifting fields of sun-flowers appeared in the distance. The train's speed increased, and Tara could feel the thrum of the movement low in her belly. "I've got a feeling I'm headed toward something…something big. Yes, I want more time with Garrett and Dylan. I love being with them. But it's more than that. My father's here and he's alive, and I'm on the verge of locating him. I just know it.

The woman occupying the seat in front of her turned and gave a sympathetic glance, so Tara lowered her voice. "I only have nine addresses left. My odds have got to be getting better."

"Now I remember why we only went to Vegas once." The train was quiet enough for Tara to hear the sigh all the way from Kentucky to France. "I'm just jealous. Garrett's getting your whole summer. By the time you get back, we'll be heading back to work, and there won't be time for any of those things we'd planned to do."

"We'll still take that road trip to Memphis," Tara promised. "Graceland's on the to-do list this summer, no matter what else comes up."

"Thank you. Thank you very much."

Emma's barely recognizable imitation of Elvis sent Tara into a fit of the giggles. "That was god-awful."

"Yeah? Well, you ought to try it with drool running from a totally numb bottom lip."

Tara rolled her eyes. "One little filling, you baby. Try cutting off half your hand."

"I'll leave that to you."

The words were blotchy, and Tara realized they were about to lose reception. "Hey, you're cutting out, but before I lose you, do you think my mom and dad are doing okay?"

The line went silent, and Tara checked her phone. Call Ended was soon replaced by No Service.

She let out a frustrated sigh. Dad went fishing July Fourth. The family had a picnic at the cabin and had included Emma. Things were back to normal; she just needed to cool it with the worrying.

For the millionth time since she'd arrived in this country, she imagined how it would be when she met her father. He would smile, embrace her, introduce her proudly to his family. It seemed strange to think other siblings might be waiting in the wings to make their appearance on her life's stage.

She pressed her forehead to the train window, turning her attention to the landscape outside.

This trip was the most important journey of her life.

She didn't want to miss a single detail.

"We missed you at Ladies' Prayer Group, Faith. And the prayer meeting Wednesday night."

The voice behind her caused Faith's teeth to clench involuntarily. She'd known that Sue would make a beeline to her if she stepped even one foot outside. But she was tired of feeling like a prisoner in her mother-in-law's house. Besides, she could hardly do the gardening at night.

Faith tossed the handful of weeds into the bucket without turning around. "I didn't feel like going." She grabbed another clump of chickweed.

"All the more reason you should've been there. When we're at our lowest, we need to be lifted up. You need prayer right now more than anyone else I know."

Faith could swear she heard a smile in Sue's condescension. "Prayer I need." The chickweed broke loose. She tossed it away and turned to face her neighbor. Yes, indeed, the woman had a smug, mule-eating-briars grin on her face. "Gossip I can do without."

"Avoiding people isn't going to stop the gossip." Sue wrinkled her nose and sniffed as if the clean air harbored some kind of stench.

"Maybe not. But it gives me a rationale for avoiding people I don't like." Faith gave a fake grin of her own. "Like you."

"Don't blame me for your personal problems." There was the anger that always lay just below the surface of Sue's insecurity. It never took much scratching to bring it to the top. Fact was, Faith had always suspected Sue enjoyed being mad. She seemed to delight in telling people off, and this morning she was going to get a chance to start her day on the upswing.

"I'm not blaming you for *my* personal problems.

I'm blaming you for leading the charge against my husband." The words left Faith's mouth in a much calmer state than they'd been formed.

"*Somebody* has to take the reins in a situation like this."

Faith snorted. "You mean, somebody has to stir the *pile*. So tell me, Sue, just what kind of situation are you making this out to be?"

Sue's fisted hands rested on her hips and her head wobbled as she spewed her venom. "One where the preacher and his wife are having serious enough marital problems that they separate, yet they won't tell even their closest friends what's going on. It looks bad. Real bad. And I'm not going to sit around and wait until the Taylor's Grove Church becomes the laughing stock of Marshall County."

Faith pulled off her gardening gloves. "Have you and Ed ever had problems, Sue?"

"Well, of course we've had problems. Every married couple has problems."

Faith leaned forward and used a stage whisper. "Did you want those problems talked about?"

"*I* didn't put them on public display by moving out of the house." The smug smile came back out to play at the edges of her mouth.

"And neither did Sawyer." Faith took the gloves in one hand and slapped them against the other to knock the dirt off, imagining the hand was Sue's smirk. "But he's who you're going after."

Sue's chin lifted. "He's the leader of the church."

"Or maybe he's the easier of the two targets." Faith opened the cage on her own anger. "You know if you come after me, I won't take any of your crap."

Sue gasped and Faith rolled her eyes at the drama. "Oh, like you've never heard the word before. Your daddy started the church and you control the purse and therefore you *think* you control Sawyer." Maybe Sue had been right all these years. Telling somebody off *did* feel good! "What you may not realize is that Sawyer doesn't just put up with your *crap* because of your position. He genuinely likes you, Sue, which isn't true of most of the people in this community. He somehow manages to see through your hateful, mean ways to some goodness inside you—though goodness knows where. Did you know that? Sawyer's your staunchest supporter. 'Sue has a good heart,' he always says. 'She means well.' Well, look at where *that* faith in humanity has gotten him."

Sue's face was the color of the beet Faith had unearthed a few minutes earlier. "I'll make you sorry you ever crossed me, Faith Franklin. I'll get to the bottom of this secret you're harboring, and when I do, I'll have you run out of town on a rail. And your husband, too. He'll never lead another church in this county or anywhere near here, if I have my say."

"Oh, that's what you do best, Sue. You have your say...whether it's the truth or not." Faith took a menacing step in the woman's direction, brandishing the weeding fork she still held. "Now, get out of my yard before I throw you out. Lacy's plants don't need any more of your…fertilizer."

Sue nearly ran from the yard.

Faith watched with amusement, breathing hard and thinking the woman might actually vault over the gate in her haste to leave.

She gathered up the gardening tools, the task having suddenly lost its appeal. Guilt tightened her chest for participating in such an ugly scene in Lacy's lovely place of tranquility.

She needed to finish the calls she'd started two days ago, and then she'd go see Sawyer and tell him what had just happened. He'd been sure the Board of Fellowship would follow Sue's lead. Well, her tirade had pretty much put the last nail in that coffin.

The house was cool and stepping inside was like putting a soothing balm on her temper.

Faith sat down at the table with the list of numbers she'd jotted down in her quest for Jacques Martin and picked up the phone.

The placement office at Murray State didn't have any information on the former student, nor did the Office of Alumni Affairs. But the woman there had been most helpful. She'd suggested Faith use the yearbook from her college sorority to help contact her sorority sisters—one of them might have information on Jacques Martin.

It was a splendid plan, and had kept Faith busy the past two days catching up with old friends and rehashing old times.

She dialed Tina Lofton's number and listened to it ring. No answer. No answering machine. No voice mail. She'd try that one again later.

On to Mary Jane Mitchell. She had only the first three numbers punched in when the phone vibrated in her hand.

"Faith? It's Cheryl Wheeler. Cheryl Gates Wheeler. I got your message."

An image of Cheryl Gates as she looked thirty years ago settled in Faith's mind. "It's so good to hear from you, Cheryl. Thanks for calling me back."

They chatted for a while, catching up on the years that had been swept away like they'd been caught in a flash flood.

"So, Cheryl, do you remember Jacques Martin?" Faith tried to modulate her voice so it didn't sound too full of excitement...or trepidation.

"That hot French guy? Nobody could forget him." Cheryl laughed. "Didn't you two hook up on graduation night?"

Hearing the secret she'd harbored for so many years spoken aloud as if it were common knowledge caused Faith's throat to tighten. When Cheryl said it, it sounded so worldly and modern, So opposite of the real her, but perhaps the woman she might have been if she'd not spent the past twenty-nine years as the preacher's wife in Taylor's Grove.

"Yeah, just that once, though." She forced a smile, trying to borrow that worldly persona. She'd practiced what she would say and fell easily into the lie.

"But my husband and I are thinking about a trip to France, and I thought I might try to look Jacques up. Would you happen to know if he's still in Paris?"

"He *is* still in Paris," Cheryl answered, and Faith tilted the phone away from her mouth and nose to keep her sporadic breathing from sounding creepy. "Or, at least, he was two years ago. Kay and George Yancy had dinner with him. You remember Kay and George? George and Jacques were fraternity brothers."

Faith swerved the phone down to her mouth. "Yeah, I remember Kay and George well." Her hand shook as she grabbed the pen and notepad.

"Well, they live in Frankfort now. George is a state congressman." That came as no surprise. "But we see them occasionally. I'm sure they could put you in touch with him."

Her? In touch with Jacques? Lord, no! "That would be great. Could you give me their number?" Faith's throat felt as tight as her grip on the pen.

"Sure, just let me get Kay's personal number, one second."

A few seconds later Cheryl returned to the phone with that fateful number and Faith jotted it down on her notepad.

"Just so you know, Faith, I tried calling Kay a few days ago and found out she and George are on a cruise. They won't be home until Sunday, so, if I were you, I'd wait until Monday or Tuesday to call."

"That's no problem. I'm not in any hurry." Faith's

throat relaxed a little, knowing she had a few days' reprieve before she had to act on this. "But thanks for the number, Cheryl. I really appreciate it."

"Oh, you're welcome. We should get together sometime."

"Yes, definitely, when life isn't so hectic," Faith answered. *Which is never.*

"I hear you." Cheryl paused, and Faith didn't pick up the conversation. "Well, I'll let you go. I hope you enjoy your trip."

Trip? Oh, the made-up trip to France. "Yes, thank you. Hopefully we'll actually end up going." Adding the qualifier softened the lie in her mind. "Thanks again, Cheryl."

After the goodbyes, Faith stared at the number she'd scribbled. Her hand had been shaking so much, it would be difficult for anybody but her to make it out.

Kay. Tara. Jacques.

Now, with the possibility of Jacques being as close as three calls away, Faith's courage began to slip.

She hadn't thought about the possibility of Jacques Martin's return to *her* life. She'd imagined Tara meeting him. Coming back to Taylor's Grove, thrilled with the new discovery. She'd never considered that the man himself might show up, too.

The air conditioner kicked on, and the vent above her head directed a cold breeze down her back, causing a shiver to course through her.

What would it be like to see Jacques Martin again?

Would she have heart palpitations? Yeah, but not because of any attraction to him.

Because of Sawyer.

With everything else he was going through, could she do this to him, knowing it could be the end of the marriage she wanted so desperately to save?

The choice had come down to choosing her daughter's happiness or her husband's and therefore her own.

A tear fell on the paper, smearing the ink and obliterating the last two numbers.

She might have considered that as a sign not to start the sequence of actions if the number wasn't already etched into her brain.

CHAPTER TWENTY-ONE

THE MATTER WAS out of Garrett's hands now. He could only hope things went as he'd planned and that he hadn't made a mistake.

It all seemed a little surreal that Saturday morning had come at last. That they were strolling hand in hand toward a bench where, unbeknownst to Tara, they would await the meeting with her birth father. He, with his heart in his mouth, hardly able to concentrate enough to put together a coherent sentence. She, in her yellow dress, smiling and bright.

"You look like a freshly picked sunflower...or maybe a drop of the sun." He kissed her hand as they walked. "You've certainly brought light and warmth into my life...and Dylan's."

The smile she rewarded him with both soothed his heart and made it ache.

For the millionth time, he wondered if Tara would pick up a familial vibe or notice a resemblance between her father and herself.... Though he'd exaggerated the similarity in looks in order to appeal to Jacques Martin's ego, it definitely existed. Her mouth was an exact copy, but her eyes and nose belonged to her mom.

As they approached Place des Vosges, another worry niggled at his brain. Why in the hell, with Paris's abundance of parks, had he chosen *this* particular place for their meeting? It seemed a cruel twist of fate.

Paris's oldest square, beautiful in its symmetry, had drawn its share of famous residents, and Parisians and visitors were still drawn to its beauty.

But it was also a well-known place for dueling, for God's sake, and *that* irony caused the sweet morning air to leave a bitter taste on Garrett's tongue as he spoke.

"King Henri the second was wounded here in a tournament." Garrett guided Tara to an empty bench. A quick glance around the immediate area turned up no Jacques Martin, which relieved and agitated Garrett at the same time. "He died of the wounds."

"Poor Henri."

"Yeah." He tried to ignore the irony in that statement, too, and changed the subject by pointing to *maison* number six. "Victor Hugo lived there. It's a museum now that houses some of his things. Did you know he went mad?"

He watched Tara's mouth curve down at the corners. "No, but I can believe it. I've never cared for *Les Mis.* I mean, it was uplifting, but the story was so sad."

"It must not have given him much joy, either. He

took to carving furniture…with his teeth, earning him the nickname Beaver Hugo."

Laughter rippled out of her. "You're kidding, right?"

Garrett held up three fingers. "Boy Scout's honor. Well, not about the nickname, but the part about carving out furniture with his teeth. Or, at least, that's what I've read." He grinned. "Probably started out as a pencil chewer."

"So maybe the madness was caused from all the lead he ingested." She said it with a straight face that dissolved into a giggle. "Nope, I don't believe you."

"God, you're beautiful when you laugh." He nabbed her smile with a kiss that she returned with enough enthusiasm to make him wish they were home in bed.

She jumped, then her lips tore away from him, and she leaned over. "Oh, look!" she cooed.

A small blue ball lay at her feet with a tiny Yorkie rushing toward it in pursuit.

Garrett looked up to see Jacques Martin watching them intently, and his breath froze in his chest.

He counted the man's steps as he approached although instinct had already told him the distance between them.

Ten paces.

TARA PICKED UP the ball as the Yorkie skidded to a halt at her feet.

He didn't bark, just looked at her with bright, expectant eyes, twitching with excitement. The ball she held matched the dog's turquoise collar, which was set with jewels that sparkled in the sunlight like real diamonds.

Surely not. But the man who approached them— the dog's owner—had an affluent air about him that screamed "Money!" and changed her mind to *maybe so.*

"Bonjour, madame...monsieur." He rattled off something she didn't understand, and, as she had gotten used to doing, she turned to Garrett for a translation.

His eyes cut to the stranger and back. "He said he's sorry for the clumsy throw."

"Ah, English?" the man asked.

"American." Tara leaned over to allow the dog to sniff her hand. He rewarded her with a couple of licks. "Can I pick him up?"

"But, of course." The Frenchman nodded toward the dog's continued licks. "Attila likes you."

She chuckled at the name. "Attila the Hun?" The tiny dog felt almost weightless in her hand and barely made an indent on her dress when she placed him on her lap. He had way too much energy to just lie there, though, and scrambled up to lick her face. She laughed as he covered her nose with doggy kisses. "More like Attila the Honey, if you ask me."

A wide smile split the Frenchman's face and his dark eyes brightened. "You make a good joke."

Nice-looking for a middle-aged guy, the man was

of medium height and build, with dark hair combed back from his face. Heavy brows framed dark brown eyes with a keen and perceptive gaze that seemed to miss nothing. His pink shirt was crisp and tucked neatly into trousers that appeared to be of black silk. Expensive-looking black leather shoes and belt. A leash that matched the dog's collar dangled from his hand. His whole demeanor exuded elegance—something she'd grown used to in Paris.

Attila flipped around, looking at her over his shoulder, and wagged his almost nonexistent tail.

"He wants you to throw the ball, but not too far."

Tara waited for a strolling couple to get past and then tossed the ball a few yards away.

Attila shot from her lap, catching up with the ball before it stopped rolling. He stretched his little mouth wide to pick it up and skipped his way back, jumping on the bench beside her and placing it back in her lap.

"What a good boy you are!" Tara scratched behind his ears, and he closed his eyes and tilted his head to give her full access to his favorite spot. "He's so adorable. How old is he?"

"Seven months." Pride showed in their visitor's eyes almost as if he were talking about his child.

Tara scooted closer to Garrett and pointed to the empty space beside her. "Would you like to sit down?"

The man gave a slow nod. "Thank you. You are very kind."

"Yes, she is." Garrett gave her leg a pat. Attila

added his approval by stretching over Tara and licking his hand.

When the gentleman sat down beside her, the pleasant fragrance of his cologne filled her head. Unlike the light, clean aroma that surrounded Garrett, this was a heavier scent, exotic and mysterious. Perhaps a good match to the man who wore it. But the two extremes dueled for dominance in the air around her, with a distinct advantage determined by the way she tilted her head.

She picked Attila up and buried her nose in the soft fur, finding a third scent that was decidedly feminine. "You smell good." She rubbed her nose against him again, and he licked her cheek in response.

"My wife's *parfum*." The man rolled his eyes. "I tell her a dog with such a name should not smell like a woman, but she puts a little on her hands and strokes it into his fur."

Tara fought back her own eye roll. She couldn't imagine her mom putting perfume on a dog. And never in her wildest imagination could she imagine her dad walking a dog that wore a diamond-studded collar. The absurdity almost dislodged a snort she kept at bay only through sheer will.

She tossed the ball again, and the dog sprang from the bench.

The Frenchman's laugh was low. "He already has you trained. Now he will allow you to throw the ball for him all day."

"That's okay." Tara clapped when Attila grabbed

the ball and held it up like he was showing off his prowess. "We don't have any place we need to be for a while."

"So you are American?" The man gave her a side-long glance and passed a hand over his brow. The heavy Rolex on his wrist glinted in the sun—another thing she couldn't imagine ever seeing on her dad. If Sawyer were ever given such a thing, he would sell it and send the money to some mission.

"Yes, I'm from Kentucky," she answered.

"Ah!" Attila jumped onto the bench between them and the man took his turn at throwing. "I have visited Kentucky, I believe. But only once, and that was many years ago."

Garrett jerked beside her, coughing hard several times.

"You okay?" she asked and he nodded. She turned back to the stranger. "You should go back there sometime." Most of the French people she'd talked with on this trip weren't familiar with Kentucky. It was nice to converse with someone who had some familiarity with the place. "It's really beautiful on Kentucky Lake in the summer."

The Frenchman shrugged. "Perhaps I'll return someday."

Garrett coughed again, this time louder and harder. She hoped he wasn't coming down with something.

"Hey, babe." Apparently he'd gotten the coughing under control enough to speak. "I'm going to find a bottle of water. Be right back, okay?"

She nodded.

"You want anything?"

She shook her head. "No. I'm good."

"Your husband?" The man nodded toward Garrett as he left.

"Boyfriend." The words felt good on her lips. She couldn't keep from smiling, waving bye to him when he glanced back over his shoulder.

The man pointed to the half hand she'd waved with. "You have had an accident."

"A wreck on a motorcycle." She ran her fingertip up the scar on her arm. "But I've since sworn off those things." She held her hand out for a shake. "I'm Tara O'Malley, by the way."

"I am—" he paused to throw the ball for the dog whose energy didn't seem to be waning in the least "—François Martin."

All of the moisture in Tara's mouth abandoned her at the sound of the man's surname. "Martin?" The word came out as a croak.

"*Oui*, Martin. It is the most common surname in Paris." He gave an apologetic shrug. "Much like Smith or Jones in the U.S."

Tara nodded mutely. She already knew that, but to have an actual Martin sitting beside her seemed an amazing coincidence. She'd been feeling like she was getting close to finding her father. Maybe this man was here to help.

"I, uh." She sucked in a breath. "I've been looking for a friend of my family while I'm here, and *his* name is Martin. Jacques Martin. You wouldn't happen to know anyone by that name, would you?"

A hint of laughter lit the man's eyes before he gave her a small smile. "*Oui,* Tara O'Malley. I know two men who have the name of Jacques Martin." He held up two fingers and ticked the names off. "My father's name was Jacques Martin, though he died many years ago. And my son is also Jacques Martin. He is fifteen years old and could not be the friend of your family, I think."

"No." Tara's chest heaved with disappointment. She tossed the ball for the waiting Attila. "You don't know of any others. Cousins...?"

The man shook his head, his heavy brows drawing in and nearly touching. "No, but as I said before, there are many Martins, and Jacques is also very common."

Garrett headed back toward them from across the park, and a spark of joy lit Tara's insides at the sight of him. Thankfully, he'd ignored her when she declined the offer of a drink. He held a bottle in each hand.

"Are you originally from Paris?" She continued to make conversation.

"Yes. I was born here and have lived here most of my life although I also travel extensively." The touch of pride was evident again.

"It's such a beautiful place." Tara rolled her shoulders to loosen the muscles that had tightened when the man told her his name. "I'm glad I got to come see it for myself."

The Frenchman's eyes met hers directly. "Yes, she is a beauty." He swallowed hard before he glanced away, obviously moved by his love for the city. "I have much to be proud of."

The wistful timbre of his voice and the sudden serious tone the conversation had taken made Tara a little uncomfortable. A shiver scampered up her spine, though there was no logical reason for it. But Tara sensed sadness in this person. Perhaps he'd experienced a recent loss…or maybe he was the type of wealthy person who was never quite satisfied no matter how much he had.

"Here you go."

Garrett's familiar voice wrapped her in instant warmth. She took the Orangina he proffered, enjoying the solidness of him as he settled down beside her again. She downed the small bottle of liquid in two gulps, the cool drink soothing her parched throat.

Garrett laughed. "Thought you weren't thirsty."

"I'm glad you knew better than I did." Pointing to her companion, she added, "I should introduce you two. Garrett Hughes, meet François Martin."

She should have timed it better, should have allowed Garrett to swallow what was in his mouth. Instead, she watched him choke when the name Martin left her lips. He managed not to spew Orangina, but his face turned so red she was afraid he was going to burst a blood vessel. His body jerked with spasms and he finally gave in to a series of long, loud coughs.

"Sorry." At last, he got himself under control enough to extend his hand. "*François* Martin, is it?"

"Yes, that is correct." François's hand dropped to caress Attila's head, his several-carat diamond ring glinting sunlight into Tara's face.

She turned to face Garrett. "His father and his son are *both* Jacques Martin."

Sympathy softened Garrett's features as he brushed the back of his finger to her face. She gave him a soft smile and kissed the finger.

The weight of his arm settled on her shoulder and he pulled her to him in a quick hug. "I'm sorry, baby," he whispered into her hair and then kissed the same spot.

She winked to let him know everything was okay.

Attila's energy had finally run out, and he snuggled into Tara's lap. A tiny snore escaped, which made them all laugh.

"Ah, the excitement of the day has tired out the great Attila the Honey." François stood and held out his arms. Tara handed the sleeping dog to him, and François gathered him to his chest. "I think it is time for us to say *au revoir.*"

A sudden restlessness spurred Tara to her feet. "It was nice to meet you, Monsieur Martin." She gave Attila a final scratch, her eyes tangling with François's dark gaze. "If you're ever back in Kentucky near Paducah, please look me up."

"Thank you, lovely Tara." François's hand rested briefly on top of hers. "I shall remember your generous invitation. *Au revoir,* my dear."

As he left them, Tara tracked his movement until he was completely lost from sight, then she plopped back down beside Garrett. "Can you believe that? A Martin. Right here beside me."

"Yeah, that was quite a coincidence," he said, but without any enthusiasm. "C'mon, Tara." He stood up and held his hand out. "Let's go see the crafty stuff Hugo cut his teeth on."

She let Garrett take the lead, her mind still occupied by the new acquaintance she'd made.

Allowing her hopes to get too high would be a mistake. But her growing love for the Hughes guys and the conviction that nothing happened by chance made her heart feel like it could soar with happiness.

Luckily, Garrett's grip on her hand kept her firmly grounded.

FAITH HAD CALLED to tell him she was on her way, so Sawyer was waiting for her at the back door when she arrived.

She hadn't been back to the house since she'd left a week ago yesterday. It felt odd to be welcomed into her own home. She glanced around, relieved to see he was keeping the place clean. But, of course, he would be. Sawyer's standard of clean living reached into even the tiniest crevices of his life.

A faint aroma of burned food hinted that his cooking skills hadn't improved, though.

"I was glad to see you at church tonight." He handed her a glass of iced tea, their fingers touching as she took it. If he felt the jolt from the touch like she had, he gave no indication.

"You preached a good sermon." She took a sip, finding the strong brew sweetened and *lemoned* exactly the way she liked it. "You always do."

She'd skipped the morning service for the second week in a row, but Ollie had come by on his way this evening and talked her into accompanying him. He convinced her that a show of confidence and solidarity with Sawyer might encourage the Board of Fellowship to stop and consider what they were doing.

She was glad she'd taken his advice. It also put that first-time awkwardness behind her, although the stares and whispers had sent her into the mother of all hot flashes.

But she'd survived.

And now she knew she could.

Sawyer nodded toward the den. "Let's go in there where we'll be comfortable."

Finding her favorite spot on the sofa, she slipped off her shoes and pulled her legs up under her, making herself at home. Sawyer sat in his recliner, but he didn't kick it back.

"You first," she said.

When he'd invited her to come by after church, she'd hoped he was going to ask her to move back home. If he did, it would make what she wanted to talk about much easier.

But the distance he kept didn't bode well that reconciliation would be their topic of conversation. She steeled herself against whatever the purpose of this visit turned out to be.

"Well, I'm sure you've already thought about it, but we haven't talked about it." Sawyer leaned forward and rested his elbows on his knees. "If I lose the church, we'll have to put the house up for sale. I've been studying our finances all week, and I just don't see any other way. Selling Mom's house and the cabin will help, but it won't pay off the mortgage." He leaned back and passed a hand across his eyes. "Of course…if another church will have me… it would mean a move anyway."

If another church will have me. If was the definitive word. Their future together was not so definitive though—*have me*, not *have us*.

Before all this, he'd always referred to them as a team.

Guilt pushed a heavy finger into her chest. The house they'd planned and built together. The place where they'd raised their family. Their sanctuary from the world.

All of it would be lost.

Because of her lie?

Yes. But what it actually came down to was her lack of faith in Sawyer's love.

If she'd trusted his love enough to tell him the

truth all those years ago, they wouldn't be going through this now.

She would never make that mistake again.

"We'll do whatever we have to do." She deliberately chose the plural form and felt some of the guilt seep away with her words. "Sell the house. Sell both houses and the cabin. I'll get a job. I'll get two jobs. It's not like I have kids to stay home for anymore."

His tired eyes regarded her for a moment over the rim of his glass. He opened his mouth to say something, and then closed it, setting his drink down with a shrug. "Thanks for not going all emotional on me. I don't think I could've stood that."

"I'm giving up emotional…except with Sue." She saw his chin buckle at that admission, but Faith wasn't here to mince words. They'd already been through yesterday's argument with Sue. No use pretending it hadn't happened. "I've decided that logical's a better fit at my age."

"It looks good on you." Her heart fluttered as she watched the corners of his mouth turn up, and the tiniest light of interest flare in his eyes. "But then, everything looks good on you."

His tender smile and flirtation made her heart race. But she couldn't let herself get carried away. The news she bore would douse that flicker in a hurry.

And there was no use letting the flirtation go any further. Building hope only to dash it again was cruel to them both. So, without preamble, she blurted, "I've found a promising connection to Jacques Martin, and I think I can get his address for Tara."

Sure enough, all the emotion drained from his face and the flame went out, leaving behind a white mask, devoid of expression.

"I got it Friday." She plunged ahead, just wanting to get this—all of it—over with. "But I didn't bring it up because I can't do anything about it until tomorrow, and I wasn't sure what to do about it anyway."

"What do you mean you're not sure what to do about it?" Sawyer's fingertip brushed his lip, back and forth.

"I have the number for someone who may be able to give me his number and address." She took a fortifying breath to help her get through this next part. "But I think I need to leave it up to you whether or not I make the call."

His head tilted in question. "Me? Why?"

"Because you appear to be the one with the most at stake."

His lips pressed together into a thin line. "Because, if she finds her birth father, she may push me out of her life."

"I don't think that's going to happen. But it's possible he could visit if they hit it off. She might bring him here to show off where she grew up. Next to Tara, you seem to be the one who could be the most affected, so the decision of whether I call or not has to be yours. I refuse to do anything else that might screw your life up worse than I have already."

"You haven't screwed my life up, Faith." The voice was flat again, almost robotic, so the words, placating as they were, didn't live up to their intention.

She snorted in return. "Well, I haven't made it a rose garden lately."

She wasn't interested in debating the issue. It was all water under the bridge, and she dismissed it with a wave of her hand. "I'm not here to discuss that. I just need to know whether to make the call in the morning or not?"

Sawyer leaned forward again, studying his tightly clasped hands. "The whole time she's been over there, I've been praying that she wouldn't find him. That's selfish, I know. It was me I was worried about." His eyes drifted up to meet hers. "What kind of father would I be if I put my happiness ahead of hers?" He paused and shook his head. "Not the kind I *want* to be." He sat up straight, opening his hands to rest them on the arms of the chair. "Make the call, Faith. She needs this, and in some weird way that I don't understand, maybe I need it, too."

His fingers brushed at the corner of his eye, and Faith's throat constricted. "You're sure?"

"I'm committed," he answered. "But the truth is that I understand a little better how Abraham must have felt when he was leading Isaac up the side of that mountain."

She nodded. "I'll call first thing in the morning."

CHAPTER TWENTY-TWO

GARRETT WATCHED THE FIRST light of dawn break through the bedroom window and catch in Tara's wild curls. Snuggled against his side, her naked breasts rising and falling to the rhythm of her soft breathing, she had the countenance of an angel—or so he'd been thinking. But the fiery glow suddenly surrounding her reminded him what a she-devil she could be in bed—a tempting red-haired seductress whose magic brought out a passion that he'd buried years ago and had all but forgotten.

She stirred in her sleep and he felt himself stir in response, despite his lack of shut-eye the past two nights.

Since Saturday, he'd been waiting for the call that hadn't come—the invitation he'd been sure Jacques Martin would extend to Tara to join his life after their encounter.

Seeing the fulfillment of her quest sitting next to her, while she remained so blissfully unaware brought out a protective instinct in Garrett that he'd thought was reserved for only Dylan. He wanted to grab Martin and shake him until he loosened the part of the man's brain that would allow him to think clearly instead of filtering everything through his wallet.

Just wake her and tell her the truth. Lay out the entire story about Martin's fears of losing his wife and his fortune, his threat to Soulard. Make her promise never to approach the man.

Tara stirred again, shifting her head slightly. The sunlight had eased over enough to catch in the ring that decorated her thin brow line. It flashed like the beacon from a lighthouse, warning of dangerous waters.

Warnings he'd ignored from Angie.

I hate you.

His insides coiled into a hard knot pulling from his stomach to his throat.

He closed his eyes, taking long, deep breaths, and ran a hand over his sweat-drenched face.

Tara was nothing like Angie, and he couldn't continue this asinine habit of allowing his guilt over his wife's death control the workings of his heart.

If any warning was truly flashing, it was the one in his brain to guard against broken promises.

He'd promised Henri to keep his secret safe. He'd, also, given Martin his word he wouldn't interfere.

A man was only as good as his word.

And he'd learned the hard way that he had no business trying to control other people's lives.

But he had to believe that Jacques Martin would

make that call. It might take a few years, but it would happen. And, when it did, he would be there with Tara in his arms, holding her, protecting her, dancing with her in her time of joy.

He opened his eyes to find her watching him, sunlight on her face and lovelight in her eyes.

"Good morning." She slipped her arm around his waist and her leg moved subtly between his. Not quite as subtly, she pressed against him in unspoken invitation.

"Good morning." He kissed the brow ring and then let his lips wander to her nose, her mouth and on to her neck.

Her contented sigh feathered around his ear. "I love you, Garrett."

The words spread through him like wildfire across a dry plain. He moved lower, covering her with kisses, igniting her heat with his mouth and hands, fanning the flame.

The blaze raged hotter, an inferno that burned away any lingering doubts of whether true love could grow in such a short span of time. Garrett allowed it to consume him, reaching for only the slightest protection as the combustion moved toward their collective core, shattering them both in a simultaneous cataclysm of passion.

He held her tightly until the delicious spasms subsided and her breathing returned to normal. He loosened his hold then, but only with his arms. His heart gripped tighter than ever.

"Wow," she whispered. "I never knew it could be like that. Like this. Just...wow."

The room was bright now with a light that Garrett wasn't sure originated from the sun. An ember from the wildfire continued to burn in his heart, waiting for the next piece of kindling—a touch or a whisper—to make it burst into flame.

Wildfire could be destructive, he knew, but it could also be beneficial in the larger scheme of things. Though its uncontrollable blaze moved through an area with thoughtless destruction, the final result was ultimately freshening.

Wildfire had wiped the area of his heart clean, destroying the leftover debris from times past. It had burned away the rubble of that which was dead.

It had cleared a space for new growth.

At 9:07 A.M. Monday, Faith made the call to Kay Yancy, whose only recollection of Faith was that she'd slept with Jacques Martin graduation night.

A reluctance in Kay's tone had Faith doubting whether securing Jacques's number was going to be possible—even with the plausible lie about the intended trip to Paris.

"Jacques's very different than he was at Murray." Kay's voice held a hint of warning. "He's very private. And very wealthy. A bit of a snob, actually."

"Oh, what a shame. He was such a neat person back then." Faith's heart quivered at the thought of what she might be putting Tara through, but she pressed on with her made-up story. "I'll give him a call and feel him out before we make the trip. If he doesn't seem interested in getting together, I won't push it."

"Well." There was a long pause on the other end. "Here's his address and phone number." Kay quickly relayed the information. "But this is his place of business. We've never been invited to his home."

"Oh, this will be just fi-fine." Faith's throat went dry as the nonchalant attitude dissolved. The numbers and letters she'd written down were scrawled across the page as if the hand that wrote them belonged to someone recovering from a stroke.

She didn't press Kay to chat. They had little in common. So she thanked her acquaintance, said her goodbyes and hung up.

Then she punched in Tara's number before she lost her nerve.

"So, IF I GET home on the second, I can sleep all day on the third, make the meeting the morning of the fourth and spend the rest of that day getting things ready for the kids on the fifth. What do you think, Ethel?" Tara made some quick notes in the back of her journal. When she finished this call, she'd contact the airlines and change her returning flight, so she wanted to make sure she had her dates correct.

Ethel, the school's ancient secretary, gave one of her trademark cackles. "You can do that at your age, doll. I'd have to sleep for a week to recover from the jet lag."

"I'm actually gaining time coming back," Tara explained. The phone beeped and she glanced down before she spoke again. "Hey, Ethel, my mom's calling, so I'm going to let you go now. I'll see you August fourth."

"See you, doll. Have fun."

Tara was all smiles as she retrieved the other call. Three more weeks with Garrett and Dylan! "Hi, Mama."

"Hi, sweetpea."

Her mom's voice sounded off, and Tara gripped the phone a little tighter. "You okay? You sound upset."

"I have…I have Jacques Martin's business address and phone number…if you still want it."

A violent shudder echoed in Tara's speech. "You— you have it? H-how?"

She heard the deep intake of breath on the other end of the line. "One of my sorority sisters from Murray knew someone who's been in touch with him fairly recently."

"That's unbelievable." Tara was thankful for the chair beneath her as she felt her legs go weak. But she wished she hadn't just drunk that double espresso. Her heart was galloping at a scary pace. "Yeah. Yeah, I still want it."

"Kay says that he's really wealthy, and quite a

snob." The warning in her mom's tone was clear. "Are you sure you want to go through with this?"

The pounding in Tara's temples said she wasn't sure of anything at that moment, but her mouth ran ahead of her brain. "I'm sure."

"Do you have something to write on?"

Tara glanced down, a little surprised to find a pen already in her hand and her journal opened in front of her. Oh yeah, she'd been talking to Ethel and jotting down dates.

Was that only a minute ago?

"Gah." She swallowed, trying to wet her parched throat. "Got it."

Her mom spoke slowly, spelling out the name of the street. "Do you know where that is?"

"No." Tara pulled out her map. "I can find it, though."

"First make sure it's not in a bad part of town, and don't go by yourself. Take Garrett with you." It was unclear if she meant for safety or moral support. "Kay said he's very private."

Tara flinched. "So, you're saying he might not welcome a long-lost daughter from Podunk, Kentucky."

"I'm saying just be careful, precious. Guard your heart." Tears were evident in her mom's voice.

"I will, Mama." Her own eyes blurred, and she wasn't sure if the tears were joy, fear or something else entirely.

"And call me afterward. Okay?"

"Okay." Tara glanced at her watch. It was after

four. She couldn't let this wait until tomorrow. "I need to go now."

I need to go now!

"Okay, baby. I love you, and I'm praying for you."

Tara found comfort in those words. "You always are. Thanks, Mama. I love you, too. Bye."

Tara ran a shaky hand over her face. She needed grounding. Without a second thought, she called Garrett. It went to voice mail, which meant he was in a meeting. She knew the protocol. If it was an emergency, call the business line and the secretary would get him out of the meeting.

She hung up.

This wasn't an emergency. If the secretary interrupted the meeting, he would panic and think something had happened to Dylan.

She opened up the map and found the street. It wasn't too far away from the café where she sat. Too far to walk maybe, but a cab would get her there in ten minutes. Fifteen tops.

Her breathing became erratic.

In fifteen minutes, she could be meeting her birth father!

He might not want to see her.

If she called, he might turn down a request to meet. But if she went to his place of business, she had a good chance of at least seeing him.

She looked at her blue sundress. It was classy and went well with her coloring. Her hair was fairly tame today since the humidity was low.

She dug in her purse and found a tin of strong mints, popping a couple in her mouth.

Coffee breath taken care of.

She took a few bills out of her wallet to cover her check and laid them carefully on the table.

She was ready. She could do this.

Her knees felt weak, but she willed them to hold her up long enough to hail a taxi.

The driver nodded that he understood the address, and then she was whizzing through the Parisian traffic…on a magic carpet ride to meet her father.

She punched Garrett's number into the phone again, and once again listened as it went to voice mail.

"Garrett, it's Tara. Mama called and she's managed to get Jacques Martin's address and phone number from somebody she knew in college." She was giddy with excitement now, and the words rushed out. "I'm…I'm going to see him! Right now! I decided not to call first. It's his business address, so I figure I'll at least get a glimpse of him if…if nothing else." She knew she was rambling. "I'll tell you all about it when I get home. Wish me luck. I love you."

She put the phone away. Then, on second thought, she got it back out. She needed to think about what she was going to say, and she didn't want anything interrupting her thoughts the rest of the way there.

Not even Garrett.

She turned off her phone.

GARRETT CHECKED HIS phone as he headed back to his office.

Two calls from Tara. Odd. But the meeting hadn't been interrupted, so there was no emergency.

He dropped the legal pad on his desk.

The last call came in four minutes ago, and she'd left a voice mail that time.

"Garrett, it's Tara. Mama called and she's managed to get Jacques Martin's address and phone number from somebody she knew in college. I'm...I'm going to see him! Right now!"

Oh, God. No.

"...his business address, so I figure I'll at least get a glimpse of him if...if nothing else. I'll tell you all about it when I get home. Wish me luck. I love you."

Garrett's head spun, and he leaned on the desk with both hands.

Tara was on her way to Jacques Martin.

Bloody hell!

He had to talk her out of this.

Her phone went to voice mail.

Damn it.

Think!

He pressed a hand to his forehead, vaguely noticing that both were covered in sweat.

Call Martin and warn him she's on the way.

But he didn't have the number. He'd given Henri the original back and destroyed his copy, like he'd promised.

The sound of panting echoed in his ears, and he realized it was his own.

Where was Tara? Was she out in the city somewhere or had she gone from home?

Either way, she had a head start. He couldn't ask Henri for the number again. Too great a risk. And there was no time, besides.

Garrett rushed from his office, stopping just long enough to let the secretary know he was leaving. Then he was hailing a taxi and spewing Jacques Martin's address from memory.

His only hope—Soulard's only hope—was to make it there before Tara did.

He called her number repeatedly during the ride, giving up, finally, and leaving a voice mail.

"Tara, if you get this message before you get to Jacques Martin's address, please don't go in. I'll explain everything. Just wait for me outside. I love you."

CHAPTER TWENTY-THREE

TARA STOOD IN front of the imposing building, trying to bring her breathing down to something that resembled normal rate.

The taxi ride had taken longer than she'd anticipated with a couple of fast sprints through harrowing tunnels that had her clutching her seat and thinking of Princess Di.

Amazingly, several times the fact that she was headed to meet Jacques Martin slipped from her mind as she feared for her life. Then, the purpose of the taxi ride would pop back into her mind and she would clench her teeth and hope that meeting her father would still remain an option in this lifetime.

She should probably spend some time in contemplation of the fabulous architecture of the building, but later seemed like a better time for that activity. Right then, she needed to get on with the task at hand before she lost her nerve...or her chance.

And she had no guarantee Jacques Martin would even be in, or that he would welcome her unannounced visit.

She opened the massive door and stepped into a huge corridor whose pink granite floors cast a rosy hue to the ivory walls—an effect she found both charming and soothing. What appeared to be suites of offices lined the sides of the wide hallway. A large lobby opened up the center of the first floor, and beyond it was another corridor, identical to the one she was standing in.

She felt as if she'd just fallen down the hole with Alice and needed one of those mushrooms that made her larger—and more significant.

At least one breath came easier when she located the directory on the wall, but when she came to the name, it went erratic again. *Jacques Martin, le concessionnaire, 137.* She touched her finger to the glass, leaving a smudge after she removed it.

She began walking, checking the numbers on the doors. All lower one hundreds. When she reached the lobby, dismay brought her to a halt. Seven more identical corridors. Three continued toward the back of the building. Two came into the lobby on her left, and two on her right.

She stood there for a minute, not sure which way to go next, wishing she'd waited till Garrett could have come with her and divided up the territory. Then her eyes fell on the ornate golden numbers above each corner of the hallways.

On her left, 190 and 180. On the right, 120 and 130. She walked with a purposeful gait down the right-hand 130 corridor until she stood before 137.

Jacques Martin, le concessionnaire.

She had no idea what that meant, and it made not one iota of difference to her.

The coolness of the suite hit her, as did the coolness of the drop-dead gorgeous receptionist whose crisp welcome held the warmth of a freshly dug radish.

"Bonjour, madame."

"Bonjour, madame," Tara answered, hoping *madame* was okay to use even though she was pretty sure the woman was younger than she. "Um." Tension closed her throat and her mouth went dry, causing her to pause. *"Je m'appelle* Tara O'Malley. *Je... uh...*crap!" She forgot the words. Closing her eyes, she "read" them from her frontal lobe. *"Je cherche Jacques Martin. Est-il ici?"* She opened her eyes and smiled in relief.

The receptionist, who may have been younger but had a much older air about her, didn't smile, but looked Tara up and down thoroughly, pausing at the missing fingers long enough to wrinkle her nose in distaste. Tara had seen it happen before, but coming from the embodiment of feminine perfection, the gesture made her flush. "And do you have an appointment, Ms. O'Malley?" The young woman's English pushed through a thick accent.

"No. I just decided to pop in." *Seriously? Pop in?* "Monsieur Martin is an old friend of my family's. I was in town, and I promised my mother I would stop in and say hello. They were friends in college." Tara fought the urge to cover her mouth with her hand to stop her talking.

"Jacques is very busy." The use of the man's first name, and the way she said it, made Tara think this was more than a boss-receptionist relationship. "I will see if he wants to take time for you." Her tone said he wouldn't.

The young woman rose from her seat like Venus in a red peplum halter over a black-and-white polka-dotted pencil skirt. Tara gawked at her red patent leather five-inch stilettos as she walked away from the desk.

Who dressed like that for work? Even in Paris.

The sound of a door opening stopped the young woman's forward movement, but Tara's eyes continued to where François Martin appeared in an office doorway.

"Yvette." He took a couple of steps in the woman's direction before his eyes landed on Tara.

"François?" Tara felt her face break into a smile at this happy coincidence.

For the second time since she'd entered the suite, her smile wasn't returned. François's face turned hard and cold, the look in his eyes even colder.

Tara gave a little wave and took a couple of steps in his direction. "It's me. Tara O'Malley. We met at the park Saturday. The Place des Vosges? We shared a bench and I played with Attila."

The receptionist swung around to glare at her. "You met Jacques at Place des Vosges Saturday?

And why do you call him François?" Her icy stare jerked toward François and she said something Tara wouldn't have understood even if her consciousness hadn't stalled on the first part of what the woman had said.

She'd called him Jacques.

"Your name is Jacques?" Tara's brain was slow to download the meaning behind this discrepancy, but her heart heard the message loud and clear and took off faster than the taxi she'd arrived in. She pointed a quivering finger. "You're Jacques Martin?"

"I want you to leave. Now." He bit the words out.

Tara's mind whirred, trying to make sense of what was happening while protecting her psyche from the encroaching attack. Comprehension breached the barrier quickly. "Meeting you was no coincidence, was it? You knew who I was Saturday…knew I was your daughter."

The young woman's face contorted into a mask of disgust. "Your daughter?" She pointed to Tara's hand and barked a mean laugh. "This…this freak?"

Tara recoiled from the blow as the ice queen melted into a puddle of condemnation, French words spitting out like poison from a cobra.

Temporarily forgotten by the woman and the man, whose placating words seemed to be falling on deaf ears, Tara took a moment to rise from the verbal punch that had knocked the wind out of her and take stock of what she knew.

François Martin, the man she'd had such a lovely

conversation with in the park…the man with the precious, well-behaved dog…was her father, *Jacques Martin*. He'd lied about his name because he didn't want her to know who he was.

But how did he know who *she* was? How did he find out she even existed? How did it happen that *he* found *her* when the number of people who knew of their relationship could be counted on her fingers—even with some of them gone?

Someone had alerted him.

Someone arranged the meeting in the park without her knowledge.

Someone wanted to give *him* the opportunity, but not her.

Her stomach drew into a hard knot, making her queasy. *Please don't let me throw up now.*

Who would do such a thing? Who would make such a cruel, heartless arrangement when she'd come so far and gone to such lengths?

The door of the suite opened, and the place went quiet as her companions' squabble was sidetracked by someone's entrance.

Tara swung around to face the door.

"Garrett?"

She hadn't given him the address in her voice mail, had she?

"Get out of my office." The words spewed from Jacques Martin's lips. "Both of you. Get out, and never let me see your faces again."

Tara heard the command, yet her feet stood firmly

planted to the spot. Any movement was going to take her over an emotional abyss, and so she stood motionless, listening to the growl and the shrieks from the couple behind her, unable to tear her eyes from Garrett's face.

He didn't have to say a word. The answers to her questions were all there in the grim set of his mouth.

A pain unlike anything she'd ever experienced sliced through her and lodged in her chest.

"No."

Garrett read the word on Tara's lips, and watched the question in her eyes dissolve into anguish. Her look speared him from across the room, but he ignored the warning and moved closer.

"Monsieur Hughes, I advise you to leave, and take your girlfriend with you." The threat was evident in Martin's tone. "I have lost my patience with you both."

"Give me a minute, will you?" Garrett shot a look the man's way, but continued moving toward Tara, needing to touch her, hold her. Her look chilled him and, with every step, the wall of ice between them grew thicker.

"Tara," he said gently. "I can explain. You just need to hear me out." He held out his hand, but she stepped around him, out of reach.

"You...both—" her eyes darted from him to her father "—should be ashamed."

The words brought an eerie moment of silence

to the room, and then Martin sneered. "Her mother spread her legs easily," he said in French. "The daughter of the whore should be ashamed. And you have had your minute. Now go say goodbye to your Soulard beer."

A double helix of anger and frustration spiraled through Garrett, twisting everything in its path. "I didn't tell her. I kept my word." He bit out the words through clenched teeth. "Tara, tell him how you found him."

"Mama got your address from one of her sorority sisters at Murray." Tara addressed Martin with her chin lifted, but the defiant pose couldn't mask the hurt brimming in her eyes. "I should've listened to her. Coming here was a mistake." With a dismissive toss of her head, she stalked toward the door.

"Wait, Tara," Garrett called after her, but she ignored him. He would run to catch up in a minute, but first he would have his say.

Garrett locked gazes with Martin and dared him to look away. "You've just thrown away what would've been the best thing to ever happen to you, Monsieur Martin. Something that would've given depth to your shallow existence." He pointed to the closing door. "And you may think you're all big and powerful because you can crush Soulard for no reason. But nothing you have makes you deserving of Tara. She was a gift of love, and unlike that one—" he nodded toward Yvette "—wanted nothing but love in return."

He left, keeping his dignity until the office door closed. Then he broke into a jog.

Tara wasn't in the corridor, as he'd expected, nor was she anywhere in sight. He ran through the lobby, looking this way and that. People stared at him as he jostled past groups and bumped into those standing in his way.

Where was she? His gut clenched into a knot. How could she have disappeared so quickly?

He exited the building at full speed and spotted her standing at the curb. "Tara!"

She ignored him and waved at an approaching taxi. It swept by her, giving him a chance to catch up.

He touched her shoulder and felt her flinch. When she spun around, he could see the wetness on her cheeks, and the accusation in her eyes made him flinch in return.

"How could you, Garrett?" She ran her hand through the top of her hair, sweeping off the band that was keeping the curls back. They sprang loose in a wild riot around her face that animated her speech as she punched a finger in his direction. "How could you do this to me?"

He caught her hand in midair. "I didn't mean for it to turn out like this." She winced, and he realized he'd squeezed her injured hand. He loosened his grip, and she jerked her hand from his. "When I found Martin, he didn't want to meet you. In fact, he threatened to ruin Soulard if I didn't keep you away."

"And you didn't tell me? Why?" She pinned him with narrowed eyes.

"I should have."

"But you didn't. Why?"

"I was concerned, if we ever broke up, you might retaliate by going to him anyway…." He shrugged, refusing to dig himself any deeper into the ridiculous hole he'd started.

Her look was incredulous. "You really think I could ever be *that* vindictive? That I would try to ruin your career over a failed relationship? What kind of person do you think I am?"

"I didn't think. I reacted like I would've with Angie."

"Because Angie and I are so much alike…with the tattoos and piercings and all." She shook her head in disgust and a deep breath shook her chest.

Garrett pressed on, wanting to get the whole story out so she'd have a clear picture. "Martin refused to see you, but I thought, if he could just meet you, he'd fall in love with you like I have." Her eyes filled with tears again, but she didn't say anything. "So I arranged for him to meet us in the park, and I gave him my word I would leave it up to him to contact you."

Her chin quivered and Garrett felt the tremor deep inside. "But he didn't contact me." She sniffed, fighting the tears. "And he wasn't going to, was he? Why? Would I be so terrible to claim as a daughter?"

"It's not you, baby." Garrett laid his hands on her shoulders and leaned down until his eyes and hers were even. "It's his wife. The receptionist." Tara frowned, but understanding dawned through the shimmer of her tears. "He's giving money to two other out-of-wedlock children. His wife, who is his third and younger than you, by the way, is jealous the kids are taking too much of his wealth. She threatened divorce if it happened again."

"So the freak had a price tag attached." Tara wiped a hand down her face.

"What does that mean? You lost me."

She cut her eyes away and waved her hand. "Never mind."

He slid his grip down her arms and attempted to pull her into a hug, but she shook her head and pulled away. "So you were going to let me go home…go on for the rest of my life…never knowing I'd met my birth father?"

"I thought he would come around eventually, and that, until then, what you didn't know wouldn't hurt you."

"Augh!" The sadness in her eyes morphed into anger. "How could you do that? You took the choice away from me, and gave it to him. And neither of those choices was yours to make."

Her logic made his own seem horribly flawed in hindsight. "I'm sorry. I screwed up."

Her eyes narrowed again. "How did you find him, anyway? This address wasn't on my list."

His promise to Henri flashed through Garrett's mind. Damn it! "I can't tell you. I promised I wouldn't because it could get someone in a lot of trouble."

Her eyebrows shot up, and it seemed as if her face became all eyes. "Ah! More knowledge about my father that I can't be trusted with." She threw her hands in the air, which brought a taxi to a screeching halt at the curb beside her.

When she jerked the door open, Garrett moved to join her, but she blocked the way, shaking her head. "No, Garrett. I need to be alone."

"We haven't finished talking." He held the door as she climbed in, his jaws aching with tension.

"We have for now." She pulled the door closed, and he heard the lock snap.

The sound caught in his ear, its finality jarring loose memories that ran a shudder up his spine.

He touched his phone, poised for the text message he feared might follow in the taxi's wake.

None came.

He raised his hand to hail a taxi, wondering whether Tara was going home or if she was headed somewhere else.

They would talk later when they both had clearer heads.

Right then, he needed to get back and talk to his bosses at Soulard and hope he hadn't signed a death sentence for the company.

TARA HELD HER composure fairly well as the taxi careened through the streets of Paris. She didn't go back to her flat. Couldn't. Not yet.

The hurt she felt wouldn't let her listen to Garrett's explanation again right then. Wouldn't let her get into what was sure to bloom into an argument in front of Dylan.

Tears glided from her eyes, but she held in the sobs.

The taxi dropped her off at the Tuileries—the gardens adjacent to the Louvre. The place brimmed with people, but she felt protected in her anonymity. Everyone here had cried at one time or another, and she likely wasn't the only one crying there even at that moment.

She found a small space at the end of a crowded bench and allowed the tears to continue falling, confident they weren't too noticeable behind her large sunglasses.

They slowed, and while she wasn't feeling better, she at least got her breathing under some control. So when the phone rang and she saw it wasn't Garrett but her dad, she answered with a modicum of confidence that she could handle this conversation.

Boy, was she wrong.

"Hi, lovebug."

Just the sound of her dad's voice brought all of the wicked pain to the surface.

"Oh, Daddy…" She cried, channeling her inner four-year-old with giant sobs that garnered looks of curiosity and pity from the people near her. "Jacques Martin didn't want anything to do with me. Told me to get out. And his wife called me a fr-fr-freak."

"Hey…hey," the familiar, gentle voice soothed across the line. "Calm down. It's okay."

"No, it's not okay," she blubbered. "Nothing's okay. Garrett found him a week ago, but he doesn't trust me enough to tell me *how*. And then he set up a secret meeting between Jacques and me, but he didn't trust me enough to tell me the man I met was my father. He left it all to Jacques…who doesn't want me."

"I'm sorry, sweetheart. I'm not following all this, but it sounds like you've been treated badly. Just tell me how I can help."

"You can't. Nobody can. My birth father doesn't want anything to do with me, and the man I'm in love with doesn't trust me."

"But *we* love you. Your family…your friends… your students. The people here love you and trust you. You're in a strange place with strange people, but your life is back here. Nothing about the way *we* feel about you has changed."

That made her cry harder.

Tension infused her dad's voice when he spoke again. "Tell you what…I'm going to have your mom call you, okay? I think she might be better over the phone than I am."

"O-okay. Isn't she there?"

"No, she's at Mom's. I'll call her right now and have her call you, okay? It'll just take a couple of minutes."

"Okay. Th-thanks, Dad."

"Love you, baby."

"I know." She broke down sobbing again, words not coming in response to her dad's goodbye. She waved pitifully, knowing he couldn't see her, but wishing he was there.

When her phone rang again, she answered her mom's call with another loud sob.

FAITH'S HEART ACHED as only a mother's could.

If she could've gotten her hands on Jacques Marin at that moment, she could've easily rendered him incapable of fathering any more children with just a few twists—and thoroughly enjoyed herself in the process.

She didn't pass judgment on Garrett for his part in this. It sounded as if he'd tried, though his attempts to help were obviously misguided.

She cried in sympathy for Tara's disappointment and hurt and for her own frustration that this was not in the realm of things she could kiss and make all better.

As Tara talked, her desolate tone chilled Faith's soul. It wasn't fair that Garrett was involved. Her daughter needed someone's arms around her.

She needed someone's arm around her, too. She longed for Sawyer's quiet calm.

"And he actually threatened Garrett's company?" Faith broke into Tara's lengthy blow-by-blow of what had happened, incredulous at the extent of Jacques Martin's vindictiveness. Obviously, life had changed the pleasant young man who always had a smile for everyone.

Tara, who seemed calmer now and could put several sentences together without her breath snubbing, filled in missing details of the backstory.

As Faith listened, a noise outside pulled her attention to the window.

Sawyer had pulled into the driveway.

Bless him! He knew she needed him, and he'd come to be with her.

The ache in her chest eased, knowing in a few minutes she wouldn't be alone. He would be in here with her. Would hold her. Comfort her. And together they would lift Tara up and hold her from across the distance.

This was it. This horrible incident was the catalyst meant to reunite them.

Healing would begin. Maybe already had begun.

Then she noticed what she hadn't before.

Sawyer hadn't pulled into the driveway. He'd backed in.

She watched in disbelief as he got out of the truck and gingerly hooked up the trailer to his bass boat.

He was going fishing!

At a time like this? When she needed him? Knowing that she *and* Tara both needed him?

He made quick work of the task as Tara continued to talk. Faith only added supportive, guttural phrases, 'uh-huh...right," at the appropriate lulls.

Sooner than she could've imagined, he pulled out of the drive, bass boat in tow.

Tara's story gave an excuse to cry openly, so she did.

But she cried not only for her daughter now, but also for herself.

Sawyer's action this time, even more than his inability to make love to her, screamed the message she hadn't wanted to acknowledge but which came through now with horrible clarity.

Their marriage was over.

CHAPTER TWENTY-FOUR

THE LAST TIME Garrett had endured a day this bad was when Angie died.

For the past five hours since leaving Jacques Martin's office, he'd been sequestered with the *cadres supérieurs,* the upper management at Soulard, who'd brought in the *president-directeur général* after one hour. And a couple of hours later, the owners had been pulled in via teleconference from Brussels.

When all was said and done, they'd decided to do nothing at this point. The initial panic that stemmed around the possible identity of Martin's powerful friends gave way to logic that there was simply no way of knowing who these people were without confronting the man himself. That idea was vetoed because it would push the power in Martin's direction. Plus there was always the chance he would come to his senses and not do anything.

Garrett's gut told him otherwise.

But for now, a wait-and-see attitude had been adopted.

The construction worker in Garrett's brain had a jackhammer running full bore as he made his way home. His temples throbbed, his throat ached, he was starved, and talking with Tara was still on the agenda.

He did get to utter his one bit of good news to Henri's pale expression when his friend met him at his apartment door. "You can relax, Henri. I told them a private investigator found Martin for me, which isn't a lie. You did your investigation in private. That subject never came up again."

Henri's shoulders slumped with relief. "*Merci beaucoup,* Garrett. I also spoke with Tara when she got home. I told her the truth about generating the list."

"Thanks, man." Garrett shrugged out of his jacket and tossed it on the couch. "And thanks for watching Dylan—was he good for you?"

"Dylan is always good for me. He played with the new puppy downstairs, ate a good dinner and fell asleep quickly."

"And Tara? How is she?"

Henri tilted his head with a shrug. "Sad."

Garrett glanced across the terrace. "Better than angry, I suppose." The lights of her flat were still on.

"I am not so sure of that." Henri's look was guarded and fretful, and neither boded well for what lay in store. "So tell me…what is the plan at Soulard?"

Garrett pressed his fingers into his forehead and rubbed hard. "It's difficult to know what to do because we don't know what direction Martin's strike will come from, if it comes at all. So, for now, we're going to sit tight and not do anything."

Henri's pursed lips curved down at the corners. "I suppose that is all we can do." His eyelids drooped with exhaustion. The past few hours had been hell for him, as well.

"Go on home, Henri." Garrett clapped his friend's back, trying to lighten the mood. "I'll get Tara to talk with me here or on the terrace."

"You are certain she will?"

"No," he answered honestly. "But, if she'll talk to me at all, we need to be alone."

"Je comprends." Henri laid his suit coat gingerly over his arm. *"Bon chance, mon ami. À demain."*

"Yeah, I'll see you tomorrow."

Garrett saw him out and then wasted no time heading for Tara's.

She evidently had been watching for him because she came out on the terrace and met him halfway. He hoped that was a good sign, but one glance at her red, swollen eyes told him it wasn't.

The pounding jackhammer shifted into high.

Her rigid stance, with her arms locked across her chest as if it were freezing out rather than ninety degrees, held no welcome, and the hug he'd wished for didn't come, so he shoved his hands into his pockets for lack of anything better to do and waited for her to begin the conversation. Giving her control of the situation was a must, even though it went against every fiber of his being.

The fact was he'd gone behind her back, good intentions notwithstanding. He had to face the consequences.

"Henri told me what he did." Her voice was quiet and low, her tone calm. "How he found my fa—Jacques Martin. I'm grateful for the lengths you both went to, and I'm sorry my actions put Soulard in jeopardy. If I'd had any inkling, I wouldn't have gone to see him."

Garrett pulled his hands from his pockets, opening his arms to her. But she ignored the gesture, so he rested them on his hips. "I should've told you everything. Should've leveled with you from the start."

Her eyes met his straight on. "Yeah. You should have." She glanced away, running a hand through the top of her hair, sliding the other into a side pocket on her dress.

The outfit was the same she'd had on in Martin's office. There it'd looked fresh and crisp. Now, it was wrinkled as if she'd been wallowing in it, which, he realized, was probably exactly what she'd been doing. The thought pinched his heart.

"It might *not* have changed the way things turned out, but I keep wondering if it *could* have." The wistfulness in her voice clawed at his insides. "If I'd approached him differently. In my own way. I'm good with people. With students and parents. Even the difficult ones."

Garrett recalled the conversation with their mutual

friend in the States and the guilt in his stomach took on more weight. "Josh told me that."

"But you didn't believe him because anybody with my…interesting characteristics…" a bitter note edged into her voice as she held up her half hand "…couldn't be someone others would trust."

Her words slammed into him, momentarily shattering his resolve to relinquish the control. He stepped toward her, and she stepped back before he caught himself. He didn't want her to leave. Things would be okay if he could just keep her talking. "When he told me that, I didn't know you well. Now I do, and the trust is there. Believe me."

"That's the problem, Garrett." Her voice grew quiet—ominously so—and the hairs on the back of his neck rose. "I don't know when I can believe you and when I'm being judged on the Angie scale." Tears cascaded down her cheeks, scalding Garrett's heart with their honesty. "I love you, but love can't sustain a relationship. There has to be trust, and we're just not there yet."

His heart caught on her last word and pounded it into his brain. "But we'll get there."

"We don't have time." She shook her head. "Even another three weeks isn't enough to build anything that can sustain the time and distance we're up against." She took a deep breath and he watched it shudder in her chest. The next one he took responded in kind.

"Don't, Tara." He held a palm up to make her stop

talking. Giving her control was a mistake, and he had to slow this train down and veer it away from the cliff it was hurdling toward. Then she reached out and took his hand, and the gesture came so unexpectedly...so gently and so unlike anything Angie would've ever done, it threw his game off and shocked him into silence.

"I've decided not to change my ticket," she went on. "I'm going home on the fifteenth like I originally planned. It'll be better for everybody this way."

He found his voice again and opened his mouth to protest, but she countered with her coup de grâce. "Especially Dylan."

His heart stalled in his chest, and his head felt like it would explode with the acknowledgment that she was right. This sure as hell felt like the worst that could happen, but devastating Dylan would trump everything.

"I love you, Tara," he said simply.

She nodded. "Yeah. I think you do."

Their eyes met for one horrible and tender moment that held all the passion of what they'd had together...and all the regrets of what might have been.

Then she turned and ran back to her door, flipping off the light on the terrace.

Leaving him in the dark.

TARA WAS STARTLED awake and glanced at her clock.

Six fifty-two. Someone was knocking on her front door.

Garrett. He probably didn't come across the terrace because he didn't want Dylan to know he was talking to her. On his way to work? She realized she hadn't even asked what happened when he returned to the office last night. If he was going in this early, things must not have gone well.

She lay there, listening to him knock a second time, thinking how she didn't need to begin her day like this. It was going to be difficult enough without hearing his pleas for reconciliation right off the bat.

She blinked, trying to rid her eyes of the two hours of sleep she'd managed, but sandbags had replaced her eyelids. With all the crying she'd done, she probably should be thankful they'd even open.

Garrett knocked again, more persistent this time, and she resigned herself to the fact that he wasn't going away. She stumbled from the bed still in yesterday's clothes, grimacing at the achy feeling that suffused her entire body.

She'd caught a bad case of heartbreak flu.

"I'm comin'." Her voice crackled as if she were ninety.

She stopped at the door and took a deep breath to brace for the onslaught of emotion. Then she swung it open, and her chin hit her chest.

"Dad!"

"Hi, lovebug."

Sawyer O'Malley didn't look quite as bad as she did, but he was running a close second. Tired and rumpled and unshaven, he was the most wonderful thing her eyes could've beheld at that moment.

He dropped his small bag and held out his arms, and Tara fell into his warm embrace, sobbing her joy and anguish.

"What are…you doing…here?" She jerked her way through the obvious question.

He didn't let go. Just kept holding her while he spoke, rocking back and forth in a soothing motion. "You sounded so miserable yesterday when I talked to you. I couldn't stand the thought of you facing all of this alone."

"But, Dad…this is Paris. It's…not like driving… from Taylor's Grove…to Paducah. How'd you get here…so fast?" Her tears were leaving a wet spot on his shirt, but she didn't care. Her dad was there, holding her, and suddenly her topsy-turvy world had righted a bit.

"I bought a ticket, drove to St. Louis and got on a plane." He kissed the top of her head. "The seven-hour difference helped. It was still morning at home when I talked to you."

She loosened her grip so she could lean back and look him in the eye. "You shouldn't have come. But I'm so glad you're here."

"Me, too." He gathered her to his chest in a tight squeeze. "But if I don't get some coffee soon, I'm going to collapse."

She pulled away with a smile, the first one she'd felt in what seemed like forever. "I can help with that."

She showed him around her apartment and let him freshen up while she prepared breakfast. Her appetite still hadn't returned but she forced down a few bites of bacon, eggs and toast to help ease her splitting headache while she shared all the gruesome details of the visit with Jacques Martin.

Pain radiated from her dad's eyes as he listened, and every so often he'd shake his head in disgust or sympathy or whatever the appropriate emotion was at the time.

She didn't say too much about Garrett—only that she'd ended the relationship and how that seemed to be the smart thing to do. And, for the most part, her dad withheld advice.

"It just felt so right, Dad."

Her tears turned on again, and he took her hand, his touch as gentle as his voice. "Maybe it *is* right."

That certainly wasn't what she'd expected. "But not if the trust isn't there."

"No, trust is important." He swallowed hard. "It has to be earned, and that takes time."

"Time Garrett and I don't have." She shrugged. "I'm leaving Saturday." She paused, realizing she'd been talking only about herself since he'd arrived. "Are you staying till then?"

He smiled, but sadness darkened his eyes. "No. Actually, my return flight leaves at three, and I have to be back at the airport at one, so I'll need to leave here by noon."

"What? It's seven already! You're only here for five hours?"

"I have an important meeting at the church tomorrow. I have to be back for it."

"So you came all this way…?"

"To show my daughter—" He looked at her then with an intensity she'd rarely seen except when her dad was preaching. He tapped his chest at the place over his heart. "To show *my daughter*…who is more precious to me than life itself…how much she's loved and treasured. And that I'll *always* be there for her."

Tara's heart swelled so large it pushed the air from her lungs and for a moment she couldn't speak. "I'm sorry for what I've put you through, Dad," she managed, at last. "I'm not sure I deserve you."

"None of us deserve the blessings we're given. That's what makes them special."

She glanced out the window and saw Garrett and Dylan stirring in their apartment. They'd blessed her life. She could only hope that in some small way she'd blessed them, too. And the best way to assure that she remained a blessing, at least to Dylan, was to leave while things were good between them.

She made her mind up quickly. "I'm going to call the airlines and see if I can move my flight up to today. I want to go home with you."

Her dad's eyes widened. "Are you sure you want to do that?"

Her heart, which had grown so large a minute ago, started to wither. She knew if she stayed, it would shrivel up to nothing in no time flat. "I came to Paris to find out who I am, and now I know. I'm Tara O'Malley from Taylor's Grove, Kentucky…and I'm proud of that," she said more to herself than to him. "I need to go home, need to get back to my life."

"But…?"

"No buts." Resolve brought her to her feet. She had a plan of action. It may not be the best one, but at least she wouldn't be wallowing in sorrow here for four more lonely days.

She could wallow at home just as easily…surrounded by people who loved her.

"I'm going to shower and pack."

"Can you be ready by eleven-thirty?" Her dad's eyes held a strange glint.

"Yeah. Why?"

"I have one thing I want to see during this whirlwind trip to Paris."

She gave a small laugh. He was so predictable. "Notre-Dame's not far. I'll hurry and maybe we'll even have time to walk there."

He shooed her in the direction of the bedroom. "Go on. I need to call your mom."

Tara grabbed her luggage from the hall closet and hurried to her room to begin stuffing it with clothes.

IT WAS JUST after midnight, but Faith wasn't asleep. She wasn't even in bed. She'd been staring at the same words on the same page for a long while, debating with herself whether to call the sheriff and report Sawyer as missing.

He'd texted her around five saying he'd talk to her tomorrow. She'd been so hurt and angry he'd gone fishing, she hadn't texted him back.

But an hour or so ago, she swallowed her pride and called him because he still hadn't returned from the lake and all sorts of scenarios had started messing with her mind. Most of them centered around him falling out of the boat and being knocked unconscious and drowning.

Of course, he'd specifically texted tomorrow, so he could be ignoring her calls or might even have his phone turned off. He did that sometimes when he needed to think.

She picked up her car keys. She would just drive over to the house. He might've taken the boat home since her car wasn't taking up the extra space in the garage. She could run over there and peek in the garage window....

Her phone rang, shattering her thoughts. The caller ID said it was Sawyer, but what if someone had found his phone in an empty boat?

Panic flooded adrenaline through her system. "Hello?" she practically screamed into the phone.

"Whoa!"

"Don't whoa me!" she snapped. All of the frustration that had been bottled up since morning came spewing out. "Where are you? It's after midnight and you haven't brought the boat back and you haven't been answering my calls and I've been imagining your dead, unconscious body floating around some dark cove on Kentucky Lake."

He laughed? How dare he?

"Dead *and* unconscious, huh?"

"You know what I mean. I've been scared out of my wits."

"I'm in Paris, Faith."

"Well, you could've at least told me you were going down there." She huffed. "Is there a tournament?"

He chuckled again. "Not Paris, Tennessee. Paris, France. I'm with Tara."

Faith's knees buckled, and she plopped down on the floor. "You're in France? With Tara?"

"I couldn't stand the thought of her being over here alone, dealing with all she's going through."

Faith winced at the raw emotion in his voice. "Oh, Sawyer. How's she doing?"

"Hurting. Depressed."

Shock began to dissolve her brain matter into a mishmash of relief and worry, releasing a flood of questions into her brain. "How'd you get there so fast? Why didn't you tell me you were going?"

"I left as soon as I could get the arrangements made, and I didn't tell you because I knew you would try to talk me out of it."

She nodded, even though he couldn't see her. She would most definitely have tried to talk him out of such an extravagant trip, especially with their income on the chopping block… Oh, Lord! "Did you forget the meeting with the Board of Fellowship tomorrow night?" With him not there to defend himself, Sue would ramrod her way through the process in record time.

"I didn't forget." The weariness in his tone caught in her chest and squeezed her heart. "I'm booked on a return flight this afternoon. Tara's decided to come home with me. She's going to try to change her ticket to that flight."

"Ah…" A worried gasp escaped from Faith's lungs. "How are we going to pay for all this, Sawyer? If you lose the church…?"

"Don't worry about the money. Everything's already taken care of." The gentle voice lowered. "Love always finds a way."

The reality of the situation finally rooted in Faith's mind, warming her through and through. Sawyer, bless his heart, had gone all the way to Paris, France, to take care of his daughter. *His* daughter, regardless of the circumstances surrounding her conception. He'd used their savings, no doubt. But that didn't matter because he was there for Tara, taking care of everything…like he'd always done. And Faith could feel his steadfast love holding *her* up, too.

"You're a wonderful man, Sawyer." Faith hoped her voice could convey a tiny part of the pride she felt. "Tara's so blessed to have you in her life."

"I'm the one who's blessed, Faith."

She couldn't stifle the sob that sprang from her lips.

"Hey, don't cry." His soothing voice caressed her from across the miles…across an ocean. "I'm going to let you go now. I'll call you when we get back into St. Louis. But adding in the four-hour drive, it might be late when I get home."

"I don't care how late it is. I'll be up."

"Yeah, I figured that." She heard the smile in his voice.

A final question popped into her mind. "But if you drove the truck to St. Louis, what did you do with the boat? It's not here."

There was a long pause, and then an even longer breath. "I sold it."

Faith felt another blow to her system that shook her to the core. "You sold your dad's bass boat? Why?"

"I used the money to come to Paris."

"But, Sawyer, you loved that boat." Faith couldn't stop the tears now if she wanted to, and her voice started to blubber as her nose and throat clogged.

"No, the boat was nice to have, but I love my family. Trust me, it was a small price to pay for the love I get in return. I'll talk to you later."

He hung up quickly, and Faith understood he didn't want to hear her cry. But that didn't stop her. She cried for Tara, for what she was enduring. And for the bass boat, the family heirloom…gone now.

But, most of all, she cried for the conclusions she had jumped to that morning.

Sawyer loved their children. All three of them.

And he loved her.

He proved it day after day...had proven it as long as she'd known him.

He would get home, and they would work out their problems.

"'Love always finds a way.'"

She branded his promise on her heart.

GARRETT FELT THE tension as soon as he walked in the door at Soulard.

Far from the usual morning bustle of activity and conversations, people were scurrying around like scared mice, speaking in hushed whispers, eyes wide with alarm or narrowed and tight with agitation.

Through the conference-room window, he saw the same group he'd met with last night, but two others had been added to the group. Adrienne Goffinet, Soulard's brilliant young attorney, and a middle-aged man he didn't recognize, but who was speaking and had everyone's attention. Adrienne's face was ashen and drawn into a scowl.

It took only a quick glance for the solemn atmosphere in the conference room to creep into Garrett's gut and chill him to the bone...only another few seconds to know that Jacques Martin was behind it.

He'd barely had time to set his briefcase on his desk before Henri came in and closed the door. His friend held no coffee. This was even worse than he'd thought.

"What's happened, Henri?"

"*C'est mauvais, Garrett. C'est très, très mauvais.*"

"Tell me what's happened, damn it!"

Henri unbuttoned the top button on his shirt and loosened his tie. "An official is here from *le CFE.*"

An official from the *Centre de Formalités des Entreprises* was here? Henri was right. This was very bad. "What does he want? Do you know?" Garrett empathized with Henri's loosening of his tie. His own felt like a noose around his throat now.

"I hear the rumor there is a threat to close the company temporarily. Important documents are missing from the Soulard file."

"Shit!" Garrett's ability to stand left him in a rush and he dropped into his chair. The terror he felt was reflected in Henri's eyes.

How long was temporarily?

Adrienne had often complained of the hellish number of documents the CFE required to start up the company. But it was beyond belief that the attorney, who was meticulous to the point that Garrett suspected she might have OCD, could've missed anything. It had taken her months to complete all the required paperwork. That was three years ago. How was it that missing documents were just being discovered today? "This is Jacques Martin's doing." The coincidence was too great for Garrett to attribute the crisis to anyone else.

Henri nodded gravely as he pulled up a chair and sat down. "I fear you are correct."

Neither of them said anything for a long minute. What was there to say? What was done couldn't be undone. He'd screwed up royally, and they both knew it.

Henri rested his arms on the desk and leaned forward, his voice low and sympathetic. "What about you and Tara?"

Garrett glanced away, unwilling to share the full depth of the grief churning low in his belly. "Well, let's just say if bad news was counted like hits in baseball, this morning I'd be batting a thousand."

CHAPTER TWENTY-FIVE

"ARE YOU READY?" Her dad gave the living room one final inspection.

Tara had contacted the landlord and made arrangements for the cleaning service to come by. They'd assured her they would take care of any food left in the cabinets and refrigerator. She'd stripped the bed and left all the linens on the washer, and checked under the bed and in the closets for anything left behind. And she'd taken care of the trash.

Everything was done.

Well…there was one thing left to do. The most heartbreaking thing. But it was inevitable.

"Just one more thing, Dad. Come here. I want you to meet somebody."

Dylan looked up from his book when they stepped onto the terrace. He was all smiles and boyhood charm, and, for a few agonizing seconds, Tara thought her heart would stop for good.

She called on all her teacher reserves that kept her from bawling whenever she read a sad story to her classes.

"Hey, Dylan." She motioned him over. "I want to introduce you to someone."

He placed his book on the bench and came running at her invitation, stopping by her dad with a big grin that said "See how fast I am?"

Tara stooped down and put her arm around his waist. "You remember I told you I was looking for my father?" He nodded. No use complicating this more than necessary. "Well, I found him," she said simply.

Dylan's expression of wonder made him look so much like Garrett, she had to cut her eyes away to breathe. She pointed. "This is my dad from Kentucky, Sawyer O'Malley. Dad, this is Dylan Hughes."

Dylan's face turned somber for a moment, and he stuck out his hand. *"Bonjour, Monsieur O'Malley. Comment allez-vous?"* The formal facial expression gave way to a wide grin. "That means hi."

Tara could tell by her dad's smile that the child had already won him over. He laughed and grasped the little boy's hand. "Well, bone jur to you, too, bud."

"Hey, my dad calls me bud sometimes!"

A tremor shot through Tara at the mention of Garrett. She stood up and patted Dylan on the back. "My dad has come to…uh…" Lord, this was even harder than she had imagined. "To take me back home. So, I guess I have to say bye."

In a nanosecond, Dylan's happy expression went south. "But I don't want you to go."

Tara knelt down again and took his hand. "I know it's hard. It's hard for me, too. But remember when we talked that day at the Luxembourg Gardens, and

I told you I'd have to leave sometime soon?" His bottom lip protruded as he nodded. "Well, everything I told you that day is still true. Your dad—" She paused and swallowed. "Your dad has my number, and I want you to call me anytime you want. As often as you want."

"But talking on the phone's not the same as being with you."

Tara shrugged. "I know. But it's the next best thing for people who live so far apart. And I have something for you that will make it seem like I'm still here, sort of." She reached into her tote and pulled out the purple Crown Royal bag containing the GPS locator and all the homemade tokens. "I want you to keep this so you and your dad can do lots of geocaching and find lots of treasures. And I want you to call me every time you find one."

"Wow!" The surprise brought a smile to Dylan's lips and Tara's heartache eased a smidgen when he took the bag. "Thanks!"

She pulled a card from her tote. "I wrote down the addresses of some geocaching clubs that meet here in Paris. I thought y'all might consider joining one."

"I wish you could be here to join it with us." Dylan's eyes grew cloudy. She had to get this over with quickly or it was going to be a major trauma for them both.

She raised her chin. "I wish I could, too." A sob was building in her chest. Its weight pulled at her heart. "But I really have to go now, so give me a hug, and let me get out of here."

He grabbed her around the neck with such force she struggled to stay upright. "I love you," he said.

She nodded. "I love you, too."

She let him break the hug first, and then she stood up. "Call me tomorrow, okay?"

"Okay."

When they turned away, her dad's arm came around her shoulder and she leaned into him, appreciating the support.

"Hey, Tara," Dylan called.

They stopped and turned back around as the little boy came running to her, holding out one of the tokens they'd made together. "You'll need this in case you find a treasure." His innocent grin told her he didn't realize the devastating consequences his parting gift would wreak on her emotions.

She took the token and squeezed it. "I think I've already found one." She gave him a quick peck on the top of his head and somehow managed to hold her outburst until she and her dad were safely back in her flat with the door closed.

Then the dam broke, rendering her amazed at the volume of tears her body could still produce. They had to be nearly all gone by now.

Her dad held her, silently rocking back and forth again, until this wave passed.

"What a great kid," he said.

She nodded and blew her nose on the tissue he handed her. "Dylan's the best."

"I was talking about you."

His joke brought a wan smile to her lips.

"Are you ready now?" He glanced at his watch as she flipped out the lights.

"Yeah." She opened the door to let him pass. "But we'll have to take a taxi to Notre-Dame. There's not enough time to walk."

He took the handle of her duffel and rolled it out the door. "I don't want to go to Notre-Dame. I want to meet Jacques Martin."

Tara's startled movement slammed the door behind them, and its echo surrounded them in the dark corridor. She slapped the light switch on to find her dad's calm expression looming in front of her.

"No, we can't." She wasn't about to face the jerk or his condescending wife again.

Her dad nodded calmly. "Yeah, we can." He punched the button to call the elevator.

"He was mad yesterday, Dad." She had to make him understand. "And he threatened Soulard. No telling what he might do if I or anybody connected to me shows up again."

The doors opened and they stepped inside. "I've made up my mind," he said matter-of-factly. "You can either give me the address, or I can call Faith and get it."

Tara sighed dramatically and didn't answer. She seethed in silence the rest of the way down, her brain whirring to come up with a way to talk her dad out of this absurdity. As they stepped off the elevator and made their way through the myriad passages, she tried to fight her growing anxiety by pointing out the items she used as markers to help her find her way through the building.

When they finally made their way to Madame LeClerc's post, the woman seemed truly sorry to see Tara go and hugged her, muttering things in French Tara didn't understand, but they sounded kind.

Something niggled at Tara, though, and when they stepped into the open air, she narrowed her eyes to look at her dad. "So…how'd you get past Ironpants LeClerc this morning? The woman is a guard dog."

Her dad shrugged. "It seems Madame LeClerc might be a pushover for the American Southern accent."

Tara shook her head. "It didn't work for me."

"Let me qualify that." His grin turned positively boyish. "Madame LeClerc might be a pushover for the American *male* Southern accent."

"Daddy!" Tara was aghast. "You flirted?"

"You do what you have to do." He sped up his steps. "And I have to speak to Jacques Martin."

BY THE TIME Garrett made it into the conference room, the seats were all gone and there was standing room only. Not a breath of air stirred.

The only other time the entire staff had been crammed in like that was on opening day. Then, the atmosphere had sizzled with excitement. Today, it was sultry and stifling.

The owners, the president, the upper management—all the people he'd met with last night—regarded him solemnly when he entered. They were joined at the front table by the representative from the CFE and the company attorney, both of whom had no reason to look at him, and didn't.

He was almost grateful the less crowded area was in the back of the room, where he'd be shielded from the intensity of some of the accusing glares.

As he made his way to the back, his phone vibrated in his pocket.

Shit! In his haste, he'd forgotten to turn it off. He pulled it out to do so, but stopped short at the sight of Tara's name on the ID.

His heart catapulted into a gallop. Had she changed her mind about the break-up?

Damn! He couldn't take the call. Not now. As difficult as it was to do, he pushed *Ignore* and sent her to voice mail. Then he slipped the phone back into his pocket.

Only a minute later, he felt the vibration again. People were still filing in, filling up the empty spaces and using up what little remained of the air conditioning...and the oxygen.

He pulled his phone out and glanced at it.

A text from Tara. Nothing good *ever* came to him in a text. He broke out in a cold sweat, suddenly aware of rivulets of perspiration coursing down his back, his shirt clinging to his clammy skin as he leaned against the wall.

I called. No answer. I'm going back home today. Thanks for everything. Sorry things didn't work out and for any trouble I've caused. Please let Dylan call me anytime he wants, but please don't call yourself. It will only make the pain worse.

Garrett closed his eyes and wiped a hand down his face. A nudge startled him, and he opened his eyes to find Henri standing beside him, holding out a crisp white handkerchief.

"Is this in case I want to surrender?" he asked, and held the phone so Henri could read it.

His friend's deep sigh sucked the last good breath from the surrounding air.

Garrett turned the phone off and dropped it in his pocket as one of Soulard's owners started to speak.

CHAPTER TWENTY-SIX

TARA PAUSED OUTSIDE the door of Jacques Martin's office. "Dad." She would make one last attempt to talk him out of this, but her pleas had fallen on deaf ears in the taxi. "This really isn't a good idea, and it could make things horrible for Soulard."

Her dad placed his hands on her shoulders and leaned down to look her directly in the eyes. "Tara, I believe in a master plan. If my meeting him is part of that plan, it will happen. If it's not, he won't be here." He smiled and gave her shoulders a light squeeze. "Besides, I've prayed about what to say, and I don't think what I want to tell him will be harmful to Soulard, Jacques's wife or anybody else."

Her dad had never given her any reason to doubt that he only wanted what was best for her. She needed to trust him now. "Okay." She nodded. "Let's do this."

Sawyer opened the door and stepped back to let Tara enter first. Thank heavens, the waiting room was empty again. Just what kind of business never had any customers?

Yvette Martin's eyes widened at the sight of Tara, and she snarled something in French as she came to her feet. Pointing to the door, she raised her voice. "Get out. Now!"

Sawyer ignored the directive and pushed past Tara, extending his hand to the young woman. "Well now, there's no reason to get all huffy. Hi there. I'm Sawyer O'Malley. Tara's dad."

"I don't care who you are." She spoke through gritted teeth. "This is a private office, and I am instructing you to get out now."

Sawyer shifted his look between the two women and grinned. "Whooee! There's no use getting all worked up like this. I just want—"

"Jacques!" Yvette turned toward the closed door down the hall and shouted.

While she continued shouting in French, Sawyer gave her an innocent shrug. "See there. You already knew what I wanted without me even having to ask."

The office door flew open, and a red-faced Jacques Martin marched out, shoulders squared and obviously ready to tangle.

Sawyer rushed to meet him as Tara gawked, rooted to where she stood.

Her dad extended his hand once more, and again it was ignored. "Hello, Mr. Martin," he said calmly. "I know this is a surprise, but I couldn't pass up what might be my only opportunity to ever meet Tara's birth father."

"She is *not* my daughter. Now get out."

Her heartbeat, which was already fast, didn't accelerate. Her stomach did no additional churning. In fact, his words had no effect on Tara this time. Perhaps the tears had done their job and left her numb… or maybe having her dad there with her made all the difference.

Sawyer turned to Tara and held out his hand to her.

She moved to where he stood, taking the hand he proffered, relaxing in his firm but gentle grip.

He turned back to Martin. "You're right. She's not your daughter. She's *my* daughter, and I thank God every day for her."

Tara's face heated, but she noticed Martin's had lost some of its earlier color.

"And I want to thank *you,* Mr. Martin. Without you, I'd have no Tara." Her dad's voice lowered. "You see, my wife and I produced two other children whom I love very much, but nothing I could ever have done would've allowed me to produce Tara. Only you could do that."

Sawyer looked at Tara, and the smile he gave her held so much love she thought her heart would burst from it. She smiled back through eyes that brimmed with happy tears.

He tightened his grip on her hand before turning back to Martin while Tara stole a quick glance toward Yvette. The young wife was perched on her seat, arms crossed tightly, eyes boring into nothing but the top of the desk.

"And so I came here today," Sawyer continued, "simply to let you know how much you've blessed my life, and I've asked God to bless you in whatever way he sees fit. Rest assured, you'll be in my prayers often."

Martin said nothing, but just for a moment, Tara thought she could see a resemblance to the kind man she met at Place des Vosges.

Her dad faced her. "Ready?"

A chuckle floated out of her on a bubble of joy. "Yep."

She kept her arm linked through her dad's as they left the office, carrying in her heart a certainty that she was bound to this man with a bond even deeper than blood.

GARRETT HAD ALWAYS heard that 95 percent of the things you worry about never happen.

Just his luck that this incident lay in the remaining 5 percent.

The owners had announced, to the groans of shock and dismay from the audience, the immediate, temporary closing of Soulard until such time as this crisis could be resolved. Because most of the missing forms were those dealing with the labor force, it would be inadvisable to keep the brewery open until the documents were back in place.

Guilt that he had caused this whole, nightmarish fiasco was eating Garrett's insides like acid. Bile had actually risen into his throat when the official announcement was made.

He'd made up his mind to offer his resignation as soon as the meeting adjourned. It might not help anything, but if there was a chance it would call off the jackal that was Jacques Martin, it would be worth a try.

He and Dylan could make it for a while. He'd never touched the insurance money from Angie's death, which was tucked away in savings for Dylan's future, but he could borrow against it if a crisis arose.

Damn, he was going to be sick if he didn't get out of this room soon. He wiped his face with Henri's handkerchief. The walls were closing in on him, squeezing the breath out of his lungs.

The CFE representative was droning on and on with his apologies and reiterating the importance of having all required paperwork complete, and how he couldn't accept the copies on hand because all official documents must be originals.

It was a highly unusual breach of protocol for the receptionist to interrupt a meeting, especially one of such magnitude, and a nervous titter moved through the crowd when she pecked on the door and entered, waving a piece of paper.

She handed it to the man from CFE, who frowned and apologized, but then pulled out his cell phone and stepped from the room to make what was assumed to be an urgent call.

People remained oddly quiet, maybe wondering what else could possibly have happened that would rank high enough to interrupt this meeting. There were a few nervous whispers around him, which Garrett didn't try to discern. Instead, he studied the grim faces of those who sat in silence. He, at least, had some income to fall back on. Some of these people were the sole providers for their families. They wouldn't be able to wait around for months to be called back to Soulard.

The man from CFE returned to the front of the room. The room fell silent, and he cleared his throat.

"I have just received a call," he began in his smooth French, which Garrett had no trouble following, "and I must offer my personal apology to each of you for the turmoil you have been through this day." He paused and cleared his throat again, and Garrett wondered what else could be so difficult for him to say that he hadn't already said.

"Just say it," Garrett muttered under his breath, causing several people around him to look his way.

"It appears a grave error has been made. The documents for Soulard Brewery have been located and are all accounted for. The brewery is in no danger of being closed. You may all return to work immediately." He stopped and gave the owners a sheepish look. "Or as soon as you are instructed to do so."

The loud cheer that filled the room soon gave way to a myriad of mixed emotions. Some people cried tears of joy. Others laughed and hugged. Still others spoke in harsh, angry tones that they'd been made to suffer for several hours over what turned out to be nothing.

Garrett slid to the floor in a sweaty heap of happiness, anger and frustration.

Had Jacques Martin gone to this extreme just to flex his muscles and show his strength?

What a bastard!

Tara was fortunate Martin didn't have a part in her life. Perhaps someday she would realize that.

Garrett pulled his phone out and switched it on, hoping to find another call from her, but there wasn't one.

Perhaps, if *he* was fortunate, he might have a part in her life again.

They had been good together.

Perhaps someday she would realize that, too.

FAITH RUSHED TO meet Sawyer when he pulled into the driveway, getting there even before he could switch the motor off. To her surprise, Tara was waking up in the passenger seat.

Faith opened the door for her sleepy daughter. "I didn't expect to see you, sweetheart. I thought Sawyer would drop you off in Paducah."

Tara shook her head as she lumbered from the truck and grabbed Faith into the tightest hug she'd felt from her eldest child in years.

"I didn't want to go to my place tonight. I wanted to come *home*." Her heavy emphasis on the word brought a warm glow to Faith's heart. "Oh, Mama, I'm so sorry for everything y'all have been through. Dad filled me in, and I feel just awful." She started to whimper, and Faith recognized that it was exhaustion coupled with jet lag speaking. Tara had been through a lot the past couple of days.

They all had.

She cooed soothingly while Sawyer came around the truck. She'd never seen him as disheveled as he was right then, but he'd never looked sexier. When their eyes locked, she recognized the flame burning in his gaze, and felt the spark from it deep within her.

He spread his arms and pulled them both to his chest, voicing a quiet prayer of thanks.

It was just after eight, and the sun hadn't set yet, so they were very much on display to the people that passed. A few passersby waved or tooted their horns in greeting.

"Let's go inside for a bit." Faith tilted her head toward the door.

"I'll wait for you out here." Tara staggered back to the truck and crawled into the backseat.

"I don't want to go inside." Sawyer pulled Faith against him and locked his arms around her. "I want the world to see me kiss my wife." His lips captured hers in a knee-weakening kiss, and his obvious erection pressed boldly against her. It went on far longer than she would've ever imagined, his tongue blissfully exploring the deepest reaches of her mouth, and Faith became vaguely aware of the loud blaring horns, catcalls and applause from the residents of Taylor's Grove.

"Sawyer, we're becoming a spectacle," she gently chided when they finally came up for air.

"I don't care." His eyes remained locked on hers with a burning intensity that said he wasn't aware anyone else was around. His arms loosened from around her back, moved up her arms and shoulders to cup her face. "Forgive me, Faith. I've been such a fool these past few weeks. Come home with me, now. Let me make love to you. Let me show you how blessed I am to have you as my wife and the mother of my children...my three precious, wonderful children."

"Jacques Martin...?" The name pushed from her lips on a rush of air.

"And *you* gave me a blessing beyond value. And I want to spend the rest of my life showing you how grateful I am." He lowered his lips to hers slowly this time, and hers trembled at the tenderness in his touch.

No longer caring who was watching, she slipped her arms around his neck and pressed her cheek to his when their lips slid apart. "Take me home," she whispered. "I'll get my stuff tomorrow."

He growled hungrily in response, and she laughed at the pleasant shiver the sound sent through her.

He led her to the truck and gallantly opened the passenger door for her. A soft snore came from the backseat as she buckled her seat belt.

Faith breathed a deep, lung-filling breath. What tomorrow would hold for them was a mystery, but the happiness she felt right then was enough to sustain her for a long while.

As Sawyer backed the truck out of the driveway, she glanced toward her neighbor's house to the north.

Sue Marsden had come outside, no doubt checking to see what all the commotion was about.

And if her crossed arms and angry glare were any indication, she wasn't at all happy with what she'd observed.

CHAPTER TWENTY-SEVEN

GARRETT WALKED INTO his office and slapped a han
to his backside. Yep, his ass was still there. After th
chewing it had just received, he was surprised ther
was anything left.

The president and the upper management ha
pretty much ignored him yesterday after the ho
rendous threat had passed. Spirits had been muc
too high to do anything that would bring them dow
But this morning, the president had wasted no time
He couldn't be sure the incident had been Jacque
Martin's doing, but he needed someone to blame, an
Garrett seemed like the logical choice.

He'd been lambasted for his actions and told h
needed to keep his girlfriend "under control."

Garrett didn't bother to correct his boss abou
his now-defunct relationship. He was having a har
enough time accepting that himself.

God, he missed Tara.

He shut his door and went over to stand by th
window, looking out on the city.

Control Tara, indeed. He snorted and gave his hea
a shake. There was no controlling Tara...nor did h
have any desire to control Tara.

He *had* wanted to control Angie, and, damn it, she'd ended up controlling him.

And still was.

He balled his hand into a fist and hammered the butt end into the wall.

Tara was right. Angie haunted him. He lived his life in fear of Angie, running from memories that dredged up guilt, so afraid of making the same mistakes again.

This time it had cost him plenty—almost everything, in fact.

Well, no more. He couldn't keep putting Dylan—or himself—through this.

The time to stop running was now. He had to face his fears and put Angie's ghost to rest at last.

He drew a deep breath and felt his head clear completely for the first time in four years.

And for the first time in four years, he knew exactly what his next move needed to be.

He strode from his office to Henri's with a purposeful stride, barging in on his surprised friend without bothering to knock.

"Henri," he said. "We need to talk."

THE CROWD WAS so large for the Board of Fellowship meeting, it had to be moved from the pastor's study to the Fellowship Hall of the church.

Remains from the Wednesday night potluck had to be cleaned up first, but, with so many hands there to help, that task didn't take long.

Faith knew she should be upset about the single item on the agenda, but she wasn't. Her breath came easily, her heart beat at a normal speed. Her family was all there together—Tara on one side of her, Thea on the other, Trenton between Thea and Sawyer. Even Emma was there on the far side of Tara. They were a loving, united front and nothing that happened tonight would change that.

Ollie had stopped by for a few minutes as they were leaving for the church. He asked if he could play them one song, then he'd pulled out his violin and played the old hymn "Wherever He Leads, I'll Go."

The song had been playing in Faith's head ever since.

Like Sawyer always said, there was a master plan, and they were all part of it. If that plan included a move away from Taylor's Grove, so be it. As long as she could be with Sawyer, she'd go to the ends of the earth.

A hush fell over the group as Arlo James began the meeting with roll call. All five members were there, and, as Faith considered each one, she was pretty sure she knew how four of the votes would go.

Sue Marsden played Duane Abell like a puppet. He always voted with her on everything. On the other hand, Arlo and Sawyer were fishing buddies, and Johnny Bob Luther treated Sawyer like a son, so it was doubtful either of them would vote against him now.

That left Miss Beulah May Johnson, a matriarch

of the church, who sometimes threw out pearls of wisdom the size of golf balls, and other times was sillier than a pet coon.

Her flights of fancy hadn't come on with old age. She'd always been that way, and everybody accepted what she said with a grain of salt.

But how Miss Beulah May would vote was anybody's guess.

Sawyer was listed on the agenda under New Business, and because there were no Committee Reports and no Old Business, his position came up quickly.

It was Sue, of course, who made the motion to "relieve Pastor Sawyer from his duties due to gross lack of leadership and lack of transparency in his personal life as behooved a spiritual shepherd."

Faith felt her hackles rise at the ridiculous drivel, but as expected, Duane seconded the motion.

Then came the call for discussion.

Tank Wallis was the first to speak. "Sue's motion seems to be based on old facts," he said. "Not current ones. Everybody in town knows Sawyer and Faith are back together. And their actions in Lacy's front yard last night were pretty transparent to anyone looking on. I think the motion should be withdrawn."

Sue butted in without being called on. "Their actions in Lacy's front yard last night make my point. A preacher and his wife shouldn't behave in such a vulgar manner."

"I'm kinda sorry I slept through it," Tara whispered, and Faith gave her a wink.

"And," Sue continued, "I believe they only made a show of reconciliation because they knew what was coming. If we let him off tonight, she might still move her things out tomorrow. They're just trying to buy some time and weasel the church out of his salary for another month."

"Oh, that's ridiculous, Sue." Faith recognized Ivadawn's loud voice from the back.

"It's not ridiculous. We still have no idea what any of this separation was about, and why everything suddenly became so hunky-dory when Tara got home. If we don't know the reason, how can we be sure it won't come around again?"

Tara had flinched at the mention of her name, and Faith felt her own spine stiffen. Her child had been through way too much lately, and it had shown in her mood today.

Faith had never seen Tara so down—not even when Louis had come home from Honduras with a wife on his arm. It hadn't bothered her to speak of Jacques Martin, but any mention of Garrett Hughes made her mood plummet lower than a snake's belly.

Faith reached for Tara's hand too late. Her daughter was already on her feet.

"I can't believe this has even gotten this far." Tara shook her head in disgust as she addressed the crowd. "What business is my parents' separation to anybody here except them? And y'all know my dad is the finest example of a loving spirit Taylor's Grove has ever known. I was in Paris, alone and sick at heart, and as soon as he heard that, he sold his bass boat—you know...the one that belonged to Grandpa Ian?" There were a few gasps from people who knew what a sacrifice that was, and Faith's throat tightened. "Yeah, that one. He sold it in order to have the money to come see about me. If that's not love, I don't know what is." She looked directly at Sue. "And neither do you."

A bubble of pride swelled in Faith's chest. Her daughter had become quite a woman.

"Well, of course, you're going to be on his side," Sue snapped. "You're his daughter."

"Yes, I am." Tara turned a beaming smile toward Sawyer. "And proud of it."

"I understand Sue's point," Randall Lively called out. "The preacher needs to be somebody you can go to with your troubles. If he's too worried 'bout his own, he ain't likely to be too interested in mine."

A few nods and grunts of agreement followed.

"Everybody's got troubles, Ran," Tank growled.

"And maybe that's what we need to think about." Ollie stood up from his seat in the front row. "We all have our troubles—that's no secret and it shouldn't be a big deal. So why keep secrets?"

Where was he going with this? For the first time that evening, Faith squirmed uncomfortably in her seat.

"Let's just let it all out." Ollie swept his arm dramatically. "You see, I have the mother of all secrets."

Faith felt herself blanch. *No, Ollie. Please, don't.*

"Years ago," Ollie said, "when I was a much younger man and had just been told I was probably gonna lose my sight, I was depressed. Mightily so." Faith clasped her hands together to stop the trembling. "I couldn't sleep at night, so I took to walking the streets of town. I was trying to memorize everything so I'd have the images in my brain when I couldn't see them with my eyes anymore."

He paused and looked around slowly. "Y'all have no idea the things that happen in this town after the sun goes down…but I've seen them all. I have the mother of all secrets because, you see, I *know* the secrets."

Ollie's gaze shifted from one side of the room to the other, but he couldn't see who was sitting where, so his eyes held no accusation. "I've seen the cars driving into garages at night, occupying the space where the out-of-town spouse's car usually sits. I've seen the clandestine meetings in the dark parking lot behind the school." He smiled. "Yes, kids, I've known for years about the smoking and drinking that goes on down by the marina when it's closed for the night. And the skinny-dipping, too."

An embarrassed laugh passed through the crowd.

Ollie shook his head sadly. "I've heard the arguments and seen the abuse through windows that weren't quite closed and shuttered all the way." He sighed. "And I'm here to tell you tonight, that if you demand complete transparency from the preacher, I'm gonna unload everything I know about everybody. If the preacher can't have secrets, ain't nobody gonna have secrets."

There was a long, anxious moment of silence before Nell Bradley stood up. "Y'all are just turning this meeting into a big gossip session, and I for one won't stand here and listen to it."

"Yeah!" A number of people shouted their agreement while Nell excused her way across the row of people sitting by her.

"We don't need this!" one particularly hostile voice shouted from the back. Faith thought it was Bobo Hudson, but she couldn't be sure.

"You're right," Ollie agreed. "We don't need this. Maybe we don't need transparency. Maybe all we need is love. We all have secrets, and we love each other in spite of them. If we knew everything about each other, I don't think we'd love each other nearly as much."

That brought a much-needed laugh of relief.

Miss Beulah May stood up. "I think we just all need to relax. And I believe I'll go home now and pour myself a good stiff shot of bourbon."

"Miss Beulah May!" Sue's chin dropped to her chest. "You can't say things like that in church!"

Miss Beulah May gave a smile and a pageant-queen wave to the crowd. "I think I just did." She looked very pleased with herself as she moseyed her way to the door.

"You just lost your swing vote, Sue." Tank gave a delighted laugh.

Johnny Bob Luther stood up in the middle of the aisle. "I reckon the preacher ain't gotta be perfect. He just needs to be better'n me." He slapped Sawyer on the back as he passed him. "And I reckon he is."

The meeting dissolved with that. People started talking, moving about and leaving.

"Sit down!" Sue snarled, but everybody ignored her. "This meeting's not over yet."

"Yes, it is," Arlo shouted over the noise. "The motion's withdrawn. This meeting's adjourned."

Sue slammed her palm to the table. "You can't do that!"

Arlo smiled at her and did a good imitation of Miss Beulah May's wave. "I think I just did."

The outpouring of love Faith felt from the congregation filled her heart to the brim. This was why they'd stayed in Taylor's Grove all these years. It was a good place. A loving place. It wasn't perfect, but, like a successful marriage, you took the good with the bad, for better or worse.

Sawyer's arms slid around her waist in a hug from behind. "I love you." He kissed her ear. "I've been too lax about showing it in public, but that's all changed."

Palming his cheek, she pressed his face to hers. "I'm never going to get tired of it, either." As he moved away, she held her arms out to Ollie, who had moved within reach of her, and hugged him across the folding chair. "You said what nobody else could, Ollie. I'll never be able to thank you enough."

"I only spoke the truth. We're not made to be perfect. The blessing lies within the fact that we're loved in spite of our imperfections."

"Amen," she agreed.

"You have a good man, Faith."

She glanced at her husband, who, at the moment, was hugging all three of his children at once. "The best," she said.

"Don't ever forget to tell him that."

"I won't," she promised.

And she never did.

CHAPTER TWENTY-EIGHT

TARA OPENED HER eyes to the bright morning sun. *Eighty-nine days.*

"Stop it!" She wrapped the pillow around her head as if that could stifle her thoughts.

Since the day she'd returned home from Paris, the first thought to pop into her mind every morning was how long it had been since she'd seen Garrett and Dylan.

It was crazy, but despite her best efforts, she just couldn't get beyond the man and his little boy. It was like her brain wanted to move on, but her heart remained rooted in the concrete of that terrace in Paris.

The first couple of weeks after she'd left, Dylan had called every day. But toward the middle of August, his calls became fewer and fewer, eventually dwindling to none. She supposed it was a good sign that she'd been forgotten.

The pillow made her feel like she was smothering herself. She uncovered her head.

One day she'd want to date again, and she would allow herself to love someone else.

Today just wasn't that day.

But she did at least have a plan that would keep her

busy for the next three days—the annual O'Malley Columbus Day weekend at the cabin.

She'd stayed up late last night getting all her students' essays graded, so the entire weekend would be work-free.

She hurried through breakfast and a shower, anxious to get to the lake, where there would be so much laughter and talk that her mind would have little chance to wander.

She grabbed her phone on the way out the door, listening to the voice mail from Emma as she walked to the car.

"Hey, I got booked into a much-needed massage today, but it's not until eleven. Go on without me. I'll drive up later."

"Darn," Tara muttered. She'd looked forward to having Emma with her on the drive. She reached over and tuned her radio to a heavy metal station, setting the volume to a few decibels below painful.

The changing foliage with its stunning array of crisp golds and fiery reds filled the roadside, and she tried to lose herself in the passing images. But her thoughts kept diverting back to Paris and how the city would look in autumn…how much Dylan would have grown…how Garrett's eyes could set her on fire with a simple glance.

The cabin came into sight, drawing an audible groan from her. She was the first to arrive. Where was everybody?

She pulled out her phone and punched her mom's number. Her mom picked up after just one ring.

"Morning, Tara," she said brightly.

"Hey, Mom, where are you? I'm the first one here." She unlocked the door and tossed her bag on the floor of the front bedroom.

"We're on our way. I took food up yesterday, so everything's there. Start a pot of coffee, would you?"

"Okay. See you in a bit."

She made coffee the O'Malley way—extra strong. The aroma took her back to mornings in Paris when Garrett would bring her coffee in bed. She sighed and stepped away from the coffeemaker…and the memory.

A car door slammed, which probably meant either Trent or Thea had arrived. She headed to the front door to greet her sibling, and was barely halfway across the living room when the screen door opened and Garrett stepped in.

Tara's brain stalled as her feet came to an abrupt halt. An unseen force knocked the breath from her lungs, and she stood there gaping and mute.

His hands went to his hips and he filled the doorway, barring escape in that direction if she'd been so inclined, which she wasn't. "Hi," he said, and she could read the wariness in his eyes. The scar on his upper lip disappeared as his lips pressed together tightly.

The momentary numbness passed and feeling

rushed back through her extremities. Her first inclination was to run to him, but she held herself motionless.

"Hi," she answered. "What are you doing here?"

"I came to talk to you. Can we do that?"

"I guess so." She tried to right her world, which had been jerked completely off its axis. "How did you know where I was?"

His face relaxed enough to allow a small smile. "This weekend has been planned for…well, for a long time. Your dad and I started talking on the phone the week after you left Paris, and your parents invited me here for this weekend."

"You came all the way from Paris for the weekend?" And her mom and dad had encouraged that?

"No." He shook his head and the smile disappeared. "Look. Can we sit down? I'll explain everything."

His presence filled the room…the whole cabin, and Tara needed fresh air to clear her wobbly thoughts. "Let's walk down to the lake." She tilted her head in the direction of the back door. When she moved, he followed, but she noticed he was careful not to touch her. Was that for her benefit or his?

"You want coffee?" she asked as they passed through the kitchen.

"Not yet. My heart's racing enough without it."

She smiled at his honesty, knowing exactly how he felt, although she didn't say so.

They stepped into the brisk autumn air coming

off the lake. Tara breathed it deep into her lungs, hoping it would clear the conflicting emotions this man's presence caused.

"Where's Dylan?" She cast him a sidelong glance, still not trusting a direct eye-to-eye gaze.

"He's with your mom and dad. We stayed with them last night."

Her parents had invited Garrett and Dylan to stay with them in Taylor's Grove…and hadn't called her? Hadn't warned her they were coming? They knew how heartbroken she was over Garrett. Did they think closure would get her over her depression?

That brought her around to face him straight on. "Garrett…please tell me what's going on."

His chest heaved as he took a breath, then let it out, and his gaze bored into hers, pinning her to the spot. "Tara," he said. "I love you."

It probably wasn't the best place to start, but it was the truth, and Garrett wanted her to know where he was coming from. No secrets. No ghosts.

She tilted her head in question and slid her hands into her back pockets—a stance that kept her elbows back and placed her heart right out there. An encouraging sign. "Did Mama and Dad know you were going to say that?"

He nodded. "They told me that to win your trust, I was just going to have to lay it all out there."

"Go on." She started to gnaw on her bottom lip.

"After you left, I did some soul-searching, and I

realized you were right. You *couldn't* trust me. Hell, I couldn't trust myself. I was afraid. Running away from my past. Running away from Angie. I'd pulled Dylan away from the family he needed…the family who needed him and me…at the time when we all needed each other the most. And I'd done it because I didn't want to deal with the memories and the guilt." He paused.

Her nod was encouraging, but a shrug followed in its wake. "Great. But I'm still not getting it."

"Dylan and I moved back to St. Louis last month."

An audible gasp rushed from her lungs as her eyes widened.

"I quit Soulard, sublet the flat and we moved back home. A friend from college had been in contact with me for several years about starting a new marketing firm in St. Louis. I'd always turned him down before, but this time, we decided to go for it."

For the first time, he edged closer to her. She didn't move, but her eyes clouded. "What about Henri?"

His heart twinged at the mention of his best friend, who he missed like hell. "He wasn't happy about it, but we both knew it was for the best. We'll visit." He held out his hand, and when she placed hers in it, his heart twinged in a different way that he didn't dare stop to analyze. It felt promising. And, if it wasn't, he didn't want to know yet. "I was hoping you and I could do that, too. Take turns visiting on weekends and during school breaks. Dylan and I can come down here. You can come up there. I just want you back in our lives, Tara. We can take it as slow as you want. Or as fast. Just give us a chance."

The words had barely left his mouth before she was in his arms. Her hands clasped around his neck and she kissed him with a fervor he hadn't allowed himself to think about for months.

"I'm so glad you're here! I love you, Garrett." The words poured out, straight from her heart to his. "And I love Dylan. But things happened so fast, and I was so upset and confused. Trust takes time…I learned that from a very wise man. I knew in my heart that I'd screwed up by not giving us the time we needed to work through the trust issue. And I've been *miserable* for the past eighty-nine days because of it."

He laughed at her exactness while she laughed and cried at the same time.

He kissed her again then pulled her to his chest, against his heart. "God, I missed you. Your parents kept telling me you were miserable, but I didn't think there was any way you could be as miserable as I felt."

"At least you had Dylan." She sniffed. "All I had were memories." She gave him a squeeze. "But not anymore. I can't believe you're here."

He kissed the top of her hair where the morning sun was burnishing the copper tresses. "Believe it."

She leaned back in his arms and he brushed back the damp hair that had stuck to the tears on her cheeks, brushed the eyebrow ring with his thumb and kissed it.

"How'd you get my dad's number?" she asked.

That brought a chuckle. "As opposed to your other elusive father, Sawyer O'Malley was listed in the on-line phone book."

She narrowed her eyes and gave him a pretend pout. "I don't know who you're referring to. I only have one dad."

The sound of car doors slamming came from the front of the cabin. She grabbed his hand and took off running in that direction.

They rounded the corner as Dylan was skipping up the sidewalk, chattering excitedly to Faith and Sawyer.

"Dylan!" Tara called.

The unbridled joy on his son's face when he turned and saw Tara would stay with Garrett for the rest of his life.

"Tara!" Dylan ran to them, and they swooped him off the ground in an ecstatic, three-way hug.

Garrett's arms were full, but his heart was fuller. If he let go of Dylan and Tara right then, he would float away on happiness.

Over Tara's head, he watched Sawyer stop and eye them for a moment, then he nodded, and Garrett nodded back.

The exchange was brief, but its meaning unmistakable.

Sawyer O'Malley had just given his daughter away.

EPILOGUE

June of the following year

"FAITH, YOU LOOK STUNNING."

"Thanks, sweetheart." She smiled at him, and Garrett watched the soft blush rise from the round neck of her pink dress.

"And the pink is perfect." He pointed to the hot pink streak of hair that swept through her bangs.

She fingered it self-consciously and shrugged. "Hey, this is Paris, right?"

"I think it's lovely."

Garrett turned at the sound of his mom's voice as she slid her arm around his waist.

"And you are a vision of beauty in that blue," he told her.

She slapped her chest in mock horror. "Oh God, it's getting deep, and I'm in open-toed shoes." She grinned up at him. "But Henri's shoveling it out more than you are."

Over her head, Garrett could see his friend talking with Thea and Emma, most certainly in his element. Garrett had warned Tara that taking Henri up on his offer to have her sister and her best friend stay with him might be a mistake, but she'd insisted everything would be fine with Trent there.

Garrett sighed. They were all adults, and today, he wasn't going to worry about anything.

His phone vibrated and he pulled it out of his pocket and read the text.

I'm ready (again). I love you.

He smiled at their private joke. Switching off the phone, he clapped his hands loudly.

"All right, people. It's showtime."

The few guests took their seats as the wedding party found their places.

Garrett nodded to the harpist, and she began.

THE STRAINS OF "Ode to Joy" floated through the open door.

Tara took a deep breath and gave her dad a smile.

"Ready to make this official in God's eyes?" he asked. He was the only one in on the secret that, because of French law, a civil ceremony had already taken place.

"I've never been more ready, Dad."

She took the arm he proffered, and they stepped through the door onto the terrace.

Her eyes locked with Garrett's, and her heart swelled at the look on his ruggedly handsome face. "I love you," he mouthed, and she felt her answering smile spread across her face.

She shifted her eyes to Dylan, who was standing in front of his dad, and kissed the air in his direction. He giggled and blew her a kiss in return. It caught in her throat, lodging on a bubble of joy her heart had released.

When she reached the wedding party, Emma took her flowers as her dad kissed her on the cheek and then moved to stand beside the French minister.

Garrett reached for one hand and Dylan for the other, and, as the three of them exchanged their vows, she recalled the first time she'd stood on this terrace during the raging storm.

She'd sought shelter, and she'd found it in the hearts of these two guys.

She understood how her dad felt now. Dylan wasn't hers by blood, but that didn't make any difference to her heart.

Garrett was hers, and Dylan was hers.

They were a family.

And they would stay a family forever.

* * * * *

LARGER-PRINT BOOKS!
GET 2 FREE LARGER-PRINT NOVELS PLUS
2 FREE GIFTS!

HARLEQUIN
super romance®

More Story...More Romance

YES! Please send me 2 FREE LARGER-PRINT Harlequin® Superromance® novels and my 2 FREE gifts (gifts are worth about $10). After receiving them, if I don't wish to receive any more books, I can return the shipping statement marked "cancel." If I don't cancel, I will receive 6 brand-new novels every month and be billed just $5.69 per book in the U.S. or $5.99 per book in Canada. That's a savings of at least 16% off the cover price! It's quite a bargain! Shipping and handling is just 50¢ per book in the U.S. or 75¢ per book in Canada.* I understand that accepting the 2 free books and gifts places me under no obligation to buy anything. I can always return a shipment and cancel at any time. Even if I never buy another book, the two free books and gifts are mine to keep forever.

139/339 HDN F46Y

Name _____ (PLEASE PRINT) _____

Address _____ Apt. # _____

City _____ State/Prov. _____ Zip/Postal Code _____

Signature (if under 18, a parent or guardian must sign)

Mail to the **Harlequin**® Reader Service:
IN U.S.A.: P.O. Box 1867, Buffalo, NY 14240-1867
IN CANADA: P.O. Box 609, Fort Erie, Ontario L2A 5X3

**Are you a current subscriber to Harlequin Superromance books
and want to receive the larger-print edition?
Call 1-800-873-8635 today or visit www.ReaderService.com.**

* Terms and prices subject to change without notice. Prices do not include applicable taxes. Sales tax applicable in N.Y. Canadian residents will be charged applicable taxes. Offer not valid in Quebec. This offer is limited to one order per household. Not valid for current subscribers to Harlequin Superromance Larger-Print books. All orders subject to credit approval. Credit or debit balances in a customer's account(s) may be offset by any other outstanding balance owed by or to the customer. Please allow 4 to 6 weeks for delivery. Offer available while quantities last.

Your Privacy—The Harlequin® Reader Service is committed to protecting your privacy. Our Privacy Policy is available online at www.ReaderService.com or upon request from the Harlequin Reader Service.

We make a portion of our mailing list available to reputable third parties that offer products we believe may interest you. If you prefer that we not exchange your name with third parties, or if you wish to clarify or modify your communication preferences, please visit us at www.ReaderService.com/consumerschoice or write to us at Harlequin Reader Service Preference Service, P.O. Box 9062, Buffalo, NY 14269. Include your complete name and address.

HSRLP13R